DEMON'S REVENGE

Emily Book 2

By
Ashley McCook

ISBN: 978-0-9571255-1-3

Also by Ashley McCook

DEMON'S DAUGHTER
(Emily Book 1)

Crooked
Halo
Publications

www.ashleymccook.co.uk

DEMON'S REVENGE

By
Ashley McCook

Published by

Crooked Halo Publications

www.ashleymccook.co.uk

ISBN: 978-0-9571255-1-3

Graphic Design by Nigel Johnston

For Shauna

Thank you for your wonderful friendship...
and for reading absolutely everything that I put in front of you
with an open mind and an open heart!

CHAPTER ONE

We were waiting for a train.

The last train of the day, in fact – the one that most normal people try to avoid in case there are junkies, drunks or (heaven forbid) teenagers on it. The train would be virtually empty which, when you're on the run from Demons, makes it a darn sight easier to watch your back. And I'm not kidding about the Demon thing.

My travelling companion, Sariel, was standing a few feet away having a discussion with another of his seemingly endless supply of 'contacts'. Using my awesomely sharp powers of deduction I figured that the conversation wasn't exactly going swimmingly – Sariel's hand waving, glaring and the narrowing of his lips, which I knew from past, but brief, experience were soft and hot and tasted like…

Sariel looked up at me sharply and widened his eyes in a 'too much information' glare. I sighed. I have a tendency to think much too loudly for Sariel's liking, which wouldn't be a problem if Sariel and I didn't share this freaky psychic-link type thing. Sometimes it's cool, like when you're about to be eaten by a Demon and want some help to talk your way out of it (been there, done that, seen the film, read the book and bought the t-shirt) but generally having someone read your thoughts at inappropriate moments sucks. Sariel's teaching me to block my thoughts and stuff like that but believe me – having to think about not thinking too loudly is tougher than you might think.

I decided that concentrating on Sariel's contact, Ron, might be the way to go. Ron was, hopefully, going to provide us with transport to the channel tunnel in the morning so that we could make our escape to a safe place that Sariel knew in Italy. Ron seemed to be a fairly average guy – a little overweight, graying at the temples and with the bizarre habit of sucking on his bottom lip (something it seemed he did a lot if the angry red scourge mark beneath it was anything to go by). As I studied him he looked my way several times, pulling his bottom lip into his mouth and releasing it with a loud squeak as Sariel fought to keep his attention. Finally, shaking his head in annoyance, Sariel motioned for me to come over.

"Ron wants a proper introduction," he told me loudly. Ron grinned and held out a hand which I dutifully shook.

"Ron Parsons," he said.

"Uh, Emily Carson," I replied.

"You stabbed him," he whispered, his eyes shining.

"Asmodeus? Yeah, I did." I said aloud and grinned at him, feeling a certain amount of pride in that achievement.

"Shh, shh, shh," Ron panicked, looking around wildly.

"Jeez, Ron. It's only Asmodeus, not Voldemort," I told him, turning to grin and think at Sariel. *Geddit? Ron? Voldemort?* Sariel sighed and made an impatient twirling motion with his hand. I turned my attention back to Ron. "Nothing to worry about, Ron. I doubt if the great Asmodeus would be hanging out in a train station this close to midnight on a Tuesday. Just not his style somehow."

I caught Sariel covering a grin with his fist but Ron was still looking around in concern, his head whipping back and forth between the platforms. "He may not be here but he has his entire house looking for you," he wailed, "And some of the other houses have pitched in too."

Hard to believe but a little over a year ago I didn't know any of this stuff – Demons exist and they're organized into houses. And they have other Demons working for them. And they like to have big parties. And most of them can't sing. And they hold grudges for a mighty long time. And they're devious backstabbers who pretend to like each other. They're a lot like teenagers if I'm honest, which I'm allowed to say 'cause I am one.

"Let me guess; Lillith, Anzu and Nybbas?" I asked. Ron nodded and stepped a little closer. He smelled of stale cigarettes and sweaty trainers – not a good combination.

"The others were mighty impressed with your little act of defiance, girly. You pushed your price way up." He grinned and then his lip disappeared back into his mouth. I tried hard not to stare.

Do we really have to deal with this guy?

Si. He's one of the good guys, Emily.

He's creepy.

Play nice. We need him. And he's an amico.

Say what?

A friend.

"Yay me," I said brightly, smiling until my jaw hurt. So Asmodeus was going ahead with his plan to sell me to the highest bidder for the night of my eighteenth birthday and my trying to stab him just made me even more attractive to the others. Marvelous.

Ron studied me carefully and frowned. "You're not what I was expecting," he admitted. "I thought from the way everyone was going on about you that you'd be blonde and have…" he cupped his hands out in front of his man-boobs. I blinked but managed to keep the shiny happy smile in place. Sariel was choking on a bray of laughter. "Er, I mean, I love your accent though," Ron continued watching me closely for signs that I might consider stabbing him too. "It's very, er, nice. Australian?"

Sariel snorted. "American," I told Ron drily. "Although its kindda diluted now 'cause I've been living in England for about five years."

Ron made a face. "You traded in the good old U Ess of Ay for here? Isn't Suffolk kind of dull in comparison?"

I shrugged. "Not since I turned sixteen and found out that my dad's a Demon. I mean; I've met a Vampire who, by the way, did NOT look like Robert Pattinson; found out that ex-Archangels make fab BFF's and that the forest around Dean's Lynn is pretty much teaming with werewolves. Seems to me Seattle can't compete with all that." I folded my arms.

Ron was grinning at Sariel. "Didn't they have a problem with water sprites in Seattle a while back?" He chuckled and shook his head. "Not as sweet as they sound, right? Take your leg off as quick as look at you they would. Ever wrestled a water sprite, girly?"

I gaped at him. Water sprites?

"Er, maybe we should finalise our plans for tomorrow," said

3

Sariel, saving Ron and I from each other. "Train'll be here in ten minutes and we really don't want to miss it." He glanced in my direction and I managed to hide a shiver of excitement.

We were going to see my mum and my twin brother, Seth. It'd been almost two weeks since we'd left Asmodeus's house in the early hours of the morning. Asmodeus had been lying in a pool of his own blood in the same cave where he'd been torturing Sariel for helping me. The fact that he'd survived being stabbed was a bummer but at least Sariel had the connections to ensure my family was taken to safety before Asmodeus could get to them. We'd been lucky.

I shifted the weight of my small gray backpack, acutely aware that before we saw Seth and mum, we'd have to make another stop. Inside the bag was a knife that belonged to the Werewolves of Dean's Lynn. It had been stolen from them last year and used in a ritual to summon a Demon by one of the kids in my year at school. David, the kid who had tried to use it, had died when his summoning attempt went wrong and Adam and I had survived. Adam.

I licked my lips and concentrated on slowing the sudden racing of my treacherous heart. I'd been in lust with Adam Farlow since the first day I'd seen him striding down the corridors of Rainey High School. He was the school hero – captain of everything and gloriously blond and tousled with clear tanned skin and dark blue eyes. He was also a slave to his dad's wishes – that happens apparently when your dad's the alpha male of the local wolf pack. He'd lied to me and let me down but my stomach still did flip flops whenever I thought of him.

Bloody hormones.

CHAPTER TWO

We left Ron standing on the platform with a sorrowful expression on his round face and his bottom lip pulled into his mouth as far as he could manage it without sucking the rest of his face in there too. He'd promised transport, money and a change of clothes for both of us by mid-morning of the next day. I was skeptical that Ron could manage to find his own way back home never mind find all that we needed in such a short space of time. Sariel was more optimistic.

"Cut him some slack, Emily. Ron's on our side," he told me as we chose the middle carriage of the train and made ourselves comfortable. "You're judging him on the fact that he looks like an average Joe. Ridicolo."

For once I didn't need him to translate. "Not ridiculous and not 'Average Joe', 'Creepy Ron,'" I corrected.

"Yeah, well, Ron has no love for the likes of Asmodeus."

"Why? Whose house does he come from then?" I punctuated my question by attempting to punch my lumpy bag into a comfortable pillow.

"None of them. Ron went rogue about 180 years ago and he's managed to keep his family safe and hidden since. He's helped a lot of people along the way – people like us. Give me that." Sariel took my bag and substituted his rolled up jacket.

"Ron has a family?" I asked, stretching out across two seats and snuggling my head into my new pillow. It was still warm from Sariel and smelled delicious. Sariel sighed and busied himself with checking that the knife was still in my bag for the billionth time – why give me the thing to look after if he didn't trust me with it?

"What are you clucking about, mother hen?" I asked sleepily.

"I tell you that Ron's a rogue Demon helping others in a kind of Demon resistance movement and you're amazed by the fact that he has a family."

"Well, he just doesn't look the type," I grumbled. I closed my eyes and, just like that, I slipped into my dream world.

Snob

Sariel's complaint followed me, echoing around the house that I had built for myself. Well, technically it was the house that I dreamed for myself because my special place didn't exist in the real world – only in my mind. It was a kind of cool bolt hole that I could carry with me and I could travel to it anytime that I wanted – I didn't have to be asleep to make the journey but slipping into sleep made slipping into my imagination that little bit easier.

I ignored Sariel and opened my dream eyes, feeling my tense shoulders relax and my busy brain clear. A warm breeze gently pushed my hair back from my face and I inhaled the clean, fresh tang of the ocean.

Sariel taught me how to create this place – it was a safe escape from the monstrous reality that my, until now relatively normal, existence had become. My place was a large, low house on top of a high cliff which overlooked the ocean. Far below and to the west was a sheltered bay where clear blue water lapped onto a white sandy beach. To the north and east was the vast expanse of an ocean and to the south was the real world – the waking world. When I created my house I built a wall between it and reality so that when I thought in my house - or spoke aloud, screamed, cried, danced, sang, whatever kind of mood I was in – no-one, not even Sariel, could hear it unless I wanted them to. If Sariel spoke to me telepathically I could tune him in or out which was a skill I was becoming rather good at, much to his annoyance.

Inside, the house had white walls and elegant, modern furnishings; crisp, clean lines of colour flowing from one room to another. The ceilings were high, the lighting was muted and there were huge picture windows with views of the ocean.

The only room that was an exception to my minimalist rule was my knowledge and memory library – at the centre of the house and stretching the height of it, it was my child-hood ideal of a proper library with shelf after shelf of books, staircases from floor to floor and a fireplace complete with a huge comfy chair on either side. It was a work in progress obviously – I was only seventeen. Sariel's library was huge – 'Warehouse 13' huge – but then he was ancient so his knowledge was humungous. I probably still knew more about maths though.

Thinking about maths made me wonder how my best friends and fellow nerds were doing. Annie and Dylan had befriended Seth and me on our first day at Rainey High. I'd been so nervous and quiet, sticking to Seth's side like an Elastoplast and worrying about fitting in – we just didn't work on any level; we were twins for a start, with American accents, uniforms from the thrift shop and above-average intelligence. We were goners before the end of the day for sure.

Cue Annie – long blonde pigtails dyed red at the tips, extra-long school skirt, fringed and beaded schoolbag. She just looked like the Noughties version of a flower child. I saw her eyes widen with interest when she caught sight of Seth (yep, my brother the chick magnet even at the tender age of 12) and then she saw me beside him. Her head cocked to the side and she smiled. I smiled back (I could recognise a fellow nerd at sixty paces) and she motioned us over. Annie showed Seth and me to our next class, telling us all about the school and its pupils as she walked, her mouth working at about ninety miles an hour.

She introduced us to Dylan in History class and it was obvious straight away that we would all get along together. Dylan was a twelve year-old Einstein with a shock of dark curly hair and eyes like chocolate drops. I grinned to myself as I remembered the first words that Dylan had spoken to me.

"Why do you smell like warm sticky syrup?"

I'm sure I probably blushed several shades of tomato but I managed to keep it together long enough to respond "We had pancakes for breakfast." Not the best come-back in history but at least my voice worked.

"Homemade pancakes?" His eyes narrowed.

"Er, yeah."

"And you're allowed to put syrup on them?"

"Yeah."

He'd shuffled closer, his eyes sparkling as he licked his lips. "Are you two allowed to have friends round for sleep-overs yet?" he asked, his eyes darting between me and Seth. I might've thought he was some kind of freak with a terrible choice of pick-up lines but it soon became apparent that Dylan had a real sugar addiction. His parents had obviously discovered this too as he was forbidden from having anything with too much of the stuff in it. Our house wasn't quite so strict so Dylan eventually became part of our furniture when mum was making her pancakes.

Would Asmodeus go after my friends to get to me?

Unnerved by the thought I wandered to the living room and stepped through the open patio doors onto the deck. The sun was warm on my face, the breeze gentle and soothing. I relaxed a little and let my gaze drift across the horizon. I frowned.

Today the horizon line was broken. I raised a hand to block the sun and squinted at the speck that was marring my perfect view. It was too small and too far away for me to be certain but it looked like a little boat.

I dropped my hand and chewed on my lip. It was time to wake up – I had questions for Sariel.

CHAPTER THREE

He was sitting on the seat opposite, watching me when I opened my eyes. He smiled. "You look so innocent and peaceful when you sleep," he told me with a wistful smile.

I swung my feet onto the floor and pulled my hair out of its bobble. "I have questions, Sariel," I told him.

Sariel sighed. "Unfortunately, as always, normal service has resumed." I paused in my hair tidying duty and glared at him. "Chiedimi. Ask me." he said with a cute grin.

"There's a boat on the horizon," I told him through a mouthful of bobble.

Sariel made a face and pointed around the carriage. "As we are in a train and not on the ocean I'm going to assume that you've either lost what's left of your marbles or you're talking in code."

I finished tying my hair back and faced him. "Not here. In my special place, idiot. Usually when I look out I can see the ocean right out to the horizon. Nothing else, just ocean. But today there's something else out there. It's really far away but it looks like a boat to me."

"And you didn't put it there?" Sariel was talking slowly, as though I was about five.

"Well of course not! Do you seriously think I'd be freaked out by my own boat?" I snapped at him.

"Is it a big boat? Like an ocean liner type thing?" He asked, stroking his chin thoughtfully.

I gaped at him. "Are we really having a conversation about size? I mean, fishing boat? Aircraft carrier? Who cares? The point is that it's there and I don't want it to be. Besides," I added huffily, "I know the difference between a boat and a ship." I folded my arms and glared at him.

"Okay, okay. Don't get all Miss Stroppy Teen," Sariel said, standing up. He leaned against the window and looked out into the dark. "I'll have a think about it."

I shrugged. "Whatever. Don't tax yourself. I just thought I'd mention it." If I'd had gum I'd have blown a bubble at him in annoyance.

He turned back to me and sighed. "You nervous about facing the Weres again?" I shook my head. "Adam?" I made a face. "Your mum and Seth?"

I sighed. "If I hadn't stabbed Asmodeus then they'd still be at home. Safe and sound. Well, safe-ish."

Sariel sat down again and leaned forward, putting his hands on my knees. "I can't truthfully say that I'm sorry you did that," he said, "But I do understand why you'd feel guilty about it."

I looked up into his silver blue eyes. "I'm not sorry that I stopped him from hurting you, Sariel. I'm just pissed that it had repercussions for mum and Seth. Oh!" I remembered my other question. "I almost forgot – do you think he'll go after Annie and Dylan?" Sariel chewed on his bottom lip and looked away. Ah. He'd obviously already thought of that. "So, what, their lives aren't important?" I growled.

He rolled his eyes. "Emily..."

I bounced up off my seat, knocking him back. "You think it's okay for my friends to get tortured?" I chewed on a fingernail and was disgusted to feel my eyes fill with tears.

I felt him stand up behind me. "Of course not, Emily. But we can't hide everyone. Where do we stop? Annie's family? Dylan's? Seth's already asked about Amber and her family. Do we look after Adam and the Weres too? The priest in that church you liked so much? The guy who owns the bakery in Dean's Lynn where you got your doughnuts?"

I let my shoulders drop and turned to face him. He was right, of course, but it didn't help the gnawing fear in my gut. If anything happened to any of those people because of me, could I handle it?

"I'm sorry," I mumbled, raising my eyes to his.

He smiled sadly and caught a tear at the corner of my eye. "Anche io, so am I, Emily." He whispered and pulled me close for a brief hug. I hugged him back, loving the feel of his hot skin under the light t-shirt and his shoulder muscles shifting under my hands. He pushed me back after a moment and I resisted the urge to pout and grab him again. "Look, once we've given the Weres back their knife we could ask them to keep an eye on your friends."

I brightened up. "Do you think they would?"

He nodded. "They're not exactly Asmodeus's biggest fans." I grinned and dropped a quick kiss on his cheek. He lifted an eyebrow but I acted like it was no big deal (blocking my thoughts like crazy) and he let it go. "I know what'd cheer you up." He said and clicked his fingers.

The train's PA system came to life and Lady Gaga began to sing. "Oooh! 'Bad Romance'!" I squealed. "I love this song." One of the benefits of having Sariel as a friend is his totally cool ability to high-jack stereos, PA systems and radio transmissions – putting the music that we like on there instead of the usual boring stuff.

Sariel laughed. "Yeah, having to listen to it over and over and over when you were at home, I kindda got that impression."

"Dance with me," I said with a giggle, grabbing his hands.

"Oh, I can't…"

"Of course you can. Just move with the music," I told him and began to roll my hips. Sariel's eyes widened and I hid a self-satisfied smirk. I took dance for almost 6 years in Seattle so I knew how to move. Plus the self-defense training we'd done over the past year had given me a strong, lean, dancer's body. I dragged Sariel into the middle of the aisle and giggled as my warrior Angel attempted to find the beat.

Chapter Four

The Farlow homestead was, predictably, humungous and with something of a Gothic feel to it – large pointy-arched windows, flamboyant carvings and fairytale castle towers all in tones of gray and black. I figured it was the kind of home that had to be seen in a thunder storm to be fully appreciated and just look at all those tiny panes of glass – their window cleaning bill must be astronomical. I was willing to bet that Mrs. Farlow didn't don her wellies and head out with the Windowlene like my mum did.

Sariel and I walked up the centre of the sweeping driveway, our feet crunching on the pale gravel and Sariel whistling snatches of old 'Beach Boys' tunes. He had his hands in his pockets too which should've made him look relaxed and unconcerned but didn't fool me for a second.

Quit acting all devil-may-care. I know we're walking into enemy territory here.

Who's acting? They're only overgrown lap dogs. I could knock them down with a flick of my pinky.

Ah, you know famous 'Kung Fu Panda' Wuxi pinky hold, eh? I said in my best oriental accent. Sariel glanced at me with a look of 'that-girl-has-serious-problems' on his face. *You no see 'Kung Fu Panda'?* He shook his head. *Ah, poor Angelic being has not lived. Must go to movies velly fast.* Sariel raised an eyebrow and I giggled at the worried look on his face.

We were level with the first of three sleek Mercedes when the security lights came on and I stopped in shock.

Keep walking, Em. I don't think the rear guards are all that patient. Sariel told me.

Huh? I turned around and I swear that for just a moment, my heart actually stopped beating. Maybe ten paces behind us were two huge wolves with strange amber eyes that shone in the glare of the strong security light. The shoulders of the nearest would've reached just above my waist and their coarse, shaggy fur shivered as they crept slowly forward on paws that looked larger than my hands. The lead wolf lifted his head just a fraction, urging me on, and growled deep in his throat. I could feel the echoing rumble of that growl beneath my feet and almost launched myself out of the earth's atmosphere when Sariel took my arm to pull me on.

Are you trying to give me a heart attack?

Like I said, they don't seem like patient doggies and we're technically intruders.

I thought you could dispatch them with a flick of your pinky.

I can but you can't

Oh.

Our furry escorts directed us with a series of truly disturbing growls and snarls to the rear of the property and I couldn't help wondering how these things managed to keep out of the way of the normal people of Dean's Lynn on a nightly basis – I mean, there wasn't much you could do to hide one of them. A recessed back door was opened by a tall man carrying a real, honest-to-God shotgun. I couldn't take my eyes off it – guns look much more 'solid' in real life than they do in the movies. It was obvious that this was no toy and was big enough to do a lot of damage if the guy holding it decided that the doing of damage was necessary. I decided that it would be worth our while to be nice to him.

"Hi," I said brightly, sticking out my hand. "Is Rick at home?"

Both Shotgun Dude and Sariel turned to look at me in astonishment. Sariel's eyebrows rose into his fringe and Shotgun Dude looked first at my hand and then my face. He scowled and I withdrew my hand.

"This way," he told us gruffly and we trooped dutifully after him into the unlit house.

What exactly was that? Sariel asked, amazement and amusement colouring his voice in equal measure.

Hello? Did you not see the gun? I thought we should be nice.

You faced off against a Demon lord and now you're scared of a human with a gun?

It's a big gun!

His laughter echoed through my mind as we moved further into the house. From what I could see (which wasn't much – gothic houses are way too dark!) there seemed to be a lot of doors down

13

an endless stream of corridors which were festooned with old paintings and flock wallpaper. We moved soundlessly over plush carpets which may or may not have been hideous colours – some light would've been really good. Thankfully Sariel kept me right – steering me with a gentle hand on the small of my back when he thought I might be in danger of banging into some antique table or falling down the odd staircase.

He's taking us a round-a-bout route, isn't he? Trying to get us lost so we can't escape if negotiations go wrong. We'd be trapped in this maze for days, weeks even. I'd die of starvation and you'd be left to wander these endless corridors alone until the end of time.

Do you always get so maudlin when you're tired?

I just don't want to get lost and turned into puppy fodder by big dudes with big guns and even bigger teeth.

You're obsessing about this gun, Emily. He's not going to use it, at least not until Rick gets his little trinket back. Besides he's human.

Well, duh! I told you they were all just silly men playing at being dogs.

Huh? No, this guy's human. Rick Farlow and his family are definitely Weres.

Damn.

Scared?

No, just hate being wrong. So this guy's not supernatural in any way, shape, form or fashion?

Nope.

So do you think he knows that the Farlow's are…um…'other'.

I would imagine so. And I'd imagine he gets well paid for doing his job and keeping his mouth shut.

Escorting people around a dark, creepy house is his job?

Well, he's probably a guard of some kind rather than a 'tour-of-the-house' type. Even a Werewolf pack needs hired help, Em. And the hired help needs to get paid. They probably have a union too.

I stumbled over my own feet for the billionth time as our well-paid guard-slash-guide led us around yet another corner and then up a set of creaky stairs which were probably either antique or imported from some ridiculously expensive stair-exporting country. We plodded on with me carefully watching where I was setting my feet so that I didn't set one on top of the other again. A few minutes later and an urge that had been building could no longer be ignored.

Sariel?

Uh huh.

I need to pee. My answer was an exasperated sigh. *I really do.*

Che cosa? Emily, we're being led through a large, dark house by a man brandishing a shotgun. The house is populated by Werewolves who may or may not get violent if we blink in a way that they consider impolite to their Alpha. And you want to pee?

Maybe it's a nervous thing.

Before Sariel could stop me I leaned forward and tapped Shotgun Dude on what I figured was in the general area of his shoulder. He stopped immediately, grunting in annoyance when Sariel and I cannoned into his back.

"Sorry," I told him. "I was just wondering if you could point me to the nearest bathroom." I smiled sweetly into the darkness.

"Mr. Farlow instructed me to bring his visitors directly to him and Mr. Farlow does not like to be kept waiting." The shotgun appeared out of the darkness and disappeared again as he swapped shoulders and then his footsteps headed off again. I hurried up beside him, dragging Sariel with me.

"So you and Sariel here could keep your big date with the big boss and I could catch you up." I suggested, sweet smile still in place.

"No," grumpy Shotgun Dude threw back over his shoulder.

I slowed down, folded my arms and scowled at the place where I figured his back might be.

Have to agree with the man, Sariel told me, giving me a gentle nudge forward. *No telling what you might meet if you go wandering off on your own.*

Yeah, I agreed. *Look what monstrous horror I came face to face with last time I had to pee in a big, scary house.*

Huh? Oh, you mean me? Yes, very witty.

Shotgun Dude opened a door somewhere ahead and welcoming amber light spilled out down the corridor, making us blink and squint into the sudden brightness. Standing back, he used the shotgun to wave us past and into the room, closing the door behind us with a soft click.

Rick Farlow looked up from a large mahogany desk as we stepped into the centre of the room. He smiled pleasantly, baring his teeth just a little. "Welcome back little half-breed."

CHAPTER FIVE

The only thing that stopped me firing back a reply guaranteed to get us eaten was the fact that Rick Farlow wasn't alone in the room; in fact he was pretty much surrounded by an assortment of men and wolves. All of them seemed to have matching scowls and very white teeth. I bit my tongue and waited, moving from one foot to another as discreetly as possible to stop myself from flooding all over the gorgeous wooden floor.

Rick raised an eyebrow. "No witty retort today? My, my, we are on our best behavior aren't we? What about you, caian danje y'Eloi?"

I felt Sariel stiffen beside me. *What does that mean?*

Nothing. He's just trying to push my buttons.

Well, duh, I know that but what does it mean?

Roughly translated it means 'God's broken toy'.

Rick was talking again, standing up and walking around his desk as he spoke. "I must admit that we were most disappointed when our agreed time and date passed without the return of our property or any indication from you as to what was going on. In fact, we were all for going out there and retrieving it ourselves when we heard that you had…"

I was bored already. "Look, Rick," I stepped forward causing an outbreak of growling and snarling all around the room. I studiously ignored everyone else, although my heart was having serious palpitation problems. "Enough of the pleasantries. Take your damn knife and point me in the direction of a bathroom before there's an accident." Beside me Sariel sighed. "What?" I hissed. "I told you, I need to pee."

"Way to negotiate," Sariel stage-whispered. "You basically just told him that he can have his extremely valuable artifact so long as you can use the facilities." I made a face. "Did I mention that it's extremely valuable?"

I rolled my eyes and turned back to Rick who was watching us with obvious amusement. "Um, can I use your toilet? Then we can, er, negotiate the exchange." I smiled hopefully and he chuckled, pointing to a door set into the wall on his right.

Rick's 'ensuite' was a full sized bathroom complete with a range of built-in cupboards and a flat screen TV on the wall opposite the large claw-foot bath. Apart from the fact that the room had no windows I figured that I could quite happily have lived there and told him so, once my immediate need to pee had been taken care of and my hands and face were washed in 'tropical rain' scented soap.

Rick looked pleased with my ringing endorsement of his toilet facilities and, once I'd made my way back to Sariel's side he asked, "Shall we continue?" I nodded and, as he took a breath to start speaking again, I held up my hand. Beside me Sariel shifted his weight in annoyance. Rick lifted an eyebrow and glanced around the room at the others. "Yes, Emily. What is it now?" He asked. "Do you have a pressing need to take a nap in my bed? Or perhaps you feel the need to make a sandwich in my kitchen." There were loud guffaws around the room and my cheeks flushed with embarrassment.

He's baiting you, Emily, Sariel warned. *Don't let him rattle you.*

I took a few deep breaths to calm my burning face and then I pasted on a smile. "I'd love a sandwich, Rick. And a quick forty winks would be really welcome; although I assure you I've no interest in your bed." There were a few hastily smothered sniggers around the room. "What I was actually going to ask for is an apology."

Rick's eyes widened and another smile tugged at the corner of his arrogant mouth. His gaze flicked briefly away from me and then his eyes fastened onto mine. "What's the matter, sweet little Emily? Don't like being called a 'half-breed'?" He smiled lazily and his pack followed suit, nodding in approval.

I shook my head. "No, that's not it. I am a half breed so why would I be upset by your half-assed attempt at slander when it's the truth? No, the apology is for Sariel. You called him...let me see, what was it now?" I took a few steps forward, scratching my head.

"Emily..." Sariel whispered from the corner of his mouth. I

18

ignored him. Rick Farlow had pushed my buttons and I wasn't the type to let him get away with it.

"Yeah, that's right, you called him'caian danje y'eloi'. Wasn't that it, Rick?" I was right in front of his desk, maybe a metre away from him. "Sariel is no-one's toy, nor is he broken in any way, shape, form or fashion; so therefore that was a lie and an insult to a friend of mine. Apologise."

Rick's smile faltered for just a second and then he settled himself and moved to stand beside me, leaning in until I could feel his hair tickling my cheek. "Don't mess with me, little Emily." He whispered. "You're in a room surrounded by beasts who are a command away from ripping you to pieces. I just have to blink and your friend will be pulled apart faster than you can draw breath."

I looked towards Sariel who was looking as unconcerned as ever. I smiled and turned to Rick. He was so close I almost head-butted him as I turned. "While I was in the bathroom I put a certain artifact into my right pocket. I have my hand on it now." We both looked down at my pocket. "Sariel can look after himself, Rick. But you can't get out of range faster than I could rip your throat out with this thing. I've used it before. You may have heard." He nodded. I sighed and pulled the knife from my pocket, holding it admiringly up to the light. Rick flinched as his pack ooohed and aaahed at the sight of their beloved gold knife. I raised my voice. "I'm going to need to hear that apology very soon Rick or, much as I enjoy our little sparring sessions, Sariel and I will be forced to leave and take your lovely, sharp, Demon-slaying knife with us."

The room erupted again with shouts, snarls and snapping wolf jaws.

Have you lost your mind? Sariel stood in the middle of the room, his face calm and impassive.

Calm down. You were the one who told me they liked strength and guts.

Yes, but if you don't quit yanking his chain they'll be feasting on our guts.

He upset me.

By calling me names? Don't sweat it, Emily. It's not worth it and

19

I've been called a lot worse than that.

Not in front of me. I stand up for the people I care about.

Even when you're surrounded by Werewolves and likely to get butchered for it?

I met his eyes. *Especially then.*

Rick Farlow stepped forward and held up a hand and silence descended immediately. I tore my eyes away from Sariel and leaned back against Rick's desk. He dropped his arm and moved to stand beside me; our shoulders were touching as we surveyed the room together. Rick folded his arms and frowned.

"We have a slight problem, Emily," he said softly.

I tossed the Were knife from hand to hand, drawing the attention of everyone in the room. "What's up, Rick?"

"Well, I understand where you're coming from, I really do. I admire your commitment to your friend but even if I wanted to make some kind of apology, well," he spread his hands out theatrically. "I couldn't be seen to be weak in front of my pack. Do you understand my predicament?" He hung his head and looked at me from under his brows.

I nodded slowly, keeping my attention on the knife. "Yeah, I can see how that would be a problem. Hmmm." I jumped up abruptly, snapping my fingers and at least one of the Weres flinched. "I've got it Rick."

He raised an eyebrow. "You do."

"Absolutely. I'm not about to make you look inferior in front of your homies. I mean, you have a stellar position to uphold here and, well, I'm no specialist on Were politics or anything but I can see how issuing an apology to a female half breed Demon who almost made Demon Lord kebabs with your cute little artifact, and a Fallen Angel who survived having his innards ripped out over and over again for centuries would be really…dangerous." I met his narrowed eyes for just a moment and then pushed away from the table. "I can be flexible about this, Rick."

"Well, that's incredibly understanding of you…" he began.

"He can apologise for you." Without looking in his direction I jerked a thumb at Were goon number one whose eyes widened in astonishment.

Rick smiled and then pursed his lips. "But that would make *him* look weak," he whispered sadly.

I shrugged. "But you'd still be Alpha." He eyed me carefully and then lifted his chin.

Goon number one stepped forward and swallowed audibly. He glanced around uncomfortably and then spoke in a hushed voice. "Sorry."

I thought about making him speak up a little louder, of making a proper sentence out of it instead of just one measly word but Sariel would probably have gutted me himself if I had. I grinned. "Thank you," I said loud enough for everyone to hear. "So, are we gonna get this knife handed over then?"

The tension in the room dropped several notches as I set the knife down on the desk and stepped back a few paces. Rick laughed softly and stared at it for a few seconds before lifting his face to look in Sariel's direction. "So, you kept your promise." Sariel nodded stiffly. "Better late than never, I suppose." He rocked back onto his heels and looked around the room; his voice rose and took on a quality that I hadn't heard before. It made the hairs stand up on the back of my neck and sent a little shiver of apprehension down my spine. It was a voice full of power and authority and it rang around the room. "The agreement has been honored; Emily Carson is safe from harm."

As speeches went, it wasn't the most thrilling but it was certainly short and sweet. Rick moved back around his desk, sat down and lifted the knife reverently. His smile was self-satisfied and only slightly predatory.

Is that it? I asked Sariel.

It would seem so. I would suggest hauling ass while they are preoccupied. If we leave now, we can make the 4am train.

I nodded and clapped my hands together. "Okay! Now that we're all pals again, Sariel and I need to make tracks. Things to do, places to go, people to see and all that jazz. Been a pleasure, Rick."

Rick was still salivating over his knife. He made a vague wave

21

in our direction and one of the other goons led us from the room and took us on a much faster route through the house. He walked us to the end of the driveway and then, with a stiff little bow, left us to it.

We began walking in the direction of the train station. I checked my watch. It was just after 3:15. I yawned. "Think we'll make the train?"

Sariel shrugged. "Maybe. If you can stay awake long enough to walk that far."

I tutted at him. "I'm Supergirl, Sariel. I can walk for hours and hours and hours and…"

A car pulled out of the Farlow's drive and I blanched. "It's Adam." Sariel told me with a sigh.

"Oh, great, he's giving us a lift." I enthused as the car slowed and Adam leaned over and opened the passenger door.

Adam's giving us a lift. In his car. And his hair's all tousled like he's been sleeping. And he looks GORGEOUS. And I'm getting into his car. And he's smiling at me. And I'm just so happy I could…

Shut up? Enquired Sariel, letting himself into the back of the car.

Oops. Was I broadcasting all that?

Just a little.

Sorry. I turned on a mega-watt smile as Adam grinned at me and pulled away from the kerb.

CHAPTER SIX

Adam and I made small talk on the way to the station. It was mainly about school – what everyone was doing, how lame the teachers still were, what colour Annie's hair was now (black, apparently she was in mourning for the fact that her best friends had left without a word) – and of course all the rumours that were going around about the sudden disappearance of the Carson family en masse. Rainey High was awash with rumours; I had run off with a lover and the rest of the family had tracked me down and gone after me; I had hacked into an MOD computer and a squad of James Bond types had come in the dead of night and whisked us all away for debriefing or death; Mum and Asmodeus were getting married on Asmodeus's Caribbean island and the whole family were attending (yeuk); the Carson family was up to their arm pits in debt and, to escape the tax man, had done a moonlight flit to a far off country, starting new lives under assumed names.

"Wow," I said somberly. "Fame at last."

Adam smiled and glanced at me out of the corner of his eye. "So, how have you been?" he asked cautiously.

I shrugged. "Okay, I guess. I'm lucky to have Sariel looking out for me." Adam glanced at Sariel in the rear-view mirror but made no comment. "Have you spoken to Annie and Dylan?" I asked. "Are they okay?"

Adam made a face. "I, um, haven't had the chance to talk to them," he said and shifted uncomfortably in his heated seat.

"But they're okay, right?" I asked, leaning towards him a little. How hadn't he spoken to them?

"They seem a bit shook up that you've all just suddenly gone but they're okay."

I sat back in my seat. "I wish I could speak to them, explain. They must think we're such…gits." I said softly, looking out the window to disguise the sudden onslaught of tears. Adam touched my arm gently and I turned to look at him, brushing the back of my hand across my eyes.

"It's better that they don't know." He told me. "Asmodeus can't use them for leverage if they don't know anything." I nodded miserably as we pulled into a parking space outside the deserted station.

We all climbed out of the car and walked to the edge of the car-park. Sariel told us to stay put while he checked the station and Adam nodded, pulling me into the shadow of the concrete steps leading towards the platform. I wrapped my arms around myself and sighed, leaning back against the wall. "Where does all this leave you?" I asked.

Adam looked at me in alarm. "What do you mean?" He asked.

I chewed on my bottom lip. "I'm worried about my friends, Adam. Will Asmodeus go after people that I know to try and find us?" Tears welled again and Adam sighed and pulled me into his arms. He smelled of warmth and spices and an earthy, man smell or maybe it was a wolf smell. Whatever. He smelled good.

"Asmodeus has other ways of finding you, Emily. Demons don't just go around grabbing people off the street. They have to live amongst the population without drawing too much attention to themselves. Like us."

I snuggled into his warmth and took a shuddering breath. "Sorry. I just worry that someone'll get hurt because of me. He's bound to know that we know each other, and who you are. What if he attacks the pack because of that? Is everyone we turn to for help a target now? If Asmodeus starts to hunt down our friends he'll have a pretty short list but there's no-one on it that I want to see hurt."

"Yeah," Adam said, "Dad says that's why you and the Fallen get along so well – neither of you really belong anywhere." Annoyed, I raised my eyes to look at him and caught a glimpse of a strange expression on his face but then I couldn't think about anything anymore because Adam was kissing me. His lips were warm and moist and he tasted like caramel and spices.

Adam Farlow's kissing me! Adam Farlow's kissing me. Oh. My. God.

Adam's arms tightened around me and I could feel his

shoulder muscles bunch under my hands as I looped my arms around him. This was me. Kissing Adam Farlow and it felt…nice. Hmmm. I concentrated on the kiss, on his lips, his arms, his hands moving in lazy circles on my back and it felt…okay. But it wasn't the explosion of light and heat that I'd been expecting. This was confusing, disappointing and more than a little disturbing.

Adam pulled away and smiled down at me. In that instant he looked very much like his father – self-satisfied and egotistical.

"Look after yourself, Emily," he drawled. "I'll see you soon."

"Er, yeah. Great." I stuttered, trying hard to follow the flow of this weird encounter.

"If you two have finished making out, we have a train to catch." Sariel called from the top of the steps.

"Bye Adam," I squeaked and ran up, taking the steps two at a time. I didn't look back.

CHAPTER SEVEN

The early train was more crowded than I expected. Not one carriage was completely empty and so we ended up sharing with a young couple and their over-stuffed back packs. I watched them jealously as they entwined around each other, chatting in hushed tones and giggling together over a map of London. Every now and again the girl smiled up at her companion, the adoration clear in her eyes; in return he would kiss her forehead or brush his lips against her cheek or gently caress her arm with his hand.

Stop staring, Sariel complained.

I can't help it. Do you think they're in love?

Sariel snorted aloud, causing the young lovers to look up at him in surprise and then roll their eyes at each other. I blew out my cheeks and busied myself with staring out the window at the rapidly brightening morning. I thought about Adam (again) and about his lips, how his arms had felt around me. I sighed. If only my first kiss with him had been better. Why had it not been better? All these years imagining how it would be, how I would melt into his strong arms and feel overcome with some kind of intense passion, how he would be unable to tear his lips from mine, how our hearts and souls would entwine for all eternity and ...yeah, okay so maybe I was learning that the whole teenage romance thing wasn't quite the same in real life as it was in the movies. Damn. I sighed and Sariel shifted beside me and leaned over.

"You okay?" He whispered and I looked up at him in astonishment.

"You're speaking aloud," I told him.

"It's been known to happen." He grinned. "So what's up?"

I shook my head and stared at my hands. "Nothin'."

"Liar."

I sighed. "Hormonal stuff." He raised an eyebrow. "Adam kissed me."

He made a face. "I noticed that little detail." He folded his arms and his mouth set into a grim line. Well now. This was interesting. I sat up a little straighter and couldn't quite stop a small smile from creeping across my lips. Sariel looked...jealous. Ha! Sariel noticed my satisfied grin and frowned. "He's not good enough for you, that's all," he grumbled.

I faked a yawn. "Bored already. We've had this conversation before, remember? You wanted to know why I was wasting my time waiting for him to notice me when there are plenty of other guys around. You said that I was too pretty to be letting the other guys pass me by."

"I never said that." Sariel growled but didn't look as though he'd entirely convinced himself.

"Now who's the liar," I sat back happily.

"So, you're happy that he's finally realized you're worth some of his precious time?" Sariel leaned in again and his eyes searched mine.

"Ecstatic." I told him. "Not only is he gorgeous and muscled in all the right places but he kisses like a...like a..." I paused and chewed on my bottom lip. Like a what? A robot? A hoover? A Labrador? Where was I going with this? "Well, obviously he kisses so good that my brain has shorted out." I finished lamely.

"Sounds great," Sariel said and it wasn't hard to hear the laughter in his voice. "Almost makes me wish that he'd kissed me too."

I frowned at him. "Oh, I didn't think you were...you know. That way inclined."

Sariel shook his head. "I'm not but you just made kissing Adam sound like the best darn thing in the universe." He chuckled.

Smart ass.

Sariel sighed. "Look, if you're happy and he's not going to hurt you then I'm pleased for you. Ok?"

I nodded. It was officially time for this conversation to end. I wasn't comfortable discussing Adam's kissing ability (or lack of it) with Sariel. "I'm going to try and catch some sleep."

"Good idea. We're meeting your mum and Seth around nine so if you get some rest now then we could get some breakfast on the way." Sariel moved over a little and tugged my head onto his shoulder. "Here, make yourself comfy."

The bitchy part of my brain was telling me to pull away and lean against the window instead but snuggling up beside Sariel felt so warm and secure and yes, dammit, comfy, that I ignored it and closed my eyes.

Chapter Eight

I woke with a start and it took a few moments to figure out what had roused me from such a deep sleep. I was still cuddled close to Sariel and we were still on the train although our travelling companions had left the compartment. Daylight was streaming in through the window and making all the dust particles in the air sparkle like dancing diamonds. Sariel jumped beside me and I sat up a little.

He was asleep, his head back and rolling around on the lumpy seat as he fought a nightmare of some kind. His right arm was tight around my shoulder but I barely noticed. It was his left hand I was focused on. His fist clenched and unclenched, his knuckles were white and every time his hand opened I could see little red crescents where his nails were biting into the tender skin on his palm. Concerned, I sat back a little further and his arm fell away from my shoulder.

"Sariel," I whispered. Was it a good idea to wake someone up when they were having a nightmare? Probably not but I tried again anyway. "Are you ok?" I knelt on the seat to get a better look at his face. His brow was furrowed and his lips were pulled down in a grimace of distress. He made a noise in his throat – a sound somewhere between a growl and a moan. I took a breath and looked around the compartment for help. For the record; train décor does not offer any kind of inspiration to weary travelers whose companions have gone all 'Paranormal Activity' on them.

Okay. I was going to wake him up and hope that was the right thing to do. I stood up and was leaning towards him when he suddenly bolted up from his seat and I fell back, my eyes like saucers and my heart trying to leap out of my mouth. "No!" He shouted and turned towards me. I shrank back in shock.

Sariel's eyes were changing colour. Dark violet was spreading across his silver blue irises like ink in water and his lips were drawn back from his teeth in a snarl of rage. "They've made a bid. I should've known. I'll kill them all. Li ucciderò." His voice had changed too. It was a guttural growl that made every hair on the

29

back of my neck stand to attention.

"W…who made a bid for what?" I asked in a tiny voice. Every nerve in my body was sizzling with adrenaline. I was scared. More afraid than I'd ever been before and trying to hold strong to the belief that Sariel was one of the good guys and wouldn't hurt me.

Sariel stared at me as though he had forgotten I was there. His face contorted and I read fear there, mixed with anger and maybe even a touch of desperation. His hands fisted and he closed his eyes, taking deep breaths. I clutched the seat behind me and slowly pulled myself to my feet, watching him closely all the time. He was obviously working hard to calm himself down and I didn't know what to do to help him.

What will I do? I asked softly.

For a few seconds Sariel's mind was open to me and I almost fell down again under the assault of images and emotions. There was a brief glimpse of Rick Farlow and his smug grin, a brief glimpse of me in Adam's arms (wow, we made a pretty cute couple), a dark room with a screaming Angel strapped to a stone altar and then a red curtain was drawn across it all as anger descended and Sariel forced me out of his head.

He opened his eyes for a moment and I saw how dark they had become, almost pure black with just a tiny swirl of silver blue left at the edges. "Run," he growled.

I shook my head and fought to hold on to the Big Mac I'd had for dinner last night. This was insane. He was telling me to run and yet, here I still was. I shook my head, harder this time, telling myself as well as Sariel. *I'm not leaving you. What can I do to help you?*

Sariel made a sound of frustration and sank to his knees, holding his head in his hands. "Mio Dio. I don't know if I can control it. I don't want to hurt you. Please, Emily. Run." His voice was strained and my heart constricted. This was really happening. This wasn't some weird dream that I could just pinch myself and wake up from. I was suddenly very calm. I could die here, I thought. This could be it. But Sariel was in torment and my legs just wouldn't obey my brain. Besides, we were on a train. Where was I supposed to run to?

"I'm not jumping off the stupid train so tell me what to do." I told him loudly.

He stood up in front of me and his eyes opened. "Damned stubborn woman," He growled. "Distract me then. Aiutami."

Distract him. Right. How do I do that? Tickle him? Tell a few knock-knock jokes?

Sariel hissed and I could see the tendons standing out on his neck. Nope, I needed to do something fast. Something unexpected. Something that would jolt him out of...whatever this was. So, what to do - break a window? Strip off? I made a face.

"Per favore, Emily. If you're going to do something then do it soon. I can't..." His eyes were tightly closed again, sweat was beading on his brow and I made up my mind, leapt in front of him and put a hand on either side of his face.

I was braced for impact, waiting for him to turn me into Emily pancake and, when that didn't happen I leaned in a little closer to him, whispering softly. "Sariel, please, you have to stay with me. Help me here; I don't know what's happening to you. I'm scared." No response. Wait, his left eye twitched ever so slightly. Was that a good sign or not? I wrapped my arms around his neck and pulled myself up tight against him, felling the heat of his body against mine. He felt like he was on fire, burning from within and I bit my lip before continuing. "You have to snap out of this or I'm going to die and I'm not ready to die yet. I want to see my mum and Seth." I gulped and a tear slid down my cheek. That was true. I kept talking, my words coming out faster and faster. "I want to make sure they don't hate me for bringing all this down on them. I want to check on Annie and Dylan and I want to get us away from Asmodeus. I want to find out why we can hear each other's thoughts. I want you to tell me what you were dreaming about and I want to give Adam another chance to kiss me 'cause, and I'm being honest here, he wasn't all that..."

I didn't get any further. I felt Sariel relax and he leaned forward, touching his forehead to mine. "You're crying," he said in that weird growly voice that seemed to have been dragged up from the very depths of hell. "I made you cry. Mi dispiace." His arms dropped forward and slid around my waist and he opened his eyes looking deep into mine. The colour was lightening from black to dark purple with little wisps of blue filling in from the edges.

I swallowed a sudden burst of shyness. "Are you, um, distracted?" I asked and he chuckled.

"You could say that," he said in a voice that now bordered on husky and made my toes curl. He leaned in and, before I knew what he intended, he kissed my tears away with warm, gentle lips that left a trail of heat across my cheeks and down my neck. I sighed and closed my eyes as his lips found mine and the taste of him took my breath away.

The kiss deepened and his arms tightened, pulling me hard against him as his tongue swept across mine and little shooting stars went off in my head, making me dizzy and sending streaks of lightning through my blood. I kissed him back, loving the feel of his hands on my back and his body against the length of mine. Our bodies touched in several interesting places, making me forget where we were and why. This was what I wanted from Adam. This was a proper sweep-you-off-your-feet-and-send-you-insane-kiss!

Sariel pulled away, gasping and gave a shaky laugh. He looked down at his feet and took a few deep breaths. My legs wobbled, wanting to give way and I sagged against him for a moment until I gained control of my brain again. Why'd you stop? I wanted to ask. I was enjoying that!

"Scusa. Sorry," he said softly in a voice that was more or less back to normal. "I shouldn't have done that."

A stab of pain in the general area of my heart made me blink away a fresh onslaught of tears. "Well, I'm not sorry." I told him.

Sariel's head lifted and his face crumpled in dismay. "Emily, it's not that I…"

"You needed a distraction and thankfully we were able to come up with one. So," I made myself turn away and sit down before I burst into tears, "Are you going to tell me what just happened to you?"

Chapter Nine

In the end he managed to convince me to wait until we'd had some breakfast before we talked about anything deep or disturbing and so I chomped my way through sausage, egg and bacon with a side of beans and two slices of toast, all washed down with a mug of coffee (I was still a growing girl and it had been a long and rather eventful night!) as fast as I could and then sat back and waited for him to come clean.

"Breakfast hasn't taken the edge off your curiosity, has it?" Sariel asked, eyeing my now-empty plate with amusement. I shook my head and he sighed. "Okay, but I guarantee you're not going to like it."

I rolled my eyes. "Quit with the melodrama. I've dealt with being told that Angels and Demons exist, that I have Demon blood, that you're a Fallen Angel, that we can have a telepathic chat whenever we feel the need and that Werewolves are living in the forest near my house and go to school with me. I think I can handle whatever you care to throw at me."

He grinned. "When you put it like that…"

"Exactly. So what's the sitch?"

"Sitch?"

"Situation."

"What is the problem with teenagers constantly feeling the need to shorten every word until they make no sense to anyone?" Sariel shook his head. "I don't get it."

"That's because you're not a teenager. You're, like, ancient with a capital 'A'. Now quit changing the subject and spill."

"Spill?"

I made a frustrated tutting sound. "You know what that means. I'm not a stupid kid." *Don't kiss me like a woman and then talk to me like I'm a child.* The words flew through my head before I could censor them and we looked at each other across the table for a moment. "Ignore that. This isn't the time. I want to know about you. What happened and why. Maybe if I know more about it, I'll be better equipped to deal with it next time."

"I'm not intending to let it happen again," Sariel told me, frowning.

"So you let it happen?"

He sighed and shook his head. "Not exactly." He ran a hand through his hair which made him look very young and very cute. Not that I was concerning myself with Sariel's cuteness. No sir. "As far as we can figure..."

"Wait, 'We'? Who's 'we'?"

"I have, um, friends who are pretty clued up on the whole Demon/Angel thing. I go to them for advice when I have a concern or when something...out of the ordinary comes my way." Sariel glanced at me briefly and then looked away again. "Anyway, we think that the amount of time that I have spent in this realm and the psychological scars of such a long time being tortured by Daeshan, plus perhaps my close proximity to Asmodeus and his House and maybe also my job for Asmodeus..."

"Could we get to the juicy stuff?" I asked, tapping my watch.

Sariel chuckled. "Sorry, too much detail?" I nodded. "Okay, well we think that a number of factors have contributed to a change in my personality. Ish." I raised an eyebrow and he sighed. "Okay, basically..."

"Finally."

"Basically, unless I can control my temper I can sometimes go a bit..." he made a face, as if searching for the right word or phrase to help me understand. To help the child in front of him comprehend the physical and perhaps mental changes that she had just seen with her own eyes.

"You go a bit 'Reagan'." I finished for him.

Sariel looked at me in confusion. "As in the president?"

I shook my head. "As in the little girl in 'The Exorcist'."

"Your mother let you watch that?" He looked aghast.

I shrugged. "I'm not easily scared. So anyway. Once you're... possessed."

"Well, I'm not possessed by anything. I just kind of lose my temper. Like nuclear."

"Define 'nuclear'," I asked leaning forward. Finally we were getting somewhere.

Sariel sighed and shifted nervously in his seat. "Well, apparently my eyes change colour." I nodded. "My voice deepens." Check. "And, if I can't control it, I, well, I kind of..." He blew out his cheeks and chewed on his bottom lip. It took all my will power not to look at his lips and remember the taste of them. "I burn everything around me." He finished and I looked up, startled.

"You 'burn' everything?" I thought about that for a moment, sensing Sariel watching my reaction closely. "I take it that you aren't harmed when you burn stuff." He shook his head. "And when you said nuclear, was that an over-statement or were you being literal?"

"Well, I haven't leveled any cities or continents yet but I have pretty much burned buildings to the ground."

"And Demons? Have you burned Demons?" He nodded. I hesitated but made myself ask the next question. "And humans?" He nodded again, slowly, his eyes fixed on my face. "And they died?" I couldn't help that my voice sounded small and afraid. In front of me sat a being capable of burning me to a cinder if he got agitated. Great. As if I didn't have enough things to deal with. I made a deal with myself that if I ever met up with God, I was going to have some serious words with Him about the number of things a teenager can handle and not go insane.

Right then, however, Sariel was waiting. I took a breath and smiled at him. It came out crooked, I could feel it, but I kept it on my face. "So, we just have to make sure that you don't get pissed off then," I told him brightly.

He nodded again and returned my smile but his eyes were sad and I wanted so much to try and make him feel better; to tell him that it was okay, that I still trusted him and knew that he'd never hurt me; but the words wouldn't come, I just couldn't find a way to say what I was feeling and the moment passed.

Sariel paid for our breakfast and we walked out into the sunshine of a glorious spring morning in central London. I pushed everything to the back of my mind and concentrated on the fact that in just over an hour I would see mum and Seth again. That was something to look forward to. Wasn't it?

CHAPTER TEN

The store that Sariel had chosen as a meeting place was busy and noisy. Dance music was playing at ear-splitting volume and the aisles were packed with a variety of shoppers ranging in age from a three year old tugging on his mother's hand to an elderly couple browsing the Country Music section. The majority, however, were teenagers and I felt instantly at home.

Sariel glanced around as we entered the store, checking out everyone on the ground floor with us in a single sweep. Taking my hand he dragged me past the endless displays of current top ten singles, albums, movies and posters and up a set of metal stairs onto the mezzanine floor where he would have a good view of the entrance. A quick check of our fellow browsers upstairs showed zero Demon activity and so we settled to wait at a display of music compilations which overlooked the steps and ground floor.

I was excited and nervous about seeing my family again – a dangerous combination for a seventeen year old – and it was easy to fall into the kind of bantering conversation with Sariel that I might have had with Annie and Dylan on a day out shopping in Ipswich. We compared compilations – slagging off each other's choices with relish, nudging each other when we found a song we liked, looking for something that we thought might annoy or embarrass each other. In short, we acted like a normal teenage couple.

"Damn." I said softly. "I'm so sorry, Sariel, but they don't seem to have any Gregorian Chants in this section. Would you like me to ask them to look some out for you?" I looked at him with puppy dog eyes and he grinned.

"That's okay Emily, they have something for your age group. Here you go." He reached me a compilation of something called the 'Mini-pops' which seemed to be five year olds singing pop songs. I rolled my eyes and slotted it back into place.

"Juvenile." I told him. "Ooh, look they have our song on here." I waved my choice in front of him excitedly.

"We have a song?" He took the case from me and scanned the

list on the back of it.

"Of course we have a song," I told him, pulling another cd out to look at it. "Everyone has a song."

"Isn't that just for couples?" His voice sounded odd.

"No, Annie and I have a song, Dylan and I have a song. Seth and I have a song. Mum and I have a song. I even have a song that reminds me of Adam."

"Yeah me too – 'How much is that doggy in the window?'" He chuckled and then made a face when I glared at him. "Okay, okay. Wait, you and SETH have a song?!" Sariel's eyes were round in amazement.

"What? Just 'cause we're brother and sister and we fight a lot doesn't mean we can't have a song." I admonished.

"So what's the song? Does Seth know about this?" Sariel was looking at me with interest.

"I don't care if Seth knows or not. He should do but then he's an idiot boy so he'll probably not catch on 'till he's in his nineties and walking with the aid of a Zimmer frame." *If we live that long*, I pushed that train of thought firmly away. "You know that Terrorvision song, 'Tequila'?" Sariel nodded and I found myself grinning just thinking about it. "My mum played it loads when we lived in our apartment in Seattle. Seth and I must have been about 6 and we used to totally rock out every time she put it on. Every time I hear it it's like being back then. I get such a warm feeling here." I rubbed my stomach absentmindedly. "I remember us giggling and laughing and dancing and singing at the top of our voices. Mum was worried we'd start singing it at school and they'd think she was feeding us tequila instead of juice or something." I laughed, a tight little sound that made my throat suddenly close up and tears spring into my eyes. I blinked them away. "I miss my brother." I said with a crooked grin. "But if you ever tell him I said that I'll have to kill you."

Sariel laughed. "So," he waved the cd in front of me. "Which one of these do you think is our song?"

I leaned over and pointed down the list, very aware for a moment that we were standing close together, our arms touching, and my head close to his shoulder. "This one." I pointed it out and he chuckled. A second later the dance music was gone and The Plain White Tees "Delilah" was blasting around the shop and heads were lifting all around the shop in confusion. I laughed. "That's it. Our song."

Sariel grinned and cocked his head to the side listening. I looked at him; his dark hair was getting long again, curling below his ears and at the back of his neck. Even his fringe was longer – down below his brows – and I had the urge to reach out and push it back so I could see the incredible silver-blue of his eyes. Should Fallen Angels be beautiful? If the bible was to be believed then God had made them and us in His image so did God look something like Sariel? Or did he look like Pee Wee Herman? Phillip Seymour Hoffman?

Sariel was staring at me. *What are you thinking about?* He asked.

I frowned. *Can't you hear?* He shook his head. *Nothing important.* I told him. *Just wondering what God looks like. Brad Pitt or Pee Wee Herman?*

Sariel spluttered with laughter. *Oh, that's good. You'll have to ask …* He frowned.

Ask who?

He took my arm and pulled me behind him. *It mustn't be safe for them to come. Looks like we'll have to go to them. Stay behind me.*

Cold fear settled over my heart. Not safe? How did he know? Gulping down a wave of panic I followed Sariel down the stairs as the shop staff gained control of their PA system and retro dance music began to blast again.

CHAPTER ELEVEN

Sariel pulled me back outside and into the flow of people-traffic. We hustled from one side of the pavement to the other, dodging and weaving around mothers with push-chairs, suited executives, a tight knot of retro-punks (with hair colours that Annie would've loved), several pensioners and a young priest resplendent in cassock and collar. I had time to wonder if Londoners ever did anything at a leisurely pace – everyone seemed to be in a hurry to get somewhere and not all of them could be on the run from Demons!

We turned right into a side-street and then left down an alley behind some shops. We practically flew the length of the alley, Sariel dragging me along behind him and me feeling ridiculously out of shape as I puffed and panted behind him.

Back onto the main thoroughfare, Sariel turned right again into the stream of pedestrians and we began the whole process again.

Where are we going?

We're following Liz.

Who's Liz?

A friend. She's been looking after your family.

Oh. What does she look like? I craned my neck around a city slicker busily talking on a hands free kit that made him look like a bizarre alien creature from 'Star Trek'.

Sariel turned to grin at me. *She looks a little like the queen.*

Right. So we're running through London hot on the heels of a woman called 'Liz' who looks like Queen Elizabeth?

Yep. Although Liz is a few centuries older than the monarch and looks a few decades younger.

I sighed. *Well, being on the run with you is never dull, Sar.*

We reached the entrance to Caledonian Road Station and ran down the steps, stopping briefly to buy tickets from a machine and then heading through the turnstiles and down another corridor to wait for another train.

I couldn't see anyone who looked like the Queen standing

at the side of the tracks and after catching the eye of a cute guy standing a few feet away for the fourth time I gave up trying to find her. The train arrived with a wheezing growl and a blast of warm subway air and I began to walk forward to join the queue of eager travelers. Sariel's hand on my arm stopped me. He was looking across the station towards the exit. I followed his gaze and my breath caught in my throat. Standing there and watching everyone who left the station was a tall thin male of about nineteen with copper hair and hard, feverish eyes. Even from across the station I could sense his wrongness.

What is he?

Vampire. Nybbas must be covering London.

Oh, crap. Vampires. Remembering Nybbas made my skin crawl. He was one of the majorly creepy Demons that Asmodeus had introduced Seth and me to at the birthday party held in our honour last August. He had, unfortunately, taken rather a shine to me. Yeuk. Just thinking about his skeletal appearance, long fingernails and the gleam of his fangs as we'd left the party made me shudder. Brad Pitt and Tom Cruise in 'Interview with a Vampire' were gorgeous, Rob Pattinson in 'Twilight' was damn fine, Nybbas and his cronies were just gross. I shook my head. *How come they get such great press?*

Sariel was pushing me into the shadow of one of the pillars behind us. *Vampires? Their mind control abilities are incredible.*

I swallowed. *Better than yours? I mean - could they work their mojo on me?*

Sariel turned to face me, glancing over his shoulder even as he shielded me from view. *Doubtful but I wouldn't like them to get close enough to try.*

So what do we do? I asked.

Sariel grinned. *We keep you safe and let Liz handle it. She's good at this stuff.*

Wait, Liz is here? Where? I craned my neck to try and see around Sariel.

Abbi pazienza, Emily. Just wait.

The train had filled and the doors were beeping to warn

passengers that they were about to close. A few late comers sprinted across the platform and slipped through and then the train was pulling away and the Vampire's eyes were on the platform instead of the exit.

Wherever she is, she's cutting it fine. If he looks in our direction he'll recognise you.

Again with the patience, Em. .

I blew out my cheeks in annoyance. *I have a slight patience problem, as you well know, and if she doesn't…*Whatever I may have been about to say was lost as a woman of about fifty with graying hair and wearing a plain navy skirt and a pale pink twinset seemed to materialise from the shadows and raced up the exit ramp, pausing only briefly to plunge a knife into the chest of the Vampire before continuing on her way. My mouth was still open in astonishment as Sariel pulled me around the pillar and across the platform. The Vampire was looking at the hilt of the knife protruding from his chest with a comical detachment. He looked up as we approached and his look of confusion was replaced by panic. He lifted a hand to strike out at us but Sariel was too fast, yanking the knife from the Vamp's chest and then loping off his head without slowing down. I gave a yelp as the head, now with a 'how-the-hell-did-that-happen' look on its face, fell a few feet in front of us and began to roll towards me. Thankfully my brain managed to figure out that jumping over the thing would be a good idea and then we were on the escalator and out onto the footpath again. Sariel kept walking, slipping an arm around my shoulders to keep me moving forward.

Are you ok? He was asking gently. I found myself incapable of even thinking straight, never mind speaking coherently and so I just nodded. *I'm sorry you had to see that but it was necessary.* I nodded again. I understood that the Vampire would have killed us without a moment's hesitation but still, seeing a guy get his head detached from his neck on a subway exit is abnormal, even for me.

Sariel hailed a cab and gave an address as we slipped into the back seat. I shook my head to clear it. This was no time to freeze up. Mum and Seth were here somewhere so I had to get with the program and leave the whole 'dead dude' thing until later.

Five minutes, Sariel told me and I took a few deep breaths.

You think they're okay?

He nodded, knowing immediately who I was talking about. *Liz wouldn't let anything happen to them. She's a tough lady.*

Yeah so I noticed. Remind me never to piss her off either.

Either?

Well you could fry me and she could stab me in the heart. Neither would be a good thing.

He tried to smile but it wobbled alarmingly. "I'm sorry," he told me softly.

I shook my head, guilt flooding my heart. "If you and Liz weren't …how you are, I'd be dead. Mum and Seth probably would be too. I'm not sorry, Sariel. I'm grateful." I reached over and squeezed his hand. He looked down at it and then opened his palm, letting me fit my hand into it. He opened his mouth to say something but the cab was pulling into the kerb and the moment had passed. He released my hand and we stepped out onto the pavement in front of a shelter for the homeless.

Sariel paid the cab and then stepped up to the door and pressed the intercom button. There was a fizz of static and then a male voice announced. "We're full at the minute, Pal. Try again tomorrow."

"Can you tell Liz that her son is here," Sariel asked pleasantly.

'Son?' I mouthed and Sariel grinned.

There was a brief silence and then a woman's voice came through loud and clear. "Come on up, sweetie."

The door buzzed and Sariel pushed it open closing it carefully behind us again. I came face to face with a dark skinned man who smiled and spoke with a lilting Caribbean accent. "She be up dem stairs now. Third door on da right."

We thanked him and headed up a set of creaky stairs past hand written signs for free clinics and soup kitchens. A few people passed us on the way down, nodding a greeting and then continuing on their way. There was a heavy smell of pine and

42

sadness in the air and everyone we saw looked weary and slightly confused – but the place felt safe to me, calm and quiet after the press of bodies on the street and the noise of traffic and stale reek of exhaust fumes. Passing the rooms on the left of the corridor was an education – each room had maybe five beds in it and they were filled with people sleeping, reading dog-eared paperbacks, talking and laughing quietly or just sitting on the beds staring into space. We had gone for almost three weeks now without a permanent address – staying with friends of Sariel's mostly, sleeping rough just three times – and until now I hadn't imagined never having a proper home again. I felt suddenly close to tears and was glad when Sariel, perhaps sensing my mood, reached over and took my hand again.

We stopped at the door and knocked.

Chapter Twelve

The woman from the station opened the door and waved us in, pointing to the phone at her ear, then walking back across the floor of her office and slipping back in behind the desk. "Yes, Alistair," she was saying, "I totally understand and of course we would love for Sir Elton to visit at any time that is convenient to him. I'm simply asking if we should expect the press or if this is going to be a personal visit?" She listened for a few moments, nodding and absentmindedly twirling the phone flex around her index finger. "Absolutely. When were you thinking? Let me just check the schedule…"

Sariel and I sat down on a small camel coloured sofa that smelled vaguely of citrus air freshener and I had a chance to study 'Liz'. Sariel was right; she had a remarkable resemblance to her rather more famous crown-wearing namesake – same perfectly coiffed steel-coloured hair, same understated elegance, same charming old-lady smile. I was pretty sure that the queen didn't go around stabbing Vampires, although I had to admit that stranger things had happened recently so it was probably best not to discount the idea.

Liz finished her call and set the phone down. She regarded us across her desk for a moment. "Tea?" she asked. Sariel shook his head but I found myself nodding. What is it about elderly people and tea? Liz pressed an intercom button. "Joan, could we have two cups of tea please? Thank you." That done she folded her hands on the desk in front of her and smiled. "Now then. Where shall we start?"

"Are they okay?" I asked quickly as Sariel tried to speak.

Liz raised an eyebrow. "Well, of course they are. They're in my care, aren't they?"

Sariel opened his mouth but again I was quicker. "So why didn't you bring them to the store?" I asked, ignoring Sariel's glare.

Liz unfolded her hands and sat back in her chair. "As you probably noticed, Nybbas and his children are patrolling the city, day and night. Taking them out unnecessarily would be folly." She glanced at Sariel, "I take it you finished it off?" Sariel nodded and she smiled. "We shall have a cup of tea and then I shall take you to them." She turned her blue eyes to me. "Will that be acceptable?"

I wilted under that piercing gaze and felt immediately like a nine year old caught passing notes in class. "Yes, of course. I'm sorry. I just miss them. Thank you for keeping them safe. I don't know what I would have done if anything had happened to them."

Liz's eyes softened. "Of course you miss them, dear. And they've been missing you too. I've been keeping them up to date with where you've been and what you've been doing but it's not the same as seeing a loved one in the flesh, is it?" I shook my head. "And you have had quite a time of it, haven't you?" She clucked her tongue. "Such a shock all of this, isn't it? Finding out the truth of things. I'm told you've handled it much more calmly than most," her gaze flicked to Sariel and then back to me, "Still, you must still feel a little as though you're in a dream and can't quite wake up."

I was thinking about that when the door was knocked and a woman came in carrying a tray. Liz jumped to her feet and cleared a space on her desk. "Wonderful, thank you, Joan."

Joan smiled widely and left the room again, her gaze lingering hungrily on Sariel who pretended not to notice.

"Milk and sugar, dear?" Liz asked.

"Er, just milk." I accepted the mug which had a picture of William and Kate on it, and took a sip. It was good, strong, English tea, just like my Grandma made and I sat back in my chair with a sigh of contentment.

Liz smiled. "I suppose you're wondering what an old lady wearing a twinset is doing running around London, stabbing Vampires and harbouring fugitives?" I nodded. She took a sip from her own mug and studied me carefully. "What has he told you?" She asked and I grinned at the comical look of exasperation on Sariel's face.

"I've told her enough," he said.

Liz made a harrumphing sound. "I very much doubt that." She turned back to me. "Has he, for example, told you what he is?" I nodded and she looked impressed. "Well, that's progress. And what happened to him ...down there?"

45

"Yes, I met Daeshan." I told her with a certain amount of pride. Daeshan had tortured Sariel for centuries after catching him and ripping off his wings. "I hope I get the chance to meet him again." I couldn't quite keep the anger out of my voice and Liz's eyebrows rose above her mug. "He was horrible." I told her. "Almost as bad as Dennis." Liz choked, spluttering a mouthful of tea onto her desk. She pulled a tissue imprinted with roses from a box on her desk and mopped it up. I wondered if I should pretend nothing had happened or ask her if she was ok – what did you do in these situations? I decided on discretion and went on talking. "Daeshan looked much more like a Demon to be honest – Dennis just looked like a weedy weirdy." Liz spluttered again, threw back her head and roared with laughter. I turned to look at Sariel for guidance. He was almost purple in the face trying not to laugh too. I set my tea down on the table and folded my arms. "What's so funny?" I asked, earning a fresh eruption of laughter. I tutted and rolled my eyes. "None of you people are normal." I muttered.

Liz eventually wiped her eyes and sat back, holding her stomach and shaking her head. "Oh, my dear, you are quite the most interesting creature I've met in a very long time. A 'weedy weirdy' indeed. That's priceless." She stood up and looked into my mug. "Finished? Good. I think we should be on our way. Don't want to leave you late for your rendezvous with Ron." She stood up, dragging a light jacket from the back of her chair and lifting an oversized brown leather handbag from beneath the desk. I eyed the bag nervously. The woman had seemed to pull a knife out of thin air to stab the Vampire; God only knew what she kept in her handbag.

Liz opened her office door and we filed through, walking back down the stairs and out onto the pavement. Liz flagged down a taxi and as we climbed in I heard her whisper to Sariel, "We thought we'd lost you." I looked back at him but there wasn't time to ask questions. Liz was chatting about living in London, the price of taxi fares, the incredibly mild weather for the time of year, her favourite 'X-Factor contestant' and so on. I tuned out and stared out the window. We were on our way to mum and Seth.

Chapter Thirteen

Seth had me in a bear hug and had whirled me around several times before I could catch a breath to speak. Mum was standing watching us with her hand over her mouth and tears in her eyes. After hugging Seth back I reached out for her and she came forward to stand with her arms wrapped around both our waists. My tears fell then. I couldn't help it. One minute I was erupting with happiness at being with them again, the next I was sobbing; great gut wrenching sobs that had my shoulders shaking and my stomach muscles heaving. Tears slid down my face and landed on Seth's shoulders. Mum was crying too and gripping us tightly, her fingers digging into my waist. We must've looked a mess but thankfully we were out of sight, alone in a small terraced house down a road I didn't know the name of somewhere in London.

I disentangled myself and looked carefully at my mother and brother. Apart from all the tears (and, in Seth's case, some snot too) they looked well. Mum had lost a little weight and her face was pale above a deep plum t-shirt but she looked healthy enough. Seth was…Seth. He looked no different from the last time I'd seen him – maybe his eyes were a little more wary, a little less care-free but that was only to be expected. Guilt hit me hard and I stepped away from them both, suddenly uncomfortable and awkward. I stared at my hands.

"Emily?" My mother's voice was quiet but filled with concern I lifted my head and she was looking at me with eyes so large with confusion that I had to look away again. "What is it, baby?"

I took a deep breath. "I'm so sorry," I told them. My voice came out as a whisper. There was silence and I looked up. Seth was frowning. Mum was looking from me to Seth.

"What did she say?" she asked.

"She said that she was sorry," Seth told her. He reached out and took my hand, pulling me back into a hug. "What are you apologizing for you silly mare?"

"This is all my fault," I whimpered into his t-shirt. "You'd still be at home now, comfortable and safe, if I hadn't…" I bit my lip.

"If you hadn't stopped that monster from hurting Sariel," my mother finished. Her voice was strong and clear. I looked over at her. She was looking at me calmly now - her tears had dried and her confusion was gone. She reached out and stroked my cheek tenderly. "Never, ever, be sorry for doing the right thing, Emily. If you'd known that something was going on and didn't do anything, *then* I would've been disappointed in you. I didn't raise my children to let bullies hurt people."

"Oh, mum, Seth. I've been so worried about you guys. I've missed you so much…" She moved forward and I was back in her arms. It felt good. It felt safe.

They forgive me, I told Sariel.

Told you. I could hear the smile in his voice.

Where are you? Do we have to leave soon?

I'm not far, Em. Forget about everything else for now, just enjoy the moment.

Satisfied, I felt a little of the tension seep from my shoulders and I relaxed.

Mum made us tea in the little kitchen at the back of the house while Seth and I caught up. Liz had come to our house early in the morning that Sariel and I had gone on the run. At first mum had refused to even let her into the house but once she had broken the door down there was really nothing that mum could do about it.

"She broke the door down?" I was incredulous.

Seth nodded. "Yep, tore it right off the hinges. I don't know exactly who that lady is but I can tell you one thing; I'm sure as hell never getting on the wrong side of her!" I giggled and told him about the stabbing of the Vampire in the subway. Seth's eyes widened to the point of popping out of his head as I recounted the chopping off of the head and how I'd jumped over it. "So, you really did it then?" Seth asked shyly. I frowned. "You really stabbed Asmodeus?"

I shifted uncomfortably in my chair and then I took a deep breath and nodded. "Yeah, I did. He was torturing Sariel."

"That's what Liz said. How did you know that he was torturing

Sariel? Liz said that they were in some cavern or something and you were in the house. That you got someone to take you to the place..."

"Alexa," I told him with a smile.

"No shit?! Wow. So Alexa took you to the place and you stabbed Asmodeus." I nodded again. "So how did you know that it was all going down?" I squirmed as Seth's eyes studied me closely. "Look, Em. I know there's some weird shit going on here." He threw up his hands and laughed mirthlessly. "Hell, we've been dealing with weird shit for months now. I just don't want to be kept in the dark anymore about all this stuff. If we're in such big trouble then I wanna know about it. How can I protect myself, and mum, if I don't know what's going on?" He had a point. So I gave him the condensed version from when I first heard Sariel's voice in my head, right to the present, when not having him in my head would be odd. When I'd finished Seth shook his head and studied his hands. I wasn't sure what reaction I'd been expecting but no reaction?

"Dude, say something." I said, fake punching him on the arm. He sighed and was about to speak when mum came back into the room with a tray. Seth's eyes found mine above the plate of cheese and crisp sandwiches and the warning in them was easy to read. I gave him a brief nod to show I understood not to say anything in front of mum and we tucked into mugs of tea and sandwiches that Scooby Doo would've been proud of.

I studied mum as she poured more tea and saw the tight worry lines around her mouth, the concern in her eyes that she tried to hide, the slight shake in her hand. Seth was right – mum didn't need to know the details right now.

We played at happy families for almost an hour and then Liz came back into the house, closely followed by Sariel. Liz smiled at us. "Sorry to break up the party, folks but if Sariel and Emily want to make their rendezvous with Ron then they'll need to be going soon."

I nodded and stood up, brushing crumbs from my jeans and earning a tut from my mother about the state of the carpet. As if that was important in the grand scheme of things! She flapped around with a dustpan and brush for a few minutes until Seth gently took them from her and set them on the sofa. "It's time for Emily to go now, mum," he told her softly.

Mum turned to Sariel and Liz. "I want to go and see them off," she said loudly. Sariel's face remained impassive but Liz frowned.

"I really don't think that's a good idea, Joanna," she said. "We're trying to keep a low profile and it'll be much easier for them to scoot across the city if it's just the two of them."

Mum shook her head and swallowed loudly. "No. We're going with them." It sounded pretty final to me. Seth began arguing with her but I kept my eyes on Sariel.

Are you going to let her come? I asked.

He shrugged. *If I do they'll be in danger. If I don't I'll probably never get out of here alive.* I grinned at that. *What do you think?* He asked, surprising me.

I turned to look at mum. Her eyes were filling with tears. "Mum," I said, touching her arm. Her eyes leaped to mine. "If you come with us to the car then you'll have to come back here with Liz. No messing around." She nodded eagerly. "And on the way there, if Sariel senses danger and tells you to leave then there'll be no arguments?" Mum looked at Sariel and then back at me. She nodded. "Okay then. I need to pee before we go. Where's the bathroom?"

Liz directed me upstairs and down a narrow landing to an old fashioned bathroom complete with a heavy-looking roll-top bath and high cistern toilet. I grinned as I washed my hands – I had certainly been in and out of a few bathrooms during the past year. I wondered what toilets in Italy were like.

Pretty much like toilets everywhere-else. Sariel interrupted my reverie and I could hear the amusement in his thoughts.

Spying on a woman while she pees is gross, I told him.

I wasn't spying.

Yeah, right.

I just wanted to say that…well… you did a good job with your mum.

I paused in drying my hands. *Are you being patronising?*

He sighed. *I was trying to pay you a compliment.*

Oh, well, in that case thanks. I was smiling when I came back downstairs and, after hanging around while Seth made himself pretty 'for the laydees' (his words not mine), we left the house and piled into a taxi.

I admit it - I was excited; Mum and Seth were okay, Asmodeus and his cohorts were, for the moment, not a problem and I was heading off to Italy with Sariel. Life was looking up.

Chapter Fourteen

It should have been easy; meet up with Ron, get the transportation etc. that he'd agreed to provide, wish Seth and mum a tearful goodbye, drive to the channel tunnel, catch a few hours kip, drive to Italy. Simple, right?

Wrong.

I'd obviously forgotten the most important law known to man – 'Everything that can go wrong will go wrong'.

We were meeting Ron at the docks - and not one of the fancy moorings like we'd been to with Asmodeus. The taxi dropped us off in front of a warehouse where a lot of large pallets were being unloaded from a huge ship. I'd never seen cranes that big before, or so many men in boiler suits creating order out of what looked to the untrained eye (mine) to be complete chaos. Sariel led us around to the back of the operation and we got to view the goings on up close and personal. It was incredible – kind of like the games Seth and I had played with his trucks and vans when we were toddlers, only on a massive scale and with much better organisation. A crane lifted a large container about the size of our house back in Kings Lynn from the belly of a mega freighter called "Fernat". The containers were stacked in rows on the dock and moved by another crane to an unloading bay at the rear of the warehouse. Pallets and pallets of shrink-wrapped commodities were taken into the depths of the warehouse by an unending stream of fork-lift trucks and no doubt sorted into the delivery vans which waited at loading bays out front. It was weirdly fascinating.

Once Sariel had managed to drag Seth and me away from watching the cranes and fork-lifts, we walked along the dock in the opposite direction for maybe half a mile.

"Ron will meet us at the far side," Sariel explained to my mother.

"And we just *had* to walk this far?" I asked with a grin.

Sariel rolled his eyes. "Approaching from further away gives us a chance to check things out, make sure everything is okay."

"You think it might not be safe?" My mother was frowning as

she spoke. I wondered if reality was finally hitting her.

Sariel smiled at her. "Ron's been doing this for a long time so I trust him but we're still being hunted so I don't want to take any chances."

Mum nodded distractedly, a small frown on her face, and Seth raised his eyebrows at me over the top of her head and I shrugged. I had no idea what she was thinking about either. She reached out and smoothed her hand over my hair. "So, what part of Italy are you going to?"

I laughed at her question. "I don't know, mum. Sariel stays tight lipped about the details. I guess I'll know when we get there."

She gave me a tight smile and turned back to Sariel. "You can tell me, Sariel. I'd just like to know where my little girl will be going." Her voice had hardened and it was a tone I'd never heard before.

Sariel's smile never faltered but I felt a shiver of unease from him through our link. He blocked whatever else he was thinking or feeling almost immediately but it was enough to make me feel a little uneasy too. Seth spoke up before Sariel could, "C'mon mum. Didn't you watch 'Independence Day" with us? What was it the FBI dude said? Something about deniability…"

"Plausible deniability, Mr. President," I told him and we giggled.

Mum was frowning. As though we hadn't spoken she turned back to Sariel. "So you're not going to tell me where you're taking her? Well, are you?" Sariel's attention was on the far end of the dock and his expression was suddenly serious.

I looked in the same direction. There was a small black car with a figure leaning against it. I smiled. This was Ron with our car. It looked like a Renault Clio maybe.

"Are you going to answer me?" Mum was still intent on getting some answers from Sariel. I tuned her out and tried to make out some more detail of the car. I hoped to God it was something with air conditioning and reclining seats.

"Mum," Seth was saying, "Leave it alone. We're better off not knowing."

"I want to know where Emily is going, Seth. We barely know this...man and I'm expected to trust him with my daughter's welfare? I don't think so. Not without getting some more answers."

A radio would be good too, I was thinking, and one of those DVD player set-ups but, considering we didn't have any DVDs maybe that wasn't such a big deal and...I paused in my wish list and squinted. We were all still walking in the direction of the car and the figure had seen us and was pushing itself upright.

Sariel and I both halted in sync. "Sariel..." I whispered.

"That's not Ron." He finished and had turned around before I could blink, catching my mother's arm. "Run!" he yelled, fiddling with something in his pocket as he flashed past Seth and me.

"What?" My mum was looking at his hand on her arm. "Leave me alone. What are you...?"

"Mum! No arguments, remember. Haul ass." I shouted and then we were sprinting back the way we'd come. Seth looked back over his shoulder once and mouthed 'Oh shit'. I didn't need to look back to know that we were being chased. This kind of thing was happening way too often for my liking. Thank God for all those daft work-outs that Sariel and Akron had made Seth and I do, although I was starting to think that those should start up again soon. Preferably before I died at the hands of some Demon.

What is it? Who's chasing us?

Vampire, Sariel told me.

Well, terrific. That was just perfect. And now we didn't just have ourselves to worry about. We also had mum and Seth to deal with. Damn. Double damn. Triple damn with sugar on top. I made a mental note to teach myself some more curse words for these kinds of situations. Could I curse when I was running alongside an Angel? I glanced back at him. His face was calm as he half dragged my mum along in his wake. She was obviously having trouble running with any speed and Sariel was looking around as we ran. There were a few more warehouses but all of them seemed occupied and I knew that he wouldn't risk the lives of anyone working in them.

Can we outrun it? I asked, although I figured I already knew the answer.

No. If we can find somewhere for you, Seth and your mum to hide then I might be able to…take care of it.

The containers? I suggested. *There were billions of them.*

Might be too far. I don't think your mum's going to make it much farther.

He was right. Mum was red in the face, her feet tripping over one another. If Sariel hadn't been there she would have given up long ago. He suddenly veered left and Seth and I followed him on a kamikaze route through one of the warehouses. Angry shouts followed us from one cavernous room to another, through an office and out onto the street. Sariel didn't pause to think, just kept going. Mum was whimpering now and Seth and I were both breathing heavily.

Sariel… I was going to say that we were in big trouble. Seth and I weren't used to this sprinting lark.

It's okay, he told me. *We just need to keep mobile and stay alive for a few more minutes. Liz is on her way.*

If there'd been time I might have hugged him with relief but as it was I considered that my best course of action right then would be to keep running and thank him later.

The street that we'd come out onto was run down with most of the crumbling houses boarded up or so far gone that they barely had walls. Sariel ducked into a narrow passage beside one of the houses and out into an overgrown back garden. It was like a jungle and I hoped that it would slow the Vampire down too. We headed in through an opening that might once have been a back door and down a narrow hall, through another crumbling door, over a pile of rubble and down another hall. It was a maze and I quickly lost all sense of direction, finding it difficult enough to keep putting one foot in front of the other. My leg muscles were screaming in agony and my lungs were burning for air but somehow we kept going and came out through another garden where the grass was as high as my shoulders. Sariel veered to the right and out into an alley behind the houses. On the far side of the road were a row of garages with their door mainly still attached. He dragged one up and I grimaced as it squealed on its runners. We slid under the door and inside, covering our mouths and noses to keep the dust out. Sariel pushed to the back and broke a rusting lock on the door, then he heaved it outwards and we were in another alley. There was a screech of tires and Seth cheered. It was Liz. We headed for the car, Seth dragging mum along after him, me following and Sariel bringing up the rear. Liz was opening the doors and I turned to grin at Sariel.

The Vampire attacked from the roof of the garage. One minute he wasn't there and the next he had flattened both of us and was dragging me over his shoulder. I didn't have time to take a breath before we were airborne and then he was running along the broken rooftops back towards the docks.

My lungs found air and I began to scream.

Chapter Fifteen

We were moving so fast that our surroundings became a blur. I only got to see where we were on the few occasions that he paused to change direction. We passed the 'Fernat' a few seconds after we'd left the others behind on the road and when I next had the chance to look we were swooping onto an office block; zziipp and we were on the roof of an elegant three storey; whoosh and we were dashing through a park; zoom and we were on waste ground. I was still screaming and not very proud of myself for it but I just couldn't help it. I briefly considered giving him a wedgie to see if that would slow him down but got side-tracked wondering if Vampires wore underwear.

My voice got exhausted and my screaming stopped but that was worse 'cause then I could hear my breath whumping out of my lungs every time we took off, landed or I thudded against his back. My legs were in front so maybe kicking him would help – with any luck I might hit something that would cause him excruciating pain. Vampires still had…man parts…right? Oh, God! I was losing my mind.

And then we stopped and I was dumped unceremoniously on the ground. Maybe two minutes had passed since he'd grabbed me and I was certain that we were miles away. I sat up gingerly and rubbed my knees which were smarting from my forced landing. I'd have wonderfully multi-coloured bruises there tomorrow. My abductor was standing in front of me – I could see his boots – but he was eerily silent and, after sticking it for as long as my limited patience would allow, I slowly looked up.

He was studying me with his head to the side and a half-smile curving his lips. I stared back. This was more like it. If all the Vampires I'd met had looked like this one then I would've understood their appeal. As it was the guy in front was, so far, a major exception to the 'Icky-Like-Nybbas' rule. He had light brown hair dusted with gold here and there, skin so pale it was practically translucent, plump lips that Angelina Jolie would've been proud of and dark brown eyes.

"I'm Lucas," he said softly. "I'm here to take you home." His voice was honeyed sweetness and the smile he gave me would normally have sent my blood pressure into the stratosphere. Unfortunately I could smell him and when I say 'smell him' I don't mean that it was a good thing. He smelled like decaying apples – sweet but moldy and it totally spoiled the whole sexy 'Sherrilyn-Kenyon-hero-type' thing he had going on. I wrinkled up my nose and made a big deal of standing up and dusting myself off.

Please tell me you're on your way, I pleaded.

I'm on my way, Sariel confirmed. His voice was hard with anger.

Are you lying?

Would I lie to you?

If you had to.

Stay alive.

Well, duh.

"Your father has missed you very much," Lucas was saying. He paced around and I shivered a little when he walked behind me. Letting a Vampire wander around behind my back is not something that comes easily – it's like letting a shark share your prawn sandwich.

I chuckled nervously. "Oh, I doubt that. Besides, I didn't miss him." I bit my tongue as soon as the words were out. What did I say that for? Way to piss off the hired help.

Lucas, however, was grinning. "No, you most certainly did not. An inch further to the left and there'd be a Lordship up for grabs."

Huh?

"Oh, I didn't mean the whole knife thing," I told him with a little-girl-giggle. "I meant..."

"I know what you meant." He interrupted. He'd stopped pacing and was standing in front of me again. His dark eyes glittered with amusement. "I find you intriguing," he said softly.

"Goody," I told him, wondering if backing away would be a good idea.

As if he'd read my mind, Lucas was suddenly at my back

again, his breath tickling my ear. I squeaked and he chuckled, the sound vibrating through his chest and across my back. "Don't be running off now, daughter of the dark. It's taken me a long time to track you down and I'd be ever so disappointed if you didn't stick around for a chat." He inhaled and I felt him shudder. "You smell...incredible." His voice shook a little and sounded a little less distinct than before. I wondered if maybe his fangs were out.

Sariel?

I'm almost there. Keep him talking.

Are you listening in?

Yes, it's a good way to track you. He sounded louder so I figured he must be getting closer. Good. That was good. Lucas slipped into view again, closer this time and I gulped. Keep him talking, Sariel had said. Right.

"So, er, Lucas. You belong to Nybbas' house then." Ok, so it was a bit weak but it was the best I could do in the circumstances.

Lucas nodded and swayed forward, taking another sniff at me. That was just weird. And embarrassing. His eyes closed and his mouth opened in pleasure and yep, there were the fangs. Crap.

"You don't look much like him," I stammered.

He opened his eyes and made a face. "I was his first born. It was a long time ago and he has...changed."

I tried to wrap my head around that. "You mean he got uglier?" Lucas threw back his head and laughed. I had to hand it to them – all these Demon types had wicked good laughs. There was no polite sniggering for this lot, no sir. They found something funny, they laughed long and loud. "I don't mean to be rude," I told him carefully. "I'm just curious."

"My father is one of the ancients and since the ruling council has made so many rules and regulations about the taking of human blood, it has made it difficult for him to keep his...looks." He grinned.

"Wait, wait, wait. There's a ruling council? Like in the Jim Butcher books?" I was stunned.

Lucas shook his head and reached out to touch my hair. When had he moved so close? "Not like that. It's the Demon hierarchy that makes the rules. We exist in the midst of this human world and if we want to remain here, and get stronger, then we have to be careful. They're always talking about their long-term goals and stuff. It's pretty boring." His eyes kept straying to my neck and I shivered. This was not good.

I'm very close now, Emily. Look around and describe what you see.

"Uh, sounds like any other human business," I told Lucas.

Big, dark, empty space. Looks like lots of posts around but I can't quite see...

Inside then. Windows?

Lucas was a step away from me, his finger had a lock of my hair curled around it and he had lifted it to his lips. His tongue snaked out and licked it. I almost threw up.

Oh, that's just gross. No, no windows. There's an echo so it's a big place. It's like a... garage underground.

What's gross? Is he hurting you? What's happening? Sariel's voice had risen an octave which was as close as he got to registering panic.

No, it's fine. Lucas is just licking my hair.

Yeah, that's Gross. Wait, you two are on fist name terms now?

Jealous?

Impressed.

Lucas leaned forward and buried his head in my hair, inhaling deeply and making little mewling noises that were just downright weird coming from a tall, dark, handsome, ancient Vampire. "Er, Lucas. You know that you're only smelling the Demon whatsits right?"

"Hmmm?"

"Y'know, the pheromones that my body releases around this age to attract other, um, Demons." Yeuk.

"Mmmm."

Great. He was obviously paying a lot of attention. "So, tell me what it's like to be a Vampire," I asked through gritted teeth as his lips grazed my ear. Now if that had been Sariel with his lips near my ear I would've been feeling something entirely different. In fact

I would probably have flipped him onto his back and jumped on him by now.

Focus, Emily. Sariel sounded amused. And much closer.

I focused on Lucas again. His hands slipped around my waist and then slid up to cup the back of my head. "Er, so, the whole Vampire thing. How's that working out for you, Lucas? Lucas?" His teeth scraped my neck and I shuddered.

"So, these pheromones are making you smell like this?" He whispered into my neck and I allowed myself a sigh of relief.

"Yeah, that's right. I wouldn't normally smell this good. If you think I do, I mean. I have no idea how I smell. I could smell like blue cheese for all I know," I hiccupped a laugh.

"You smell...it's hard to think of the right words. You smell like everything I enjoy. Like my best memories and favourite people and places. Like blood and fear and tears."

Okay, perhaps the relief had been a little premature. "So, I don't smell like chocolate?" I asked weakly.

He chuckled and I could feel his smile against my cheek. I looked up into his dark, dead eyes and forgot to breathe for a moment.

I'm going to die.

No! I'm almost there.

I didn't have to tell him that he would be too late. The look in Lucas's eyes told me that death was standing beside me, holding me in its arms and looking down at me with an expression of cruel anticipation.

"You want to know how you smell?" He asked through fangs that had slid gracefully down further as he spoke. I swallowed a sob and nodded. "You smell good enough to eat." His eyes gleamed and he kept them on me as he leaned in.

"Asmodeus won't be happy if you kill me," I told him trying to back out of his grip.

Lucas smiled. "I'm not going to kill you, daughter of the dark." Well, great! That was good, right? "I'm just going to taste you and make sure you enjoy it so much that you will be the one chasing me for more." Oh, crap.

He leaned in and bit down.

Sariel!

I'm here.

The pain was intense as the sharp fangs slid into the skin covering the little hollow between my neck and shoulder. I struggled and then the pain was suddenly gone. Lucas's arms were around me and I could feel the pull of his mouth, drawing blood out of my body. I might have whimpered, I maybe lifted my hand to try and push him away but my arm would only lift a tiny amount. I couldn't be weakening that fast, could I? My head spun for a moment and Lucas made a muffled chuckling sound before the most incredible feeling spread through my body. It was like heat and utter bliss, a blast of intense happiness mingled with desire that made my toes and fingers tingle.

And then Lucas was gone taking a chunk of my flesh, and all the good feelings he'd been projecting, with him. The pain was incredible – it felt as though the whole side of my neck was on fire and I howled and tried to sit up. The world tilted and lurched around me and I fell back again, feeling warm blood dripping down my shoulder. I looked down and then wished that I hadn't - my jacket was rapidly turning red all down one side. I was losing a lot of the red stuff.

Sariel…

My head was swimming, my neck and shoulder sizzled with pain, I couldn't seem to concentrate on what I was doing and the meagre lighting seemed to be growing dimmer with every breath I took. Was this it? Was I going to die?

CHAPTER SIXTEEN

If I was dying then it seemed to be very like eating too much ice-cream too fast – there was a brief brain freeze followed by a slow return to awareness and I drifted back into a semi-conscious state wondering if I was dreaming or if I had really died and this was hell. There were several reasons for the hell concern – first (obviously) was the whole Demon-blood thing; second was the fact that there was a flickering glow beyond my eyelids along with the hiss and crackle of what could only be flames; and finally it was the heat – not pleasant summer-day-in-Brighton heat but lung burning, soul blistering, find-me-a-bloody-igloo heat.

The only thing that made me doubt my analysis was the smell – hell should smell like burning flesh, sulfur and Demon farts, not like sunshine and honey, sweet but a little spicy. And, even though Asmodeus seemed to be pretty high up on Satan's Christmas list, I doubted that the Prince of Darkness would be cradling me in his arms, his sweat-sticky hair tickling my face and his gravel and thorns voice whispering to me in a mixture of Italian and some other language that I didn't quite recognise. Hmmm.

I was vaguely aware that I knew that scent and I inhaled to get a better grasp of it. Big mistake. Pulling scorching heat as well as pleasant aroma into my lungs was damned uncomfortable but I knew who was holding me and unless Sariel had followed me to hell (unlikely but not impossible) then I was probably still alive (yippee) for the time being.

I tried calling to him though our link but there was nothing there but red – walls of red, rivers of red – and in my current weakened state there was no way I'd be able to push against that barrier and get to him. He'd obviously lost his marbles again but why? Did he think I was dead? Couldn't he tell that I was breathing, that I was very much alive and not wishing to become Emily flambé thank you very much?

It took a lot of willpower for me to force my eyelids open and when I finally managed it I almost closed them again. The place that Lucas had brought me to was a seething mass of rippling flames – they wreathed the ceiling and all the walls that I could see in yellow and orange with angry bursts of red as they licked across the concrete.

I knew that the place couldn't just have caught fire – concrete doesn't burn – so Sariel must be doing this himself and he was, so far, protecting our bodies from burning as we seemed to be in a kind of protective bubble. The heat, however, was still incredible and I wasn't sure how long my labouring lungs would be able to hold out. Oh, yeuk, my clothes were sticking to me with an icky mixture of blood from the wound on my neck and about a gallon of sweat. God knows what my hair looked like.

Sariel shifted slightly, cradling my head a little tighter against his shoulder and I had a momentary flush of joy at the sweetness of it all. At any other time it would've been incredibly romantic even though we were probably going to die. At least I was. He'd recover. Yeah, it was okay for him he'd be able to hit Starbucks for a Caramel Frappuccino in a few days whereas I'd be burnt to a crisp. I tried to speak but my mouth wouldn't work and my throat felt raw and sore. I tried to lift my hand to touch his face or move my legs to kick him and let him know that I was okay but my limbs just wouldn't seem to obey my brain. Maybe Lucas had taken a lot of blood, or maybe I was bleeding out. Right then I was practically a walking encyclopedia of ways-to-die-in-agony and a sudden feeling of utter helplessness made tears of frustration well in my eyes.

I frantically looked around for help or a way to get his attention. I couldn't see a lot from my position against his shoulder. Could I bite his ear? Nope, not close enough and lifting my head seemed to be out of the question. Could I nip his shoulder? Nope, his damn jacket was too thick.

I started to feel a touch of real despair. The air seemed to be getting hotter, as though our little bubble was shrinking, and the air going into my lungs seemed to be carrying less and less oxygen. Sariel shifted again, jolting my wounded shoulder and I moaned. *Getting a bit warm, love?* I asked, sarcasm defeats fear and pain every time as far as I'm concerned. Then I realized that, in moving, he had brought my mouth tight against neck. Without thinking about it I forced every ounce of strength I had left into opening my mouth and biting his neck.

Sariel yelped and almost dropped me in astonishment. My head rolled back and I felt the wound on my neck open again sending a fresh wave of pain through my right side and no doubt another few litres of blood onto my clothes. I bit back on the urge to vomit and whimpered as Sariel's hand came around to cup the back of my head. He lifted me slightly and then I was looking into his eyes. My stomach rolled again and I realized that my situation was even more precarious than waking up in hell.

The beautiful silver blue irises of Sariel' eyes had been replaced by a flat black that had spread across the white sclera like an oil slick - each eye had only a thin sliver of white left at each corner and I wondered what it would mean if that small crescent of colour became covered too.

He frowned and shook his head as though trying to clear it. "You're dead," he said and I grimaced at the harsh rasping sound of him. Whatever it was that he was afraid of becoming when anger got the better of him, he wasn't far from it now.

I wanted to touch his face like I'd done on the train, to pull him back from whatever depths he'd slipped into but my body was powerless and I felt a tear slide from the corner of my eye.

Sariel saw it too and those horrible dull, spiritless eyes followed its progress down my cheek and onto his arm with no more expression on his face than if he'd been watching paint dry. It all seemed ridiculous suddenly – I'd survived Asmodeus, Nybbas, Dennis, Rick Farlow and his growly goon squad, even Lucas after a fashion. No way was I going to die in some fiery underground bunker with a fallen Angel who was acting like the village idiot 'cause he didn't know I was still alive and kicking.

As always it came down to brain power which I had in spades, and anger which was rapidly overcoming my belief that I was helpless.

SARIEL! I screamed into his head. *GET US THE HELL OUT OF HERE!*

His reaction was immediate – his head snapped back as though he'd been struck, which I suppose he had. I guess I'd just given him the psychic equivalent of a bitch-slap. His eyes opened wide and the blackness shrank back immediately into his pupils.

Huh? What...? You're dead... His mind was chaotic and I was too hot, sore and fed up to care.

Think later, I told him. *Move now.*

And we did – at a speed almost equal to Lucas we flew through the flames which died out behind us, up a ramp, under an up-and-over garage door and out into blessedly cool, fresh air. I gulped in a few lungful's as Sariel gingerly set me on the grass and began to apologise. I shook my head. *It's okay, I understand,* I told him. *You came for me, you got me out. That's all that matters now.*

He was shaking his head when he glanced down at my neck and winced. *I'm going to heal it,* he told me, *it probably won't be as pleasant as when he inflicted it.* His fingers gently pulled my sodden shirt and jacket out of the way. I could feel damp, sticky tendrils of hair being moved too and felt my stomach churn again. I was definitely going to throw up before this was all over.

I don't care, I lied as he placed his hands on the wound and closed his eyes. For a moment there was nothing but our breathing in the silence and then I felt a tingle from his hands which became a buzz before heat filled the whole area that Lucas had bitten. The heat became a wave of molten pain that slipped through my bloodstream at supersonic speed, making me cry out and then scream as it intensified. I tried to arch away from it all but his hands held me down and, just when I thought that I would pass out again, he removed his hands and the pain was gone. All of the pain. There was nothing – no acid bite from the wound, so blistering heat from the healing, no scalded lungs or weak limbs. I lay there for a few moments, amazed and grateful.

Sariel leaned into my line of vision and smiled.

"Is it okay, is there a scar?" I asked aloud, surprised and thrilled to hear my voice sounding so strong and so alive. Perhaps it was shallow of me to be concerned about a Vampire leaving a scar but, hey, I've seen the movies. Damsels in distress who go around with

Vampire bite scars never ever end up living long and happy lives.

Sariel's lips grazed the place where Lucas had ripped my neck open, sending heat of an altogether different kind zinging through my body. "It's perfect," he whispered and his voice was almost back to normal – it reminded me just then of a deep, throaty, cat-like purr which was just about as close to perfect as a man's voice was ever likely to get in my humble opinion.

"Bet my hair looks like crap, though," I told him, pushing myself up onto my elbows.

"Once you get the blood and sweat out of it, run over it a few times with a steam roller and then use a mountain of product it should be almost salvageable," he told me, chuckling.

We looked at each other with silly grins on our faces until someone coughed loudly nearby. Sariel pulled me protectively against him in the blink of an eye as Mum, Seth and Liz covered the last few feet between us and the battered Volkswagen Golf that they'd followed us in. Seth was wearing an expression of delighted curiosity; Liz looked astonished and more than a little embarrassed. Mum, however, was looking at Sariel and me, lying there on the grass, with an expression of downright hostility.

"Um, hi guys," I stuttered. "How's it going?"

Chapter Seventeen

The car journey seemed to take forever and with Liz driving it was hardly surprising. For someone who can stake a Vampire and then disappear into a crowd of Londoners in microseconds, Liz drove like a…well, like an old lady. She sat hunched over the steering wheel, peering through the windscreen as though she was chronically short sighted. Hey, maybe she was. I just couldn't quite believe that a woman who could get the drop on a fanged killer would have eyesight problems but then, what did I know? The world that I thought I knew had changed beyond all comprehension. At the moment I was just going with the flow but someday something new would pop up and even my super brain wouldn't be able to deal with it.

Sariel and I sat in the back of the VW with Seth while mum and Liz shared the front. Ah, mum. Now this was going to be a problem. The weight of her disapproving glare pressed me back against the grim, grey fabric of the seat and I studiously avoided meeting her eyes – my mother was queen of the scary, silent glare which promised a lot of shouting soon. I wondered if I concentrated enough maybe I could sink through the back of the seat and sit in the boot, at least then I'd be away from the force of her judgement. I wondered what exactly she was so upset about. Me getting caught and dragged off (you know how parents sometimes equate caring with anger at you if you get hurt?)? The fact that Sariel and I had been found in a position that could totally have been misconstrued? Yes, so we were lying on the ground and wrapped around each other, but he'd just healed me and I was…grateful? Nope, not even I truly believed that. If Mum, Liz and Seth hadn't showed up would we have kissed? Rolled around in the grass a little? Just imagining that gave me goose bumps and earned me a dig in the ribs from the object of my suddenly lustful thoughts. Oops.

Ignoring the mum problem for the time being I dragged myself back into the conversation that we were currently having – Sariel and I were catching the others up on what had happened with

Lucas. We glossed over the whole fangs-in-the-neck thing and left out Sariel's melt down which had almost succeeded in me actually melting. There was a brief Q & A session during which Liz asked a great deal about the inner workings of Asmodeus's organization and Nybbas and Lucas's place in the grand scheme of things.

From what I could sense through my link with Sariel, he believed that Lucas was the most likely candidate from Nybbas' house for my...affections on the night of my eighteenth. Hmmm. Well, he was certainly much higher up my scale of hotness than Nybbas and yeah, Vampires seemed to be pretty popular in the 'potential boyfriend' stakes (Ha ha. 'Stakes'. Geddit?) but considering that I wasn't looking at any of the bidders as potential BF's ('cause, well, yeuk. I mean, they were bidding to...deflower me for crying out loud!) and the whole neck sucking thing was just...

Seth asked the same question for the third time and I left the memory of how it felt for someone to be using me as a blood flavoured slushy and answered him. What are fangs like? Pointy. How does it feel to be bitten by a Vampire? Um, probably bloody painful. (And then bloody bliss but I didn't want to think about that, thank you very much.)

And then it was mum's turn for a brief interrogation. Her clipped tones made me wince as she directed all her questions to Sariel who, if he noticed her tone, seemed completely unfazed as usual.

"How did you find them? They were gone in an instant." She asked.

"I'm lucky to have been blessed by good eyesight, Joanna, and I was able to keep them in sight even though they moved so fast and were quite far ahead."

"What happened to this 'Lucas' character?"

"I pulled him away from Emily and, er, threw him against a pillar. We fought briefly but he escaped and I had to choose between going after him and checking to make sure Emily was ok."

"And you chose Emily?"

Sariel cocked his head to the side and smiled. "Would you

rather I'd chased the Vampire?"

Mum scowled. "She couldn't have been badly hurt – I can't even see a scar – so surely it would've been better to make sure…"

Excuse me?! I couldn't let that go. "Well, the reason I don't have a big old ugly scar is because he…" I pointed at Sariel.

No, Emily. Sariel interrupted me.

What? She seems to think that it was no big deal. According to her, you should've left me lying there bleeding to death while you chased Lucas all over London. I could've died, Sariel. You saved my life. She should know that.

I thought you were dead, Emily. I caught a brief flash from his mind; a snapshot of how I'd looked lying there on the cold ground, my face white, my eyes closed and a puddle of crimson around my left shoulder. *I thought I'd let you down and I lost control. I almost burned you alive.*

. *You didn't hurt me, Sariel. You healed me.* He sounded so annoyed with himself, and so upset with the thought of what might have been that my little burst of anger disappeared as fast as it had come.

But you can't tell her that.

What? Why the hell not? Bam! There was that flush of temper again. I was going to have to start attending anger management classes if I wasn't careful.

Emily, mia cara. Do you trust me?

Ladies and gentlemen we have a winner! The award for 'Stupidest question of all time' goes to Sariel. Drum roll. Sound of applause. Big gold trophy for the mantelpiece.

His lips curved into a small smile. *I'm going to assume that means you do trust me.* I rolled my eyes. *So for now, let's just keep this quiet. Okay?*

I nodded and then became aware of the silence in the car. Sariel and I were looking at each other and grinning like two members of the silly smiles club. Mum and Seth were waiting for me to finish my sentence and I could see Liz's eyes watching us all in the rear-view mirror.

What had I been talking about?

"Yeah, he, um, dragged Lucas off before the vamp could really, er, get going with the fang, sucking, blood stuff." I finished. Lame? Maybe, but not improbable. For all mum and Seth knew Vampires might like to bore people to death with scrapbooks of their knitting patterns. Seth looked confused but said nothing and mum turned back around in her seat. The car lapsed into another silence as Liz kept driving. Still at 30mph.

At some stage I drifted off to sleep and dreamed of handsome-Vampire-type kisses that turned into cold-sweat-inducing fangs on my neck and Lucas's cold chuckle echoed through my dream. I escaped to my dream place and relaxed for a while watching the ocean. It occurred to me that the little boat I'd been so worried about wasn't in sight anymore. Maybe the rower had drifted back to whatever nightmare he belonged to. Maybe Sariel had slipped in through a side door in my mind and turned the boat into a tooth pick. Who knew? It was gone, so that was good - right?

The jolt of the car stopping woke me and I peeled myself from Sariel's side. His chin was bobbing on his chest as he slept with an arm loosely around my shoulder and I could feel the vibrations of mum's displeasure before I even woke up properly. I looked up and found her eyes on us, a snarl of displeasure on her lips and I frowned. In that moment she looked so unlike my mum that I felt a moment of dizziness, as though the world shifted around me. I shook my head. This was going to have to stop. I opened my mouth to ask mum what her problem was. (Yeah, not the best plan but I was tired, hungry, covered in dried blood and regally pissed at mum's attitude.)

Thankfully Liz chose that moment to announce that we could get a meal and stay the night here. Seth had already joined her on the gravel car park, stretching and yawning against the backdrop of an honest-to-God Coaching Inn. Mum and I glanced at each other and the promise of a discussion in the not-so-distant future passed soundlessly between us.

I shook Sariel gently. "Wake up Sleeping Beauty."

"Huh?" He rubbed his eyes blearily and then looked outside. Liz was nowhere to be seen but Mum and Seth were standing just outside the car, gesturing at the Inn and checking their watches. "What are we doing?" Sariel asked.

I shrugged. "Stopping apparently."

He frowned. "For what?"

"Food, sleep, TV-fix. Whatever. I just need to pee." I reached over him and opened the car door as he undid his seat belt. He hauled himself out mumbling about getting my bladder checked next time we were anywhere near a hospital and I followed him, stretching like Seth had done and then running my hand through my hair. I grimaced. It was worse than I'd expected. "Ewww. A shower would be good too."

Seth grinned at me. "You're expecting a simple shower to sort out that mop? It took a whole team of hairdressers and beauticians almost a week to do that before. Without them you'll need a bloody miracle." I stuck my tongue out at him and he laughed.

Liz called to us from the foyer of the Inn and we all trooped inside. She handed a key to me and one to Sariel, keeping one for herself. "I got three rooms; one for you and your mum, Emily; one for Seth and Sariel and one for me. They're serving dinner in the banquet hall at 8. That gives us…" she checked her watch, "…a little under 2 hours to have a rest and get a little more presentable." She looked pointedly at my stiff, stained shirt. I didn't need to be told twice and headed for the stairs up to our rooms and a blissfully hot shower.

CHAPTER EIGHTEEN

Dinner in the 'Banquet Hall' was quite an occasion – it was an insane place; long, heavy tables with high-backed wooden chairs; suits of armour; ancient looking flags fluttering in a light breeze from a set of ceiling fans. I loved it. I didn't care that the armour was probably plastic or paper mache, or that the flags were from a job lot on eBay. Whatever. It was charming. I was charmed.

The surroundings put me in a mega-good mood that even my glowering mother couldn't put a damper on. It just felt pretty terrific to be eating dinner in a 'banquet hall' with my family and some of my friends after so long spent worrying about them and dealing with all the weirdness.

Seth and I alternated between catching up with everything that we had been going through separately and getting back into the rhythm of annoying the hell out of each other.

"Do you know how many calories you've just packed into your belly?" I asked as he set his knife and fork down. "I'm stunned that you managed to leave any of the pattern on that plate."

Seth sat back with an expression of deep satisfaction on his face. He waved a hand in my direction. "You have obviously mistaken me for someone who cares about calories."

"You'll turn into a weeble, Seth. Seriously. I mean, look at the size of your gut already." I poked his belly with a finger. "Liz has been feeding you much too well."

Liz, who had been chatting in a low voice with Sariel, smiled over at me and then attempted to include mum in their conversation.

Seth was examining his tiny belly with a happy grin. "I'm just giving the ladies what they want," he finally commented, reaching for the sweet menu.

"And what's that?" I asked. "A fat bloke in a tight t-shirt?"

"More of Seth," said Seth, scanning the puddings on offer. "That's what they want."

I laughed and punched him on the arm. "More of Seth?" So

you're referring to yourself in the third person now?"

"Watch and learn, Emily," he whispered as our waitress plodded over to ask if we'd like anything else. She was fairly young with bleached blonde hair, an eyebrow ring and maybe six inches of make-up covering her bored expression. I squeezed my eyes shut and tried not to watch as Seth ordered teas and coffees for everyone else before asking Little Miss Grump-a-lot what she could recommend in the way of something sweet. Honestly. Surely no-one normal uses chat up lines like that anymore!

The waitress mumbled something about Pavlova, pointing to an item on the sweet menu with her pen. "Sounds good," Seth told her. "I'll have a slice of Pavlova, a coffee with milk and your phone number." He flashed a cheesy grin and she paused in scribbling our order on her note pad for just a second, glancing at him out of the corner of her eye to see if he was fooling with her. Seth kept grinning like a village idiot and she finally turned away, shaking her head.

I roared with laughter. "Oh, I do so love to watch you crash and burn, Seth." What was I supposed to be learning exactly? How to piss off every female in a thirty mile radius?"

"Emily!" Mum admonished. "Language." She turned back to Liz and Sariel and I was glad that she seemed a little more relaxed, more like her old self.

"Yes, mum, sorry mum," I said softly as Seth watched the retreating waitress with a frown.

"That usually works," he mumbled and scratched his head.

"Liar," I giggled.

"Am not," Seth told me. "Besides, I'm not the one shacked up with a guy old enough to be God's Uncle. Anyhoo, can you pass the water jug?"

I gaped.

"Um, earth to Emily, come in, Emily." Seth waved a hand in front of my face.

"What did you just say?"

"Water jug?" Seth said again.

"No, before that." I told him, glaring.

He made a face. "Oh, um, yeah. I was just fooling with you. Sorry."

I looked around the table again and caught mum's glance and brief questioning smile. I smiled back on automatic pilot. Is that what everyone was thinking? That Sariel and I were....y'know? Sariel was still deep in conversation with mum and Liz. His expression was calm and relaxed as always but I could see him glancing in mum's direction every now and again. Had she said something to Seth? To Sariel? My cheeks were burning although I wasn't sure that I had anything to be embarrassed about. Did I? Okay so we'd kissed. But I'd kissed Adam too and nobody was accusing me of shacking up with him, were they? Did mum and Seth know that I'd kissed Sariel? Well, Seth knew about the pretend-drunken-kiss-type-thing at the club and yes, he'd probably told mum about it. I turned around and gave him a scowl.

"What?" He asked in confusion.

"You know what," I hissed.

He shook his head. "No, really, what?"

"Don't act all Mister Innocent with me. I know what you did." I sat back in my chair and folded my arms, earning me a raised eyebrow from Sariel which I ignored. I was much too cross with Seth to be civil to anyone else.

Seth sat back in his chair too and leaned over until his head was practically fighting mine for neck space. "Seriously, Em. What do you think I've done now?"

"You told mum," I accused.

"Told mum what?" He obviously wasn't going to cave that easily.

"About the club, about me kissing Sariel," I growled and elbowed him.

"Ow! No I bloody didn't. She's been going off on one about what you and Sariel are up to since we left Dean's Lynn. Was even asking Liz to find out what your, er, sleeping arrangements were." Seth grinned. "That snog you gave Sariel in the club was choice though. Wish I'd had a camera so you could've seen his face," he shook his head. "He was well stunned."

"I did see his face, idiot. I was there," I huffed but I couldn't help grinning. "He was kinda taken off guard, wasn't he?" We giggled together and it was just like old times.

I heard the rich timbre of Sariel's chuckle inside my head as he answered a question that my mother had put to him. *Do you remember all the kisses you've had, Emily? Or was mine particularly impressive?* He asked and I rolled my eyes.

I'm just really glad to know that you'll never be lonely, Sariel. You'll always have your enormous ego for company.

Across the table he flicked an amused glance in my direction and mum narrowed her eyes at us both.

Beside me Seth was lying back in his chair, one hand on his throat and the other tugging at my shirt. He began to make gasping, choking noises. "Please, Emily," he rasped. "Must have. Water. Think I'm dying. So thirsty. Ehhhhhh." He rolled his eyes up into his head and his tongue lolled out of the corner of his mouth. I sighed and pushed the water jug over to him.

"Here. Knock yourself out," I told him, distracted.

Seth made little crooning noises of approval, poured water into his goblet and drank noisily. I barely noticed as the grumpy blonde waitress set our coffee down along with a slice of Pavlova that could have fed half the African continent. She beamed once at Seth and then bounded away. Seth watched her go and then lifted his plate to look for a utensil to eat his mountainous pudding with. Under the plate was a torn page from the waitress's note pad with her phone number on it. Seth waved it triumphantly under my nose and began gleefully eating his Pavlova with a tea spoon.

I ignored him. *Apparently mum's not too happy about us being together so much,* I told Sariel

Yeah I got that. Great so she had said something. My embarrassment grew.

Sorry.

For what? Having a mother who cares about you?

No, I mean for her getting at you. Especially when there's nothing for her to worry about. I mean, you were just helping me, right? There's nothing else to it. She has no need to worry about us, right?

76

Sariel turned his head and looked at me across the table. *Exactly right*, he told me. *So don't be annoyed about it.*

Yeah, right. I wondered if he could hear the disappointment in my voice. I sounded like a ten year old, all whiney and needy. I mean, what 'us' was there? I was being ridiculous. Blocking my thoughts for all I was worth I looked at Sariel out of the corner of my eye. Yes, our link was special, intimate even. I felt closer to him than I'd felt to anyone else in my life. I also thought that he was beyond hot. Total hotness. Mega hotness. Astronomic hotness. And when he'd last kissed me…well, dear Lord. My stomach flipped over several times just thinking about it. Kissing Adam had been nice but kissing Sariel was…awesome.

I frowned. If I'd kissed Adam first or if I'd never kissed Sariel, would Adam's kisses seem wonderful now?

What are you thinking about? Sariel asked and I jumped guiltily. He was taking a sip of coffee and listening to some tale that Liz was telling. My mother looked enchanted.

I was thinking that you spoiled Adam's kiss for me, I told him and then kicked myself as Sariel spluttered most of his mouthful of coffee onto the table. Liz and Mum looked at him in astonishment.

"Sorry, it went down the wrong way," he said, wiping his shirt and the table with a napkin.

"I do that all the time," said Seth with a grin, looking up from his latest prized possession – the waitress's phone number.

"There's a payphone in the foyer," I told him. "Why don't you go call her?"

His smile brightened for a minute and then he made a face. "Very funny, Em. How can I call her at home when she's still here? D'you think I'm stupid or something?"

I smiled sweetly at him and turned my attention back to Sariel who was eyeing me worriedly over the top of his coffee. *Explain*, he said.

I sighed and studied my cup which was exquisitely patterned with various brightly coloured coats of arms. *If I hadn't kissed you first then I might think that Adam was a better kisser.*

I thought you thought he was.

I lied.

Naughty.

Whatever.

So, you're basically saying that I'm a better kisser than Adam. Grazie, Emily.

I glanced at him and he was grinning behind his mug. *No, I'm saying that you maybe seem better because I kissed you first. If I'd kissed Adam first then I'd probably think he was better.*

Nah, it wouldn't have mattered. His voice was amused and he sounded extremely pleased with himself.

Again with the ego problem. Do you have to sound so…smug? I could feel my face flaming yet again.

You brought it up. I can't help it if Adam Farlow's abilities don't quite live up to his reputation or your expectations.

That was it. I'd had enough. I stood up and made a big show of yawning. "Gee, I'm so tired. I guess it's been a pretty long day."

Seth was sliding down in his chair. "Er…maybe I'll head up with you," he said slowly. "The waitress keeps waving over at me."

"Fab idea," I said, grabbing his arm and dragging him out the door after me. "Night all," I called as we left. "If you will ask girls for their number then you have to be prepared for the fact that they'll think you like them."

Would you like me to come with… Sariel began.

No thanks, I told Sariel, *I really do need some sleep and I'd like to catch up with Seth. I'm sure you won't be lonely though. You have my mum and Liz hanging on your every word and if you get bored with them, there's a waitress who might need some consoling.*

"Well, I do like her," Seth was saying as he scampered along beside me, glancing over his shoulder. "I was just…showing you that I could get her number if I wanted. But I'm kind of taken."

"You should've thought about that before you started trying to show off," I complained.

Emily…

Good night, Sariel. I blocked him out and headed to bed.

CHAPTER NINETEEN

"Okay, I'm confused," Seth told me, frowning. I'd decided in my infinite wisdom that there were some things that Seth needed to have explained in a little more depth, to help him understand why Sariel and I were so close.

I sighed. "Not meaning to be rude, Seth, but that wouldn't be difficult. Look, it's simple; Sariel thinks that he and I can communicate telepathically 'cause I was given the gift by an Archangel. Beginning, middle and end of story." Kind of.

Seth chewed on that for a bit. "Well, how did you catch this thing and I didn't?" He asked.

I rolled my eyes. "It's not the flu, Seth, you can't 'catch' it; and I dunno why you don't have it. Luck of the draw I suppose."

He made a face. "Maybe I don't do it because I've never tried. I should try thinking at you."

I nodded. "Yeah, ok." I gritted my teeth at that; I didn't want to be able to talk to Seth in my head – your twin reading your thoughts? Yeuk. Worse than disgusting. And I wanted to be the only one who could talk to Sariel like this. I immediately felt guilty. I was a horrid, selfish twin. I would go straight to hell, no question about it. Maybe Asmodeus had more to do with my genetic makeup than I wanted to believe. After all, I'd been able to lift a knife and stab someone. Okay, that someone was an evil Demon Lord who was torturing my friend at the time but who's to say that God reckons me stabbing my biological father in the back was the right thing to do, no matter the circumstances. I shook my head. That problem could wait for another time. I had to focus.

Seth was sitting on the side of one of the twin beds in the hotel room that mum and I were sharing. I sat on the other bed and faced him. "Okay, think something at me." I instructed.

Seth bit his lip and narrowed his eyes. He looked like he was in pain or having 'toilet problems' as my grandma called it. I waited. He squeezed his eyes shut and made an 'Nnnnnrrrgggg,' sound before opening one eye. "Well?" He asked.

I shook my head. 'Nothing, sorry.'

Seth shrugged. "Maybe I should try with Sariel sometime. See if he can hear me."

"He already can, Seth," I told him gently. "He can tune in to the thoughts of anyone he wants to." Seth paled. "What?"

"He knows about Rosie then," He flushed and collapsed onto his back and covered his face with his hands. Rosie?

"What about Rosie?" I slipped over beside him and pried his hands from his face. "You and Rosie…?" Seth shook his head miserably. "But you liked her?" He nodded.

"I think she liked me too but we never got time to…get any further than, well, chatting I guess." He sighed and pillowed his arms behind his head. "I feel stupid now."

"Why?" I was honestly confused.

"Well, 'cause she's a lot older than me and 'cause I'm supposed to be going out with Amber and…well, 'cause she's, well, evil." He closed his eyes.

"So that's why you were weird with Amber when we came back from London?" I asked - things were clicking into place. The whole argument about whether or not Rosie was evil could wait for another day.

He nodded. "I didn't think you'd noticed, you were so busy snuggling up to Adam." I flopped back onto the bed beside him, suddenly wanting to change the subject. Seth beat me to it. "So what is the deal with you and Sariel?" he asked.

I sat up on my elbows. "What do you mean?"

Seth rolled his eyes. "Quit looking at me like that, Em. I saw the two of you lying there on the grass together. And, like we were saying, I saw you kiss him at that freaky Demon club. And mum says he's a lot older than you so he's probably already convinced you to…y'know."

"What?!" I got up off the bed, feeling my cheeks flame and embarrassment mixed with anger flood into my veins. "She actually said that to you?"

Seth slid up beside me and settled his head on my shoulder. "She was just worried about you, Em. That's all."

"Is that why she's been looking at Sariel as though she could happily run him over with a big truck?"

Seth laughed. "Probably."

"But we didn't...we're not...he wouldn't..." I stood up and paced while Seth flopped back onto the bed.

"I should've kept my mouth shut; now you're annoyed. I'm sorry." He puffed out his cheeks and rubbed his eyes. "You're right, I'm an idiot."

I felt a sudden rush of affection for my brother and so I threw a pillow at him. "You're not an idiot, Seth, you're just a jerk. And you're always looking out for me, more than I ever do for you. You look out for mum too, I mean, she goes to you when she needs to vent 'cause she knows that I don't have patience to listen." I sighed and sat down heavily. "You guys are my family and I love you like crazy but, well, Sariel's...he's come to mean a lot to me. I'm connected to him and he makes me feel safe, hell, he keeps me safe. If it wasn't for him we'd all be living with Asmodeus and doing God-only-knows-what for his Demon pals. I owe him so much and..."

Seth sat up and slung an arm around my shoulder. "And you think he's gorgeous." He began to sing. "You want to hug him, you want to kiss him, you think he's gorgeous..." I giggled and hit him with a pillow again, starting another pillow fight which left us laughing and gasping for breath.

Straightening up the room afterwards Seth looked at me seriously. "If he ever put any pressure on you to...y'know...I hope you know that you don't have to...um.." his face flushed and I grinned.

"He hasn't, he wouldn't and I would tell him where to get off if he did," I told him.

Seth plumped up the pillows on my bed and straightened the duvet. "Unless of course you wanted to," he said, looking up at me from under his lashes. I bit my lip, torn between wanting to lie and needing to confide in someone, even if it was my twin. He sighed. "Look, I know what it's like, Emily. I mean, Amber and I..."

I held up a hand. "Please. I don't need to hear it. Amber already went on so much about your hot bod that I feel icky just thinking about what you and her got up to."

He laughed. "Yeah, Amber's got a big mouth. And yeah, we got pretty close to…stuff…but we never did it."

I sat back down, fascinated and curious in spite of the ick factor. "Why not?" I asked.

He shrugged. "I like her, I mean she's insanely beautiful but she just didn't…it just didn't feel right."

I nodded, thinking about Adam. "Yeah, I know what you mean."

"You do?"

"I snogged Adam Farlow but it just didn't feel like what I expected…he's still cute and all but kissing him didn't feel like the whole fireworks going off thing that I get with Sariel." I looked up at him and grimaced. "This is weird that we're talking about this, right?"

Seth's eyes were wide but he shook his head. "I've been wanting, no scratch that, I've been needing to talk to someone about it but there's been no-one but mum and, after hearing her rant about Sariel I kind of figured she wouldn't appreciate her seventeen year old son coming to her for advice on 'how do you know if you should sleep with your girlfriend?' Know what I mean?" I grinned at him. "So, back up a bit. You snogged Adam Farlow? When was this? Does Sarah know?"

And so I told him the full story of Rick Farlow, the Were knife and Adam's kiss at the railway. It took longer than I expected - maybe because Seth was prone to asking a lot of questions about stuff that I'd already explained or stuff that I was in the middle of explaining. Anyway, we pretty much fell asleep at the end of the story, or maybe it was in the middle. I don't remember getting to the end but I know that sleeping in the same room as Seth again was so comforting that I had the most restful sleep I'd had in ages.

Which was a good thing 'cause in the morning my world turned upside down.

CHAPTER TWENTY

I was woken up the next morning by Seth shaking my shoulder quite violently. I tried to swat him away and get back to my lovely dream – I'd been walking on the beach near my dream house, collecting shells and trying not to notice the fact that there was a rowing boat pulled up onto the shore – but he began whispering, "Emily. Emily, wake up butt-face" quite urgently into my left ear.

I opened one eye and was about to start complaining in as loud a voice as I could manage when I caught sight of his face.

Seth was pale, so white he looked like he'd be doused in talcum powder. He was also so nervous that his lips had thinned to the size of those little pencils you get in Argos, and his eyes darted between me and the door to the room. I opened my other eye and moaned at the amount of light streaming into the room – we'd obviously fallen asleep without closing the curtains.

"Wassamatterseth?" I asked, which I thought was a pretty impressive attempt at normal speech considering I'd been practically comatose until about five seconds earlier.

"Um." Seth sat down beside me on the bed, blocking out most of the light thankfully and began wringing his hands and looking back towards the door. I watched in amazement – Seth was actually wringing his hands. I hadn't realized that this was something people actually did but there was my brother sitting in front of me twisting his hands around each other over and over.

I sat up and rubbed some more of the sleep out of my eyes. "What's going on?" I asked and all the possibilities hit me at once. My eyes popped wide in alarm. "Is it mum? Is she okay? Has Asmodeus found us? Has someone died? Oh, God. Who died?" I looked towards the door. Liz was standing just outside the room, her expression sad and concerned. "Seth?" I moved in front of him, chills of alarm bringing goose bumps up on my arms, and shook his arm. "Spit it out, Seth. What's going on?"

Seth sighed. "I think you should get dressed and come talk to mum, Emily."

"About what?" I practically screeched at him. "God! You are

so exasperating. Liz?" I stood up and walked forward a few feet. "Have you lost the power of speech too?"

Liz stared steadily back at me for a heartbeat. "Your mother sent Sariel away last night after you went to sleep. He's gone."

For a moment I just stood there looking at her. I knew that my mouth had dropped open but beyond that I couldn't seem to connect my brain to my body. I turned slowly around to face Seth. "Is she telling the truth?" Seth nodded miserably. "He's actually gone?" He nodded again. "Mum sent him away?" I reached my mind out towards Sariel and found a dizzying amount of... nothing. He was blocking me. Hard.

Seth reached out a hand to me. "Emily..." For a moment I thought I might pass out. The room spun and blurred for a few seconds until every nerve ending I had seemed to spring to life and stand to attention. Anger sizzled in my veins and my body felt too small to contain it. This is how volcanoes feel, I thought absurdly. This is exactly how they feel before they blow and eradicate whole civilizations. I could almost see tomorrow's headlines 'Demonic Daughter Erupts! Takes out Entire South of England!'

"Where is she?" I asked and I was stunned at the sound of my voice. I was flat, emotionless, cold with anger.

"She's in the banquet hall," Liz piped up.

I spun to face her. "Doing what?"

Liz made a face. "Having breakfast."

I didn't even bother getting dressed; I just marched from the room in my grey and pink striped pyjama bottoms and grey vest top. I was heading for the stairs before Seth and Liz caught up with me and started talking. I knew they were talking because I could see their lips moving but if they were telling me about the weather or trying to calm me down I don't know because I couldn't hear them. There was a rushing sound filling my head, a rushing sound with a steady beat that was probably the blood flying through my veins and my heart trying to cope with the surge.

I cannoned down the stairs and barreled through the doors into the gloriously ridiculous banquet hall. There were very few tables occupied. A woman sat on her own at one. She had a laptop open in front of her and was tapping on the keys whilst talking into a mobile. An elderly couple sat a few tables away from her tucking into a full breakfast of sausages, toast, beans, egg and mushrooms. All faces turned in my direction and several mouths opened in either astonishment or disgust at my state of undress. I ignored them and headed for the back of the hall where mum sat at her own isolated island of a table, far away from the other guests. She was facing the door and watched us thread our way past the other unoccupied tables to reach her. For a moment, as she lowered her eyes and lifted a cup of tea to her lips, I could have sworn that I saw her smirk.

If she did, it was gone by the time I stopped opposite her and leaned over the table. She sighed gently and looked me in the eye, took a few breaths and then folded her hands in front of her on the table. I was vaguely aware of Liz and Seth coming in and sitting beside us, of Seth whispering something to me, of Sariel's voice saying something soothing in my head. I tuned it all out and focused on my mother.

"What did you do?" I asked in as unthreatening a voice as I could manage. It still came out as a guttural snarl and I sensed Seth take a step closer to Liz. The wuss.

Mum regarded me steadily. "Last night I spoke to Sariel," she almost spat the name out. "I wanted to know if the two of you had...had...,"

"If we'd had sex?" I asked and felt both Liz and Seth shift beside me. I spared them a glance; Liz was scanning the other diners but they all seemed more interested in their breakfasts than our little domestic dispute. Seth was watching mum and me with nervous anticipation. I rolled my eyes at him and turned my attention back to my mother. "No, we didn't." I told her, trying to control the angry tremor in my voice, "Why didn't you just ask me?"

She gave a little sigh. "Because you are not the adult, Emily. You may think that you're grown up and ready for a serious relationship but you're not and especially not with...him."

Well, this was confusing. "I thought you liked Sariel," I told her. "In fact, I thought you were glad that he was looking after me.

That's what he was doing remember? He didn't drag me away to seduce me, he ran with me to keep me safe."

She nodded. "Yes, he did his job well, Emily. And that is all you should be to him." Yeah, his job. Thanks for pointing that out, mum. "But you are my daughter, my responsibility. Not his. We can manage perfectly well without his interference. And as far as I can see his hold over you is dangerous. He could make you…do things." She shivered theatrically.

"Like what?" I asked sharply, noticing with some violent part of my brain that there were several sharp implements on the table in front of me should I decide to use them. I shook my head and focused.

"You know what I mean, Emily. Don't be insolent." Mum pointed at me. "I will not have my daughter running around the countryside whoring herself to a man who is far too old and much too experienced for her to deal with."

My head snapped back as though she'd slapped me. "Is that what you think I've been doing for the last few weeks?" Mum opened her mouth but obviously thought better of it and said nothing. "For your information, we've been running, mum. Running from all the…things that your dearest Asmodeus has sent after us. I've been scared and I've been worried about you and Seth and Annie and Dylan and Grandma and Gramps. Sariel has kept me sane and kept me safe and made sure everyone I care about is safe too. If it wasn't for him we might all be dead by now."

"If it wasn't for him we wouldn't be in this mess," she mumbled.

"Say again?" The rushing sound was turning into a roar. I had to fold my arms because I was certain that if I didn't, I would strike my mother.

"He turned your head, Emily. From the first day he appeared at our house you looked at him with that hungry look of yours."

I looked over at Seth. He shrugged.

"I thought at first that everything would be okay. He worked for Asmodeus, for goodness sake, and he was an Angel once. He was nothing but a glorified baby sitter. I thought you would be safe. But the two of you seemed to just get closer and closer. You seemed to be able to look at each other and know what the other was thinking. And sometimes when he looked at you, I could see that his interest in you wasn't purely professional. And then he went and got you tattooed." She shook her head and made a tutting sound of disappointment. Out of the corner of my eye I could see that Liz had leaned forward and was watching mum intently.

"That was for protection," I told her.

She sniffed. "I'm sure he had to make up some reason why you were lying on a table in front of him half naked."

"What? Where exactly do you think I got it done? My left butt cheek?" Seth bit back a snort of laughter and I turned around and pulled up my t-shirt. They could only see the top of the tattoo above my pajama bottoms but Seth leaned over and pulled the back of them down a little. I knew what they could see - a medium sized, upright pentagram in various shades of black and grey and in the very centre of it, a Celtic knot in colours of gold and brown. Both symbols were connected by the intertwining green stems of five white roses. Seth let out a low whistle.

"Pretty cool tramp stamp, Em," he said and I glared at him.

"Symbols of protection," Liz said. "Of secrets, and of the presence of Angels." She smiled at me. "It's beautiful."

I was so grateful to Liz in that moment that I could've hugged her. My mother however was not so easily pleased. "He didn't ask my permission, Emily. No matter how important he thinks he is, I am still your mother and your legal guardian."

I looked at her in amazement. For a blissful second my anger retreated. "Of course you're my guardian. You're my mum. Is that what this is about? Are you jealous that Sariel and I have been spending time together? That I've been listening to him more than you?"

Mum stood up and leaned across the table at me. "You are only seventeen years old, Emily. You've never had any kind of serious relationship with a boy and that man is ancient and, well, did he tell you why he fell from grace?" I nodded but she kept talking anyway. "He fell because he sinned and do you know what the sin was? It was lust, Emily. He lusted after human women, chased after them and seduced them. Angels were never meant to do that, to have children. But he did. And I won't have him doing the same to you."

I was pretty sure that if I looked in a mirror, steam would be coming out of my ears and my eyes would be glowing red. "How dare you." I growled and took great pleasure in seeing her cringe back from the cold anger in my voice. "How dare you send him away and then lecture me about his past. He told me all this and he would never push me into doing anything. In fact he's the one who steps back when I want him to take things further." Her face twisted into a grimace of disgust. "Yes, that's right. I would take things further but he won't because he wants the same things for me that you do. The only difference is that he would never send away the people I care about. We stayed away to keep you all safe. We were going to Italy to keep you all safe. And now we have no-one to protect us. If Asmodeus tracks us down we're screwed. And that's your fault, mum."

Mum began to shout again and Liz slipped around the table, trying to calm her down. I wasn't listening anymore because my link to Sariel had suddenly flared to life and he was speaking to me.

Don't be angry with her, Emily, he said and I almost cried with relief at just hearing his voice. *You don't understand…*

Where the hell are you?! I screeched at him. *Why did you leave without telling me?*

There wasn't time to fully explain. I'm sending someone to help you. Trust her and do what she says.

Her?

Seth was poking my arm as Liz and mum began to argue about what to do and where to go. "We could get guns," Seth said happily. "You can get anything if you have the money."

I sighed and rubbed my temples. "Uh, huh. Seth, three problems; first we don't have any money; second you would blow your own toes off if someone sold you a gun and third, bullets don't kill Demons." I began to pace, the anger turning into worry about our situation but not receding altogether. I was full of pent-up aggression, so up-tight that I considered kicking a few coats of armour to see if they really were plastic. Seth followed me, talking as I paced.

"Okay then. A sword. We could cut their heads off." He made a slashing motion in the air with an imaginary sword.

"What century are you living in, King Arthur?" I asked him. "No-one goes around with a sword these days."

Seth was about to retort when the banquet hall doors flew open and a girl of about nineteen flew in. "Emily? Seth?" Seth waved, looking ridiculous, and she nodded. "Who's with you? Ah, right. Let's move people, we haven't much time." The four of us stood gaping as she leaned on a long silver sword that was dripping blood onto the floor. The elderly man at the table in front of her dropped his half-eaten sausage onto the floor, his mouth open in shock. "Now!" The girl yelled and we all began moving at once.

Seth grinned at me as we ran through the foyer. "She's got a sword," he shouted.

"Yeah, you're obviously made for each other." I shouted back.

Chapter Twenty-one

D emons bleed. And die. And scream a lot while they are bleeding and dying. Until it was actually happening in front of me I had no idea that it was something I hadn't ever wanted to see.

The girl with the sword seemed to be the Demon equivalent of the Grim Reaper – she sliced through their ranks with her sword like Darth Vader with his light saber. Yep, you heard me right – ranks.

Once we'd made it through the foyer of the Inn, past the panicked employees and a couple of camera-snapping American Tourists in matching Union Jack t-shirts, sword girl dashed on ahead through the heavy entrance doors and out into the bright light of the day beyond, her sword flashing as she raised it high and then brought it whistling down. There was a 'thwack' noise, a hideous, high pitched Demonic scream and then her sword was rising and falling again. The rest of us had stopped a few steps from the entrance to the Inn and were standing in silence, our chins hitting the lumpy gravel of the car park at the shock of what was happening right in front of our eyes.

There was a crowd of around fifty people in the car park at the front of the Inn. Maybe twenty of them were Demons – some had actual horns –and the rest were humans brandishing an assortment of weapons. I saw a few more long swords, knives of various shapes and sizes, baseball bats, at least two hockey sticks and one guy in a chef's outfit aiming a rolling pin in the vicinity of a red-eyed Demon's jaw. None of the swords looked plastic and the blood spraying liberally into the air didn't look like tomato ketchup either. I swallowed thickly, suddenly delighted that I hadn't made it to the buffet breakfast. My brain was telling me that there were questions I should be asking here; who were all these humans? Where had all the Demons come from? How had the humans and Demons found each other? Was this a movie set? What the hell was going on?

An Inn employee, resplendent in a maroon monogrammed

suit with the name-tag 'Alfie', pushed past us and back into the Inn yelling at the top of his lungs for someone to 'shut the bloody doors and lock 'em, the world's gone bloomin' mental'. A loud thud behind us made us all jump and the clink-snick of a key turning in the lock told me that one of Alfie's colleagues had figured his idea was a good one and my brain calmly announced to the rest of me that we were now, therefore, locked out and going to die.

Thankfully, Liz drew my brain's attention away from my impending death before I could begin to fully process the whole I'm-going-to-die scenario as she charged into the fray pulling a set of wicked looking throwing knives from somewhere about her person. Before I could blink they were protruding from various Demon body parts, eliciting more of those stomach-churning screams and a few bellows of anger.

Seth nudged me but kept his eyes on the battle. "What the hell...? Where did she...?"

I shrugged. "She does that."

He nodded mutely as sword girl emerged from the path that she was clearing. "When you've all quite finished rubber-necking could you perhaps move your arses?" She swung her sword in the direction that we should go, decapitating a charging Demon as she did so. At the end of the almost-cleared path and on the opposite side of the road sat an ancient blue Land Rover which looked to be held together by rust and was missing at least two windows. This, it seemed, was our rescue vehicle.

Mum was standing beside us watching the goings on with an expression which managed to be both shocked and excited. Ignoring the fact that she was seriously creeping me out, Seth and I grabbed an arm each and propelled her in sword-girl's wake, stepping over fallen bodies as we went. My bare feet splashed in Demon blood and I retched and cursed my hot temper. A pair of shoes would've been a pretty wonderful idea right then. And jeans. And a jacket. Not to mention a bra.

We made it to the battered jalopy and Seth and I pushed mum into the back as sword-girl jumped lithely into the driving seat. I ignored the crimson splatters on her clothes and the warm copper smell. "Where's Liz?" I yelled over the noise of fighting and the thrum of the diesel engine. I twisted away from the car and scanned the writhing, screaming, slashing, dying crowd for someone who looked like Queen Elizabeth on a really bad pms day.

Sword-girl didn't answer for a moment, concentrating on wiping blood off her hand and onto her jeans so I repeated the question a little louder. Sword-girl looked me in the eye. "She fell," she told me. "Now get in."

I wasn't sure I'd heard right. "What?" I asked, feeling my face crumple in confusion.

"She fell. She's gone. Now get in the damn car. We have to get you out of here. It's you they want." Her eyes were hard and her expression clearly said 'this is your fault.'

I shook my head, feeling my heart constrict. "No. We're not leaving her."

"Get in the damn car!" Sword-girl screamed, glancing behind me.

I shook my head and willed my galloping heart to calm down and provide a bit of courage. "Give me a sword if you're too bloody chicken to go back. We're not leaving her."

Sword-girl's mouth opened and closed, spots of colour appeared on her cheeks and she cursed mightily under her breath. She spun to face Seth who was watching us with his mouth hanging open. "Can you drive?" Seth gaped at her. "Can you even speak?" She glared at him.

"Hey!" I shouted. "Don't you talk to my brother like that." I turned to Seth. "Get behind the wheel and keep it ticking over. We need to find Liz and you need to be ready to go when we do. If one of those…things even looks like its thinking about making its way over here then put your foot down and get mum out of here." Seth nodded, looking more serious than I'd ever have believed possible and then began climbing into the front.

"Oi!" Sword-girl shouted at me. "Who put you in charge?"

"Shut up and help me," I told her, turning back towards the car park and checking for oncoming traffic before jogging across the road. I didn't bother waiting to see if she was following, I just ran into the middle of it all; ducking past swinging weapons and great, meaty Demon arms. My bare feet seemed to find every tiny stone in the area, making me wince and hiss as I searched. "Liz!" I shouted. "Where are you? Liz!?"

Somewhere in my head Sariel was shouting at me, all around Demons were shrieking, humans were yelling, blood was flowing in steady streams at my feet and I ignored it all, checking fallen body after fallen body until finally turning around and coming face to face with a Demon who had the misfortune to almost pass for human – except for the fact that he had a long, green, scaly tongue and matching hands. "Sthtop right there!" He yelled and I immediately felt sorry for him. A half-Demon with a lisp? The poor guy was seriously messed up. "I know who you are," he told me, his oh-so-human blue eyes excited and amazed.

"Great," I told him. "I hate long introductions. Did you see where Liz went?"

He blinked a few times and then gestured to the left of the car park, near the road. "One of the K'elfi dropped her back there. Claw to the gut. It wath amathing. Man, you thoulda theen it." He shook his head, grinning happily.

"Yeah, glad I missed it to be honest, see ya." I turned away feeling time slipping away from me. Liz was injured, dying, and maybe already dead. I had to find her. Like, now!

Scaly hands on my shoulders stopped me walking and I looked back. "Where do you think you're going?" asked scaly tongue. "I've caught you. You're mine. Lilith will be tho pleathed. Ouch!" He frowned at his now smoking hands. "You have protecthon." Yay. Go protective tattoos!

I wriggled but he was obviously stronger than he sounded and I felt the first shiver of fear. I looked into his blue eyes and saw the excitement in them, as he grinned like a boisterous puppy and that scaly snot-coloured tongue slipped lazily in and out of his pink lips. Suddenly there was a flash between us and we stood blinking at each other in confusion until scaly tongue's hands fell from my shoulders and hit the ground with a wet thud. He frowned and raised his now handless arms to his face, staring at the bloody stumps in disbelief until sword-girl swung her sword again and removed his head from his body, coating me in blood splatters. Gross.

I looked at her. "Thanks. I think." She nodded and began scanning around us. "He said that Liz was over there." I pointed and began walking again.

"You asked?" She sounded incredulous, swiping at a pig-nosed Demon in a three piece suit as he got too close.

"That's how you learn," I told her, quoting my mother and concentrating on staying away from the small pockets of fighting. The battlefield had thinned out alarmingly with more bodies now on the ground than there were still fighting. I tried not to think too much about that and kept going, squelching through the gore and trying not to smell the sickly sweet, warm metal smell of death. I picked up the pace when I caught sight of a halo of grey hair and dropped to my knees beside Liz.

I had to use what was left of my willpower not to vomit as it seemed that the K'elfi (whatever they were) had more than one claw. Liz was deathly pale with blood coating the side of her head and pooling across her mid-section where three parallel slices ran from just under the swell of her breasts to the top of her thigh. I knew that she wasn't dead by the whistling sound of her breathing but I knew without being told that her chances were slim. It didn't matter. She had helped us, battled Demons for us, stood up for me and hid weapons inside her twinset. I wasn't about to leave her.

"Help me." I told sword-girl, grasping Liz beneath her arms. We struggled to lift her and I was considering setting her down again and getting Seth to bring the land rover closer when we heard the sound of a car horn. My head snapped up in the direction of the noise. Seth was leaning on the horn as a tall Demon wearing what looked like sheets of dark metal advanced slowly towards him. The Demon was dragging a long spiked club behind him, striking sparks from the road as he lumbered forwards.

"Damn. Let's go." Sword-girl lifted Liz a little higher and I tried to follow suit, my arms straining and my muscles screaming. Somehow we staggered to the road, my legs were shaking, my breath coming in explosive hitching blasts. "Faster," sword-girl ordered as Seth managed to coax the car into reverse and bunny-hop away from the Demon and towards us. I was running out of strength fast, inwardly cursing my skinny arms and weak legs, wishing Sariel had worked me harder at training. We weren't going to make it. I wanted to cry.

My mind was suddenly cleared by the certainty of failure and into the quiet came Sariel's voice. *Don't you dare give up, Emily Carson.* He sounded far away and wavering, as if his voice was coming from under water.

I can't. I told him, feeling my legs begin to buckle.

You can, cara mia. You're stronger than you think.

I'm weak, Sariel. I can't hear her breathing anymore and I can smell all the blood. I didn't get to her in time. I'm so sorry... I sobbed aloud and caught sword girl's anxious glance.

You're not alone, Emily. And you went back for her when the others wanted to leave. A weak person wouldn't have done that.

I staggered a few more feet, feeling something pop in my left shoulder. The pain was bad but I concentrated on putting one foot in front of the other. Where was Seth with the car? Couldn't he put his foot down? Sweat stung my eyes and slid down my back. I was covered in blood and stinking of sweat, I probably still had bed hair, there was a battle going on, the woman I was trying to carry might be dead, and my mother had sent away my...what was he? Guardian Angel?

Fallen, remember? Sariel told me with a smile in his voice.

Even better, I told him, grunting as the ache in my shoulders became a stabbing pain. Across from me, sword girl was breathing heavily, the hilt of her sword bouncing up above her shoulders. She glared at me across Liz's body and I ignored her. Seth had finally figured out how to accelerate and the car hurtled backwards to us. The way my morning was going he'd probably keep going over the top of us and kill us all.

Why better? Sariel asked as the car came to a jerky stop a few feet from us and Seth got out.

Because, I told him, forcing my frozen muscles to cooperate for just a few more minutes as we loaded Liz into the car, *you're more likely to be able to kick butt. And you're less likely to give a shit when I use curse words.* I hopped into the back seat, cradling Liz's head in my lap. Seth jumped into the passenger seat beside sword girl who had slipped into the driver's seat and put her foot down immediately as the Demon who'd been stalking the car finally put one huge hand on the bonnet and ripped it off.

We all screamed like banshees and then we were shooting backwards at supersonic speed, down the road and into the middle of the intersection. Brakes squealed and horns blared angrily at us as sword girl shifted into first, spun us in the opposite direction and gave the middle finger to all the drivers left shaking their fists in our wake.

All Angels can kick ass, Emily. We're warriors, remember. And I'll be cleaning your mouth out with soap as soon as we meet up again.

I'd like to see you try, I told him, smoothing Liz's blood soaked hair out of her left eye.

That sounds like a challenge, Em. I may just have to take you up on it.

I grinned and felt my pounding heart start to slow. *Thank you,* I told him. *I know what you were doing there. Giving me something else to think about, I mean. I needed the distraction.*

My pleasure. Good job we weren't relying on you for a distraction… I bit my lip, remembering the kiss in the train only too well. I didn't have to concentrate too hard to remember how it felt to have him kiss me back with real knee-weakening passion. *Major sensory overload, Em,* the he in question scolded with a deep chuckle and I blocked the rest of those thoughts with difficulty, cursing my hormones for allowing me to think about snogging Sariel at a time like this.

There was silence for maybe a minute as we all absorbed what had just happened, or tried to absorb it. Finally sword girl turned around with a mega-watt grin. "Let's start again, folks," she announced brightly. "Hi. I'm Jude. Pleased to meetcha." She shook hands with a shell-shocked Seth. "Wow. That was quite a morning, huh? Where d'you wanna go now?"

I lifted my eyes from Liz's chalk-white face. "A hospital?" I suggested.

CHAPTER TWENTY-TWO

We sat in the car-park opposite St. George's Hospital. It was an old red-brick building with a number of 'modern' cement block annexes added and a sign proclaiming the pertinent parts of the Patient's Charter in six languages. It felt like we'd maybe been watching the place for the best part of a century but Jude, it seemed, was a safety girl and wouldn't consider a course of action until she was certain the area was Demon free.

I knew that Jude's caution was probably sensible but it didn't change the fact that Liz was continuing to bleed onto my pajamas and all over the back seat of the car. I couldn't help worrying that while we looked out for our own asses, Liz's life was ebbing away. Of course, the rest of us would probably die of boredom before Liz died of blood loss.

To take my mind off it all I studied Jude. She was smaller than me with an athletic build and neat, womanly curves enhanced by her tight jeans and a clingy black t-shirt that was short enough to give brief flashes of her taut, pale belly. Her ears, nose and tongue were pierced with subtle plain silver studs and her hair was cut into a fashionable short pixie style and coloured a deep maroon. A tattoo of leaves and thorns wound its way down and around her arms and was visible across her collar bone and even the side of her abdomen. Did it have the layers of meaning that mine did? Or was it just a rebellious teen thing?

Seth, I noticed, was studying her too. He was trying to not be obvious about it but failing miserably and his half-smile told me that he liked what he was seeing. It reminded me of how he'd looked when he was lusting after Amber. Great. Just what we needed; Seth to fall for another female. And this one had a sword. It was like some weird 'Dungeons and Dragons' version of 'Chicks with Guns'. I left Seth to his sword worship (or whatever) and turned my attention to mum. She was looking out of the window beside her, unfazed by the fact that it had no glass and Liz's legs and feet were resting across her knees. I touched her hand and she jumped and then turned to me with a tired smile.

"Sorry," I whispered, "Didn't mean to frighten you."

She took my hand in hers and squeezed gently. "It's okay, sweetheart. I feel..." she frowned, "I feel very strange. Kind of disconnected or something. I mean I can't even remember..." she trailed off, frowning and looking around at the car.

I leaned over and put my head against her shoulder. "Maybe it's shock, I suggested. "I mean, it's not every day you see stuff like that. You going to be ok?"

She nodded and gave a vague, distracted smile. "Of course. If only I could remember what happened..."

I sat back and looked at her, confused. "What happened when, mum?" I asked, suddenly concerned. Was she too young for Alzheimer's? "I mean, bad stuff just seems to be following us about these days."

She opened her mouth to reply and then closed it again. My skin prickled in warning and I shrank away from her, afraid for a reason I couldn't quite understand. I was studying her closely and so I saw it happen. My mother changed before my eyes in a million tiny ways that I probably wouldn't even have noticed if I hadn't been staring right at her. Her eyes hardened, the pupils dilating ever so slightly and her brows drawing down just a little. Her posture stiffened as her spine straightened and her lips thinned as they were pressed tightly together. The tiny lines on either side of her mouth and the crow's feet at the corners of her eyes smoothed almost imperceptibly. She blinked slowly and cocked her head to the side as a sly smile slid across her lips. I had the impression that someone-else had just fitted into my mother's skin and it seriously creeped me out.

"It'll all be fine now, darling. Now that he's gone," she said in a voice so cold that I had to hold back a shiver and my vocal cords prepared themselves for a screech so loud that glaziers in the surrounding area would be doing a roaring trade for months to come.

Don't scream, Sariel whispered and I bit it all back, swallowing the rising tide of panic.

Help her, I stammered, holding my body rigid in an effort to stop myself from losing control and bolting from the car. *Help her now. Do something. Whatever's happening to her, make it stop and help my mum.*

I can't. Sariel's voice was sad and quiet. *He has her, Emily. I think he's had control of her since the party, tracking us through her, listening to our conversations, feeling out our strengths and weaknesses.*

There didn't seem to be enough oxygen in the car all of a sudden. I didn't need to ask who 'he' was and a lot of what had happened in the past few days began to make sense. *She didn't send you away.* I said, earning myself the crown of 'Queen of stating the obvious' but my heart expanded just a little with the realisation.

No, he said. *Asmodeus knows that we are...*

Close? I suggested.

Um, yeah. He obviously believed that separating us would move things along a little faster.

What do we do? I asked, feeling sick. Whatever he was going to say, I knew I wasn't going to like it.

Sariel sighed. *I have to ask you to trust me again, Emily.*

Always, I told him fiercely. And meant it.

Alright. Your mother must stay at the hospital with Liz...

But...

If she doesn't then they will keep finding you. She's like homing beacon for them. She can't help it. And by using her body at will, he has a foolproof way of knowing your plans and keeping one step ahead.

Oh, mum. I wanted to crumple right then. To find a little corner, curl up in it and cry until all this was over.

Hush, Emily. He won't hurt her. He needs her.

I can't abandon her. The thought of it made me feel nauseous.

You'll be keeping her safe while keeping you and Seth out of his reach.

I looked over at her again. Mum, or rather mum's body, had leaned forward as she spoke to Seth and Jude about travelling on and what we should do next.

"It'll take a bit of time to get to the safe house in Bristol," Jude was saying, "But we'll lie low once we leave Liz off and then I'll, er, borrow another car tonight. It'll be easier to drive at night and we should be there in a few hours."

Damn, Sariel and I said together.

I take it we need to come up with an alternative to Bristol then? I asked and he sighed.

I need to talk to Liz, Emily and you can't bring her to me so I'll have to use our link.

Huh?

It's like a conference call with me using your mind to get to Liz.

You can talk to her?

I can reach her mind yes.

Do it then.

Good girl, I could hear the smile in his voice.

Er...will it hurt?

Not much. Press your thumb against her temple and relax against the seat. Breath deep.

I did as he told me but broke contact with Liz as a stab of pain forced my head back. "Son of a ..." Everyone turned to look at me in shock. "Sorry. Bit of a headache." Seth raised an eyebrow but they soon turned away and resumed a quiet conversation about possible Demon hiding places in a hospital so I tried again, bracing myself and grunting as the pain came again. It passed quickly and I felt the cosmos slip out of kilter for a moment as Sariel's full consciousness bloomed inside my head. The sensation was incredible. My body tingled as though expecting a major pins and needles attack but I was calm and relaxed, like I was floating on my back in a swimming pool while someone pulled me gently through the water. I was in control but not in control and the feeling of 'us', of sharing my mind space with another being, was weird but not unpleasant. We were looking through my eyes, my head turned and we looked around the car, he lifted my hand to tuck a stray stand of hair behind my ear, our hearts thudded in perfect time, or was that just my heart? Sariel looked down at Liz and I knew that they were communicating but my mind was free to wander and I did, strolling through Sariel's garden again, lying on the dew-heavy grass and feeling the sun on my face. I was calm,

I was happy, I was…being called back.

I had a moment of extreme vertigo as Sariel turned towards me. Looking back at yourself through your own eyes is a bit like trying to bend over backwards and look through your own legs. I don't recommend it.

We were standing close together and he smiled at me, reaching out to gently caress the curve of my cheek. I closed my eyes, felt the butterfly-soft brush of his lips against mine and then I felt him pull away. There was no pain this time, just a terrible feeling of loss.

It's done, he told me. *She understands.* It sounded so final, and he sounded so resigned as though they had just said goodbye but before I could ask what would happen to her mum turned to look at me.

"You look pale, Emily. Are you feeling ok?"

I nodded, not quite able to meet his/her eyes. "Just tired. Feel a bit sick to be honest. Maybe I stepped on one too many corpses this morning."

Mum's lips smiled, showing way too much of her teeth and I managed to bite back a wave of revulsion, forcing myself to smile back and then turning back to Liz. I could feel Sariel's anger swirling around in my mind and knew that it must mirror how I felt. As far as I was concerned I should have stabbed Asmodeus with a few more Were knives, preferably in his black heart. Then mum wouldn't be his…what was she? His puppet?

When Asmodeus…when he…takes over her body. Does it feel like it felt when you used my mind? I asked him, wanting it to be true. I didn't want to think that my mother was trapped in there somewhere, screaming for us to help her. I bit my lip. Sariel didn't need to tell me, I felt his emotions, read his thoughts as easily as if they were my own. *Asmodeus uses compulsion, strong compulsion. He doesn't ask permission, he just takes over. Joanna isn't really aware,* Sariel told me gently, *and she probably doesn't remember much about the times that he's in control.*

Yes, she was confused there for a while. She was just mum for a few minutes before I saw him take over again and she was confused. It

102

must be horrible for her. I shivered.

When she's separated from you and Seth he won't need to do it anymore. Sariel's voice was gentle but there was a feeling of frustration in it too. He wanted to get us away from her. The clock was ticking and if Asmodeus's troops weren't already here then they would be soon.

He'll leave her alone and she'll be safe? I asked again. Sariel shielded a thought before I could catch it and I smiled wryly. *He won't let her go though, will he?*

She's good leverage, Sariel admitted.

I closed my eyes, wanting to be somewhere else; a beach hut on a Bahamian island, beside Annie in Biology class, herding sheep in Outer Mongolia; anywhere but here, making this decision. Sariel let me think it out for myself and I could feel a slight lessening in his tension when he knew that I had reached the only sensible decision that I could make. He was right. So long as mum was with us, Seth and I were sitting ducks. Leaving her with Liz still felt like desertion and Seth would fight me every step of the way but it would have to be done. I would have to trust that she was worth more to Asmodeus alive than dead.

I folded my arms. *I don't like Jude,* I told him.

She'll grow on you, he told me, his voice anxious but amused.

Yeah, like mould, I grumped. Jude was starting to organize everyone into some kind of weird Demon strike team so that we could get Liz into the hospital. Seth was watching her with an expression somewhere between bemusement and admiration.

It's time, Sariel told me.

I took a deep breath. "I have a better idea," I said and everyone looked at me.

Showtime.

CHAPTER TWENTY-THREE

I inwardly cursed myself using every nasty, evil, horrid, disgusting word that I knew. Everyone had agreed with my reasoning; Jude and I were covered in blood which would lead to way too many questions that we couldn't answer; Seth was just useless and mum was the most able to answer all the questions that would be asked when a middle-aged woman in a mauve twin-set with three deep slashes in her abdomen turned up at St. George's.

When I say that everyone agreed, I mean that Jude and Seth agreed. Mum/Asmodeus kept quiet, watching me with narrowed, thoughtful eyes. "And you'll wait for me?" she asked as we discussed exactly how to go about it.

I nodded, not trusting myself to speak.

"We'll go and ditch this car, find something else and then we'll be back," Jude confirmed. "Once this thing is on their security tapes we won't be able to drive it anymore."

"Shouldn't one of you stay with me?" Mum asked. "Seth could be useful if I need help getting her onto a gurney."

Seth opened his mouth to agree, I opened mine to argue but Jude beat us both to it. "No, if Asmodeus has his guys around then Seth could be walking into the middle of it. We have to keep him with us."

"And what if I walk into it?" Mum asked in a deadly calm voice.

Jude studied her closely for a moment. "You're an adult for a start and not as much use to him as either Seth or Emily would be." I begged to differ on that one but I let Jude carry on. "You're also much more credible if the docs start asking awkward questions. Seth'd be useless."

Seth made a face. "Everyone thinks I'm stupid," he moaned and Jude ruffled his hair.

"Cheer up, sweetie. You're not exactly Einstein but you're definitely cuter," she told him with a grin. Seth's mouth dropped open and he gave me a meaningful look.

We rolled up in front of the A&E entrance moments

after an ambulance. Mum got out of the car and Jude grabbed the first gurney that came out through the doors. An orderly, thinking that we were with the accident victims in the ambulance, helped to load Liz onto it, wincing at her injuries and looking at the rest of us with a suspicious, hostile glare. With the Land Rover missing a hood and several windows it probably did look as though it had just been in a collision. "We'll just park up and then we'll be back," Jude told mum and climbed back into the car.

Mum nodded and turned to follow Liz as I pulled myself across the seat to where she'd been sitting, feeling as though my heart was cracking open. I was leaving my mother. I was abandoning her. I was evil. I could no longer doubt that Asmodeus's Demon blood was flowing through my veins as surely as it was flowing through his own. How would I ever live with myself for doing this? How would Seth ever forgive me?

Mum turned back and her face had changed, she looked frantic. I gasped as she ran back to the car, reached in and took my hand. She reached for Seth's too and he leaned right over Jude to get to her. I almost panicked, convinced that she was about to drag us both out of the car and into the depths of the hospital where Asmodeus's goon squad was waiting to take us to hell. Instead she kissed my hand and then Seth's looking up at me with tear filled eyes that most certainly belonged only to my mother. "Get out of here," she said hoarsely. "Get away and keep driving. Don't come back for me. He has me. I know it. I love you both." She turned to Jude. "Put your foot down and look after my babies."

With that she gave Seth and I one last agonised glance and then, letting go of our grasping hands, turned back to the hospital. Jude shoved Seth away and sped out of the ambulance bay, across two lanes of oncoming traffic and drove like Satan himself was on our tail for almost three miles before pulling into a lay-by and shutting off the engine.

I had begun crying as soon as mum had started to speak. I couldn't seem to stop. I was a human sprinkler system for the back seat, my tears seemed to jet from my eyes as I gave into the anger, fear and loss, feeling despair in the very marrow of my bones. Seth sat with his hands braced against the battered dashboard and his head down. His shoulders shook with silent sobs and I wished I could go to him and put my arms around him but I knew that, at that moment, it would be the wrong thing to do.

Jude turned to look at us both. "Would someone like to tell me what the hell just happened?"

CHAPTER TWENTY-FOUR

I'd never considered McDonalds to be the best place to hole up in a crisis but there we were, knee-deep in fries and strawberry milkshakes, trying to get a handle on the fact that my mum had just sacrificed herself for us. It didn't help that Seth now knew that I'd been willing to sacrifice her anyway. Every now and again he would take a long slurp from his shake and then glare at me over the rim.

"What do you want me to say?" I asked him. "I've said sorry, I've explained everything and you heard it from mum's own lips."

"We left her," he said snagging another chip.

Jude sat back and folded her arms. "Look, it's not that I don't enjoy watching you two play unhappy families but can we just get over this? Asmodeus is hell bent on getting to you and I think it's about time you laid your cards on the table and explain what exactly is going on."

I frowned. "You don't know?"

Jude shook her head. "Sariel called my mum and told her that he needed a protection detail for four people. He gave the address of that Inn, your names and Bob's your uncle."

"You knew Liz though," the chips were getting cold but I ate another one anyway.

"Everyone knows Liz," Jude said with a grin. "She's practically a legend in Demon killing circles."

"So that's what you do?" Seth asked. "Kill Demons?" Jude nodded happily and Seth glanced in my direction. "And what about Demon Spawn?"

She wrinkled her nose. "Are we talking full Demon or half breeds?"

"Um, either." Seth looked nervous now, leaning back a little as he scanned her for possible hidden weapons.

"Full spawn? We kill on sight. Half breeds who have their sire's gifts? We kill on sight. Half breeds over the age of eighteen who have no gifts? We protect. Quite a lot of them work with us." Jude shrugged. "Demon blood is bloody dangerous shit. A half breed who gets most of his or her genes from the Demon is a killing machine. They have to be stopped."

"So, er, how do you 'stop' them?" Seth asked, paling fast.

Jude smiled. "We have swords forged with Angel blood. Lop off the head or strike through the heart and the brats won't make it to their next birthday." She made a sweeping motion with her arm and a "thwick" sound that had Seth reaching for his neck with a grimace.

You sent us a Guardian Angel who wants to kill us? If Sariel had been anywhere near us I might've throttled him (or crawled onto his lap and asked for protection!).

Her bark is worse than her bite, he laughed.

I'm not worried about her biting me...it's that damn sword she's so fond of flinging around that concerns me.

"So, you don't have a lot of love for anyone who doesn't have two human parents?" I asked, watching her.

Jude opened her mouth to reply and then closed it again. She cocked her head to the side and then studied first me and then Seth. "You're Demon Spawn, aren't you?" She said in a curiously emotionless tone.

I nodded and Seth backed his chair slowly away from the table. She looked at him and he stopped dramatically. "Where are you going?" She asked, frowning.

"Out of sword-range," he told her, backing up again.

Jude and I regarded each other across the table. "So, are you full Demon or part?" she asked, placing her hands on the table, palm down.

I wondered if the hands-on-the-table thing was her way of showing that she wasn't going to attack or her preparing to attack. Either way it made me feel damned uncomfortable. "I'm human until someone proves to me that I'm part Demon," I told her.

"You shown any signs yet?" she asked.

"Of what?" Seth was back almost as far as the ketchup stand and almost had to shout to be heard. Jude and I stared at him until he rolled his eyes and slid his chair back to the table. "Are you going to kill me?" He asked softly.

"In the middle of MacDonald's?" Jude made a face and then shook her head. "No, I'm not going to kill you ... yet ... and in answer to your question, I mean, signs of Demon abilities. Inhuman speed or agility? Retractable claws? Venom in your blood or saliva?" Seth and I were shaking our heads, our faces identical masks of disgust.

Jude nodded thoughtfully and chewed on her bottom lip. "So I know who your mum is and I take it Asmodeus is the other half of the puzzle?" We nodded mutely. "Have you always known about your... um... heritage?"

"We found out last year," Seth said, shoveling a few more cold chips into his mouth. "Mum ran away from Asmodeus, first to Seattle and then all the way back to England but he caught up again."

"So what's with all the running and hiding?" Jude asked, looking at me. "As far as I'm aware Demons look after their offspring until they find out what abilities they've inherited."

"Emily kind of stabbed him with a Were relic knife thing," Seth said before I had a chance to.

Jude lifted an eyebrow and her expression was a mixture of surprise and appreciation. "Really? Nice." I shrugged. "You decided you didn't like him or something?"

"He was torturing Sariel," Seth told her.

"I can answer these questions myself, thanks," I snarled at him and he held up his hands. "He was torturing Sariel because Sariel got me a protective tattoo." I finished lamely.

"It's not on her butt cheek," Seth told her with a grin.

"Thank you, Seth." I said shaking my head but Jude was grinning.

"Let me get this straight," she said. "Sariel worked for your... for Asmodeus but took you to get some protective ink and you caught Asmodeus torturing him and stabbed him so now you, Sariel and your family are on the run?"

Seth opened his mouth to provide a few more details but I stepped in, deciding that Jude knew quite enough thank you very much. "That's about it. Liz looked after mum and Seth, some other friend of Sariel's is looking after Gramps and Grandma so we're kind of in need of protection now. Since mum, or rather Asmodeus using mum's body sent Sariel away." Seth and I both shivered at that thought.

"And what's your connection to Sariel?" Jude asked.

I wasn't ready to get into that yet and for once Seth kept his lips sealed. "What's yours?" I asked.

Jude grinned. "What do you know about The Brotherhood?"

I gaped. "Mainly human. Well organized. No-one knows much about who runs it. Into chopping the heads off Demons and stuff." I blinked. "You're in The Brotherhood?"

Jude smiled and sat back, folding her arms and managing to look fierce and smug all at once. "My dad caught a group of Demons once, in the tunnels near London Bridge. There were men, women and several children, all Full Bloods. He came at them yelling and swinging a sword. None of them tried to fight back. He took out four of them before someone clubbed him from behind. When he came to all the Demons were gone and Sariel was sitting beside him. The Demons had been escaping from one of the Houses...you know about those right? Good...So they were escaping and Sariel had been helping them. He'd knocked my dad out but waited to explain things to him."

"What did your dad do?" Seth was leaning forward on the table, his expression serious.

Jude shrugged. "Grabbed his sword and tried to gut the dude. Thought he was one of them." I gasped. "Yeah. He left him for dead, came back to the surface and got some back-up but when they went back, Sariel was gone. He showed up at our safe house a week later, kicked ass without killing anyone and tied my mum, dad, me and my brother to some chairs until he said his piece. Then he left." She paused.

"And that's it?" I asked. 'You met him once and yet you're doing him a favour now?"

Jude swallowed. "No, that's not it. Sariel's involved with the underground system that liberates the peaceful Demons and the Fallen from the Demon Houses. He gets a lot of information from the Demons that he helps and passes it on to us. In return we protect the half breeds who don't ...y'know."

"Who don't show any signs of abilities," Seth finished. "Like me."

"You have nothing?" Jude asked and he shook his head. "And you?" She narrowed her eyes as she looked at me.

"That's for another time." I told her. "So, we can call your dad then."

Jude shook her head. "Dad died five years ago this November. Mum's our Brotherhood contact now. My brother works the Scottish region, mum's all over."

"I'm sorry about your dad," Seth told her, reaching over and taking her hand. Jude smiled at him and kept her hand where it was for a moment and then she looked up at me.

"So you got any ideas where we can go?" She asked.

I nodded. "Actually, I do."

Chapter Twenty-five

Jude 'found' us another car – in the forecourt of a small used car sales – and a change of clothes each from several unattended washing lines, before we left London using as many B roads and lanes as we could find. Jude had, thankfully, come prepared with a rucksack of useful items including her trusty sword and a tattered road map of Great Britain. Seth read the map and I sat in the back seat wondering if my idea was sensible or insane.

You're insane, Sariel had told me.

I think it's genius. Asmodeus'sll never expect it.

You're putting them in danger. That had stopped me in my tracks for a moment.

If they were in trouble I'd want to help. In fact I'd be pissed if they didn't ask me.

If they were in trouble it would probably be algebra homework not death by Demon. And the consequences of figuring out that x is equal to 4 or whatever wouldn't mean that you'd be in danger of being used as wallpaper in hell.

We stopped in a lay-by just outside Halstead and took turns getting some sleep before hitting the road again. Jude drove slowly and carefully, not wanting to draw any attention to the stolen car. We knew that we'd have to ditch it soon and find somewhere that it wouldn't be found for a while. Jude had argued that the best place to leave it would be the long stay car park of an airport but we settled for the rooftop car park of a shopping centre and Jude changed the plates with another car before we left. We started walking. It was just after seven in the morning when we stumbled into a roadside café just outside Sudbury and I made the call from a payphone.

Annie answered her mobile on the third ring, her voice thick with sleep. "Yeah. 'Lo. Whosit?"

"Annie. It's me," I said softly.

For a moment there was a confused silence and then Annie gasped and began whispering urgently into the phone. "Oh my God. Emily. Are you okay? What happened? Is Seth with you?

Where's your mum? You guys just…kapoof. Y'know. Here, gone. No warning. Why didn't you tell me? What could be so bad that you couldn't tell me and Dylan? We've been frantic. Everyone's been talking about it, wondering where you went – did your mum marry that rich guy who said he was your dad? Are you on his island in the Caribbean? These guys came and cleared out your house and everything…"

"What? Who?" I was astonished. I'd never imagined that they would touch our stuff. Never mind clear the whole house out. How dare they! Whoever 'they' were. Would Asmodeus do that? Annie was still talking and I needed to get down to the nitty gritty before the call box ate the rest of my money and spat me out. "Annie? Annie, I need you to listen."

"…so I just told her to keep her…huh?" She paused and I could imagine her sitting there in her room surrounded by her collection of classic movie posters and Stephen Hawking books. "What is it, Em? What do you need?" she asked and her voice was fully awake, calm and more than a little bit fierce.

As soon as she asked what I needed, I knew that she'd be in, no matter what I asked her to do. This was Annie, one half of the greatest best-friend tag team that a girl could have; the Annie who'd been the first to speak to us when we started at Rainey High, the Annie who stood up to the student teacher when he built a DNA model incorrectly, the Annie who was certain that the moon landing was real but that Kennedy had been taken out by aliens, the Annie who I knew I could trust.

I took a deep breath. "This could be dangerous." I warned.

"Please. Danger is my middle name," she stage whispered with a giggle.

"No, it's not. Your middle name is Lynne," I told her, smiling. "Look, does your mum still have the keys to old man Myles' place?"

"Um, yeah. I think so. It never got sold so, yeah." She sounded confused but interested, curious.

"Great. Can you get them without being seen?"

"Of course."

I moistened my lips. This next bit would be the hardest to ask. "And can you skip school and meet us there around lunchtime?" There was silence on the other end of the phone. I wondered if maybe she'd fainted. "Annie? You still there?"

"Yeah. I'm here. You're asking me to skip physics and double chemistry to take a bus and meet you on the far side of Ipswich with my mum's keys to the Myles house? And it's something dangerous?"

I grimaced. Jude had appeared outside the phone box and was making impatient 'come-on' motions. "Um, yeah."

Annie sighed. "You better have a damn good reason for this, Emily."

"I do," I promised. "I wouldn't be dragging you into this if I didn't really need your help, Annie."

"Can I bring Dylan?"

I grinned. "I'd be really upset if you didn't. Think he'll skip classes too?"

"To find out what the hell's going on? Yes. We've missed you, Em."

I ignored the sudden tightening of my heart and the threatened leakage from my tear ducts. "I've missed you guys too. I promise I'll explain everything when we meet you. Oh, and Annie? You can't breathe a word of this to anyone and you can't get caught with those keys."

Annie made a disgusted growling noise. "Well, duh."

Chapter Twenty-six

We made it within two miles of our target by lunchtime. We'd walked and hitched rides and finally pooled our last few pennies to travel the last few miles by bus. All that was left in our pockets was fluff and (in Seth's case) gum wrappers. Jude could probably have done without the bus ride but the truth was that Seth and I just weren't used to walking so far so fast. Maybe I should've asked Annie to swipe her mum's car keys too. Or meet us later. Or at least bring some Elastoplast for all my blisters.

The Myles property was situated about fifteen miles on the far side of Ipswich. There was a rusted iron gate tied with frayed rope and a few 'Trespassers Prosecuted' and "Keep Out' signs which we dutifully ignored as we clambered over the gate and began the long walk down the drive. The house had once been beautiful but now it was as abandoned as Myles' factory back in Deans Lynn. It hunkered down at the end of the drive with dark windows and lots of overgrown ivy looking as tired as we felt.

"Nice." Jude said. "Why are we here again?" She hefted her jacket-wrapped sword a little higher on her back and rolled her neck. It seemed that Seth and I weren't the only ones feeling the effects of such a long walk after all.

I pointed to the sign that had fallen onto the ground in front of the house. "Annie's mum is in property sales. She kind of inherited this place from her predecessor. One of the stipulations in Mr. Myles' will was that the house and land should not be sold to a contractor but to a private family or individual who would live in it as a home and not knock it down and build apartments."

"No takers then?" Jude said with a grin.

"Mrs. Poole has had the keys hanging up in her house for about six years. She used to keep them in the safe at work but this place has become a kind of joke and the keys were too much of a reminder."

"I reckon she wants to lose them," Seth said with a yawn. "Why else would you bring them home where your kids could nick them?"

"Won't she notice that they're gone?" Jude asked as we walked slowly around the house, examining all the possible entry points.

I shook my head. "Last time I saw them they were on a nail under the stairs."

"There," Jude said pointing to a second floor window opening that, as far as we could see from below, had no glass in it.

"Yeah but how are you gonna get up there?" asked Seth, putting his hands on his hips and leaning back to look up.

Jude rolled her eyes. "I can climb like a monkey." She shifted the weight of the sword again and moved towards the house, grasping a rusting pipe.

Seth grabbed her arm. "Wait. Why is the window out? Maybe there's squatters. They could be dangerous. Maybe I should go first." Jude gaped at him. My mouth dropped open and I couldn't quite stifle a laugh. Seth glowered at me. "What?"

"Hello? You can't climb and she has a sword!" I giggled.

"Yeah and I doubt if they do," Jude told him and then her features softened. "Thanks for the thought though." She leaned over, kissed his cheek and then began climbing. I don't know who was more surprised but Seth and I both stood looking at each other with identical expressions of astonishment.

Jude heaved herself in through the open window and we waited. Seth hopped from foot to foot. "This is insane. She could be getting splattered against a wall or eaten or anything. One of us should've gone."

"Thanks," I mumbled. "Doesn't matter if I get eaten does it? So long as Jude's safe." I folded my arms and rolled my eyes. Seth ignored me and we were both still watching the window when a hand descended on our shoulders and we both jumped six feet into the air. Seth retaliated by doing a ridiculous Jackie Chan impression, complete with hand-chopping maneuvers, and I hid behind him.

Jude almost bust a gut laughing at us.

It turned out that she had climbed in the window, made a quick sweep of the upstairs and then the downstairs before unlatching the front door and creeping around behind us. Bitch.

We trooped inside and the stale, musty smell of a house that's been closed up for almost 20 years enveloped us. It was cosy in a slightly eerie, furniture-covered-in-white-sheets kind of way. Dust lay thick on everything and, as we walked through the house, motes flashed and danced around us, making Seth sneeze and cobwebs got caught in our hair making me freak until Jude assured me that I had no spiders dangling from my ear lobes or anything.

The upstairs was just as bad – more ghostly furniture and a spread of ancient leaves coming from the room with no window. There was no broken glass and no frame lying around anywhere which was confusing, I mean, is there a market for single sash windows?

We were standing in the main bedroom looking around us with varying degrees of concern and depression when the door downstairs opened with a soft creak and a voice called out. "Emily? Seth?"

It was Annie and Dylan, delighted Seth and I scooted from the room as Jude tried in vain to calm us down and called for us to be more cautious. The two of us thundered down the stairs and for the next few minutes there was a lot of hugging and chattering in excited, squeaky voices.

"Oh, God," said Jude, standing on the bottom stair. "I have just landed in Nerd central."

Seth, Annie, Dylan and I turned to look at her in annoyance. Jude's eyes fell on Dylan and she brightened. "Oh, hello cutie. Maybe things aren't so bad after all."

Annie made a growling sound in her throat which was echoed by Seth while Dylan gulped and tried to hide his embarrassment. I glared at Jude. What a great start. Not.

CHAPTER TWENTY-SEVEN

Annie had brought food. And not just any food – chocolate. We sat on the floor in a patch of sunlight and ate a bar each, catching up on life in general. By silent agreement we were keeping the topics light; Sarah's latest piercing (yet another stud in her right ear-lobe), Adam's latest hotness (shaggier hair and a black eye from rugby practice. Yum.), Amber's constant whining (nothing new there) and how freaked everyone had been about final exams. That made me pause with a square of calorific yumminess halfway to my mouth. Final exams. I'd almost forgotten that Seth and I should have been getting ready to finish school. A stab of bitterness shot through me and I put the chocolate back into its wrapper. I'd lost my appetite. Annie looked over at me, puzzled by my sudden silence.

"Is it time for you to spill, Em?" she asked softly.

I sighed and pulled my knees up to my chin. "Yeah, I think you need to know now."

"If you guys are going to start talking about Pythagoras and shit then I'm gonna take a walk," Jude said standing up. She glanced at Dylan. "Wanna come with me, cutie?"

Dylan frowned and looked at Annie who shook her head and smothered a grin. "Er, no. Thanks all the same," Dylan said and tucked himself a little closer to Seth.

"Suit yourself," Jude wandered off, taking the bundle that her sword was wrapped in with her. We listened to her whistling for a while until it grew too faint to hear properly and then I turned to my friends and managed a smile.

"She scares me," Dylan said. "She's all hard angles and she looks at me like I'm edible."

"You are, D," Annie told him and ruffled his crazy hair affectionately.

"Ok. If you say so, but if that's how it feels to be a sex symbol then I don't think I like it." He looked so serious that it would've been a crime to laugh so I bit the inside of my cheek instead.

Seth was looking at our friends with a curious expression on his face. "What are you thinking?" I asked him, eager to stay off the subject of Demons and evil dudes for as long as possible.

Seth shrugged and studied his knees for a moment. "It's just… well, I'm not sure how to put it but you guys are so familiar but it's been so long since we saw you that I'm seeing you differently. Does that sound weird?" He grinned self-consciously.

Dylan shook his head. "No. You guys look different too. More…grown up. More serious. Your eyes have secrets."

I looked at him in astonishment. "What does that mean?"

Dylan frowned and stared at me for a moment. "Maybe it's psychological, I mean I know that you have something to tell us. Something big. So maybe when I look at you my brain is expecting to see that in you and since the eyes are said to be the windows to the soul then that's where I should see the most difference."

"And you've lost weight," Annie said squinting at first me and then Seth. "And bulked out in the muscle department." She raised an eyebrow and Seth went into muscleman pose for a few minutes which made us all laugh.

The laughter trailed away and we sat looking at each other. The moment had come and I was suddenly wary, remembering Sariel's warning. *Am I doing the right thing?*

Only you can decide that.

Will they be in danger?

You know they will.

So I shouldn't tell them.

You have to weigh up the consequences of each action. You'll make the right choice.

You should hire yourself out. 'Sariel's Special Remedy for Helplessness - Figure it out yourself.'

He laughed and the sound warmed me so I took a deep breath and turned to our friends, reaching for Seth's hand as I began to speak, needing an anchor to what was real and important as I brought two more innocent people into the firing line.

Chapter Twenty-eight

Outing the skeleton in my family's closet didn't take as long as I expected. It was, however, painfully embarrassing to suddenly be talking about Angels and Demons to my science loving, nerd friends. Why is it, I wondered, that I could discuss my inability to come up with the correct mathematical formula to work out how many flies it would take to pull a car (Yeah, okay but it was a slow school lunchtime and all our sandwiches had been eaten) without any feelings of inadequacy but when it came to talking about God and religion, I became a quivering jelly of embarrassment? Odd.

And so I stopped talking and waited, not even able to look at Dylan or Annie's faces in case they were laughing, freaking out or just plain confused. I wouldn't have blamed them for any of those reactions. What I wasn't expecting was for Dylan to turn to Annie with a completely excited grin and say, "Didn't I tell you that every human situation has a home in 'Star Wars'?"

Annie rolled her eyes. "D, Human beings did not begin with the first 'Star Wars' movie. How many times do we have to have this discussion?"

Dylan made a face. "I understand what you're saying, even though the first 'Star War's movie was technically episode four," Annie opened her mouth to complain but Dylan held up a hand and she resorted to glaring at him. "You get what I mean though, right Seth?"

Seth was still holding my hand and he gave it a little squeeze before letting go. "Let's assume I can go along with it for now. Explain your theory."

Dylan smiled a total Dylan grin of complete happiness and leaned forward. "Well, it's like this. Your...do you call him dad?" Seth and I shook our heads vigorously. "Ok, so this Asmodeus dude is Darth Vadar. Y'know all scary and evil and ..." he began to make asthmatic wheezing sounds that were obviously supposed to be scary-Vadar-noises.

"Will you stop before you pass out," Annie complained but she was trying hard not to grin.

Dylan smiled and hugged her. "Ok, so yeah. Asmowhatsit is Darth Vadar and you are his kids which makes you..." He pointed to Seth.

"Luke Skywalker," Seth said with a smile.

Dylan considered that with a frown. "Well, considering it was Emily who y'know, stabbed him and stuff, then she should really be Luke which makes you Leia."

"What?! No way! I'm not being the girl!" Seth sat up a little taller and spread his hands out, looking at the rest of us with a 'come-on' expression.

"Well, obviously it would work much better if you were female seeing as Sariel would be ..."

"Han Solo," Annie and I finished for him.

Seth frowned at us. "Will you two quit encouraging him?" He turned back to Dylan as Annie and I giggled. "So, your theory basically falls apart right there, pal."

Dylan frowned and bit his lip. "How does it? Asmodeus is evil dude, hence Vadar, Emily is the Luke in the story, you are Leia..."

"No, no, no and again no." Seth was shaking his head. "We can all see that I am not Leia and I don't have the hots for Sariel which Em definitely does so therefore I am Luke and she is Leia. Which makes you C3PO and Annie R2D2." He grinned around at us, delighted with himself.

Dylan looked crushed. "I'm a bumbling, complaining, annoying collection of gold metal and delicate circuitry?"

Annie rolled her eyes and wrapped an arm around him. "No, sweetie, you and I are the brain boxes of the operation. We move the story along, help to defeat the bad guys and look out for our friends. That's us."

Dylan smiled and bent to kiss the tip of her nose. "You're right. That IS us." They grinned at each other and I couldn't help but feel a pang of jealousy. I wanted that with someone. That sweet, romantic, ridiculous closeness. Wait, is that what I really wanted? I sighed. It all went back to the kisses, didn't it? Adam's kiss had been soft and sweet and...well, boring; Sariel's had been hot, intoxicating, exciting. Which one did I prefer? Yep, the centuries-old Fallen Angel trumped the hot teen Werewolf that I'd been lusting after for years. So maybe the Annie/Dylan type of relationship would bore me to tears.

I shook my head. This was SO not the time to be getting into the Sariel/Adam debate. "So, you guys are taking this pretty well," I said.

Dylan shrugged. "It makes more sense than your mum running off to Barbados to get married. I mean, you'd have been on the phone about that, right?"

Annie nodded. "Yeah, so we knew it had to be something really monumental to make you all up sticks and leave without telling us."

Dylan nodded. "I mean, I know Annie and I kind of left you out of things a bit for a while but we were all still buds, right?" He looked sheepishly up at me from beneath his tangled curls.

"Dylan, you and Annie didn't leave me out. It felt weird for a while, yeah, and I probably didn't deal with it as well as I could've but I'm glad you two are together, and I'm glad we're all still buds." I hugged him, feeling his bony arms link around my waist and then Annie hugged both of us and then Seth wrapped himself awkwardly around us all. We broke apart giggling and feeling goofy but it was a sweet moment that went a long way towards making me feel like a normal seventeen year old for a while.

"So," Annie began, "What happens now?" I sighed. "Well, that's where it gets complicated. Now you know what's actually going on, it kind of puts you in more danger."

"But," interrupted Seth, "It also means that you can be on the lookout for potential threats…now you know what to look for."

I bit the inside of my lip. "Maybe we shouldn't have told you."

Annie shook her head vigorously. "No, Emily. What's the best way for a scientist to produce a decent hypothesis?"

I grinned. "Information."

"Exactly," Dylan waggled a finger in my direction. "No-one can make an informed decision or reach a precise conclusion without first having all the necessary information at his or her fingertips."

"So we should get you a phone," Annie said, talking to no-one in particular. "One of those pre-pay things that can't be traced. Then we can let you know what's going on and you can stay one step ahead of Darth Vadar."

Seth and I looked at each other. "But they could be tracing your phones," Seth said, "If you buy into the whole 'they-can-do-whatever-they-want' theory." He made a face.

"I do buy that. These aren't just Demons; they're powerful Demons, Seth. We'll use payphones, a different one every time. They can't tap every phone in Suffolk." I grinned. Annie was really getting into this.

"What would they do?" Dylan asked softly. Seth and I turned to him but he was looking at Annie with concern. "If they caught us, I mean. What would they do?"

I swallowed. I didn't want to lie to him but I didn't want to tell him the truth and scare them both either. In the end, Seth saved me the trouble. "They would probably torture you first, to see if you'd tell them where we were. Or they might use you as bait to make us come and try to save you. But in the end they would probably kill you."

Dylan lifted his eyes to mine. "This is really serious shit, isn't it?" Annie came over and linked her arm with his.

I nodded slowly. "I shouldn't have brought you into this," I whispered.

Annie swung on me. "We've just had this conversation, Emily. Quit second guessing yourself on everything. If you do, then you won't last long. You have to do what your gut tells you is right – it usually is. And the consequences may not be pretty but I for one am glad to see you, to know what's going on and, well, whatever happens from here on in? We'll deal with it. Okay?" Beside her, Dylan nodded stubbornly.

I grinned and opened my mouth to say something. It would probably have been smart or funny or sweet or crazy but before the words could leave my mouth, the door behind me opened fast, banging against the wall as Jude came running into the room. "Which one of you nerd assholes did it?" She screamed, raising her sword in Annie's direction. "Which one of you led them here?"

CHAPTER TWENTY-NINE

For a moment the four of us stood frozen in shock – well, it wasn't every day that a girl pointed a sword at you.

"So, which one of you did it?" Jude asked, advancing towards us, her eyes glittering with anger. Annie took a step back and stumbled, falling into Dylan who grabbed Seth's arm as he fell. The three of them landed in a gangly heap of flailing arms and legs. "Bloody Demon Spawn and twisted, pathetic little Emos," Jude screamed at them and raised the sword above her head. Maybe a few seconds had passed since the door had opened and I felt a sickening lurch of adrenaline course through my veins as I wondered what the hell had Jude so worked up and how she could mistake Annie's flower-power dress and desert boot combo as anything remotely Emo before the look of honest, naked fear on Dylan's face spurred me into action.

"Oh, for crying out loud," I shouted, "Get a grip, you demented Xena wannabe and stop pointing that thing at my friends."

As heroic speeches went, it wasn't exactly an Oscar-worthy performance but it had the desired effect of turning Jude's attention from the Seth-Dylan-Annie beast on the floor. I had a split second to congratulate myself on a job well done before the 'Oh-crap' sinking sensation of realizing that her shiny, sharp sword had begun its downward arc just before I caught her attention and it was now heading towards my head.

I may have screamed, or that may have been Annie. I may even have held up a hand in a pathetic attempt to protect myself. Or I may have just stood there gaping like a gormless nerd who was about to get chopped in two.

The hand that actually saved me seemed to materialize from thin air. It wrapped itself around Jude's sword arm and yanked her to the right. Jude made a startled 'uh' sound and her sword buried itself in the gorgeous oak of Mr. Myles' living room floor.

There was silence for a few seconds while I patted myself down, astonished to still be in one piece. I grinned happily at my brother and friends as they clambered to their feet, and then I whirled

124

around again and punched Jude in the face. I don't know who was more surprised – me or Jude - but Jude's nose made a resounding and truly satisfying crack and immediately began to gush blood. She rocked back on her heels and grabbed for the ruin of her nose, cursing me with every colourful expletive that she could think of – she had a remarkably good vocabulary for someone who swung a sword for a living.

Allowing myself a second or two to admire my handiwork, I turned my attention to my saviour who was regarding me with an expression which hovered between amusement and annoyance. He was tall with short blond hair and blue eyes that reminded me of Sariel's. He looked like a walking advertisement for sun-kissed, all-American beefcake but there was a hardness to his pretty eyes and a haughty twist to his lips that took the edge off his attractiveness.

"Perhaps you could save your childish outbursts for a more appropriate time. We need to leave. Now." Yep, his voice matched his features – icy, smooth and shot through with a touch of sarcasm. He grasped Jude by the arm and turned for the door. Seth and Dylan made to follow him but Annie and I, obviously on the same wave length, held them back. He turned back when he realized that we weren't following and raised an eyebrow. "Is there a problem?"

I folded my arms and looked him up and down. "Perhaps you could introduce yourself and tell us where we're going and why we should follow you anywhere." Annie nodded and folded her arms too.

He sighed and rolled his eyes. "I apologise. I was under the impression that your lives were more important that any rules of etiquette." He propped Jude up against the banister in the hall and walked back to us, stretching out a hand. "My name is Armaros, commonly known as Aaron. I was sent here by Sariel to find you and escort you to your flight which he has arranged and which will be leaving in the early hours of the morning for the safety of his house in Italy. Now, if that is acceptable to you then follow me to my car. The Weres are regrouping, we don't have much time."

Sariel?

Go with him. Go now.

I started moving, motioning to the others to follow me. *A little heads up would've been nice.* Sariel's only answer was an exasperated sigh. *Yes, okay,* I told him, *We're going, we're going.*

Outside the house, the world had changed. We ran back down the drive from the Myles place through air that seemed super-charged with anticipation. The night pressed down on us, filling everyone with the need to hurry and I felt the prickling sensation of eyes watching us as we climbed, vaulted and levered ourselves over the fence and towards Aaron's waiting suv. Jude hopped into the front seat and Aaron started the car as Annie, Dylan, Seth and I squeezed ourselves into the back. We peeled away with a screech of tyres and a storm of small stones. Annie and Dylan looked pale while Seth was watching out the rear windscreen with a look of anxiety on his face.

Behind us a wolf began to howl, its mournful song joined by another and another and another until the whole world around us seemed to vibrate with sound. Annie covered her ears and Seth grimaced. "So many of them," Dylan whispered. I squeezed his hand and he squeezed mine back and smiled half-heartedly.

Jude turned around in her seat to face me. Her nose had stopped bleeding but was swollen and she was covered in blood. I felt a momentary pang of guilt, swiftly followed by the image of her sword flashing towards me. "So, who wad id?" she asked. "Who tode them we were dere."

Aaron spoke up. "No-one told them. The Alpha's son marked her. He could scent her when she was still miles away. Finding her this close to the pack was easy."

I gaped. "Adam 'marked' me. How? Why?"

Aaron's eyes met mine in the rear-view mirror. "He marked you with his scent sometime. I would imagine a Were pup would find it easy to dazzle a girl like you for long enough to mark you with his scent." I choked back a retort – 'girl like you' indeed - remembered Adam's out-of-character kiss at the station and shuddered. "Marking you like that was clever – after all, they have

126

a vested interest in making sure Asmodeus gets you back."

I frowned, confused. "What do you mean?"

It was Aaron's turn to frown. "He didn't tell you?"

"Who? And tell me what?"

Aaron's head cocked to the side and his eyes drifted for a moment, as though he was listening and I knew immediately who he was listening to.

Sariel? What's going on.

He sighed. *I didn't want you to find out like this, Emily.*

Find out what? You're scaring me.

The Weres put a bid in with Asmodeus for you. Rick wants Adam to claim you on your eighteenth.

"Pull over," I told Aaron. "I'm going to be sick."

CHAPTER THIRTY

Explaining to my two best friends why I had just thrown up into a ditch was excruciating. Even Seth looked embarrassed for me. Annie was predictably enraged, Dylan was, even more predictably, confused.

"So let me get this straight," I heard him whisper to Annie a little later while I pretended to get some sleep, "Adam's dad is the Werewolf Alpha, yes?" I assume Annie nodded. "Right, and he has promised to pay Emily's dad a certain amount of money if he allows Adam to have sex with her on her eighteenth?" Annie probably nodded again. "Well, I don't get it."

"What don't you get? They're all warped assholes." Annie sounded livid, even when she was whispering.

"Yeah, yeah, I get that but...well...why didn't Adam just ask Emily?" I could imagine Dylan sitting there with a look of ponderous confusion in his dark eyes. He was probably stroking his chin too.

"Ask Emily what?" Annie almost forgot to whisper.

"Well, you know...if Adam wanted to have sex with her she'd probably have said yes if he asked. You know what she's like about him." I cringed with shame and felt my cheeks heat up. Dylan was right – all Adam would've had to do was pay me some attention, maybe throw in some flattery and a bottle of Cherry Coke (hell, even a can of Diet Coke) and I'd probably have gone along with anything he wanted. Damn. Was I that easy?

"Well, maybe this makes it easier for Emily," Annie said softly.

"How?" That was Seth, joining the conversation.

"Well, if Adam wins the...what is it? An auction? Whatever. If their bid wins then she could convince Adam to just pretend to do ...stuff. Asmodeus doesn't need to know if they actually do the deed or not." There was a general murmuring of agreement until Aaron spoke up from the front seat.

"Sorry to burst your bubble, folks, but that's not how it works."

"Why nod?" Jude was listening-in too? Terrific.

"Well, because the winner takes his….prize in front of everyone else."

There was a stunned silence in the car as everyone digested that little nugget of information. Gross. Vile. Horrible. Disgusting. Repellent. Nauseating. Loathsome. Repugnant. Shocking. Dreadful. Horrifying. Ick of the highest ickiness. Not even my vocabulary had enough words for what I thought. My brain just couldn't seem to deal with the foulness of the situation. If Asmodeus had been standing anywhere near me at that moment I would've tried to stab him again with anything and everything close by ; knives, forks, spoons, flower pots, staples, pens, pencils, rulers, protractors, compass, photo frames, bottles. My mind went through a mental list of everything that I could've grabbed in our tiny kitchen at home. He would've been a walking weird pin-cushion by the time I'd finished. And then I'd have chopped his head off with Jude's sword. And found somewhere to stick the Were knife while I was at it.

Funny, isn't it. Just over a year ago I was a fairly mild mannered nerd going to school and rebelling at having to do the hoovering for my mum. Now I was planning the most satisfying way to murder my dad with kitchen implements. I was going to hell for sure.

My brain couldn't handle any more. I squeezed my eyes shut and willed myself to my dream house. Not surprisingly there was a storm raging outside beyond the picture windows. I watched in the darkness as jagged lightning lit up the surface of the ocean, dark clouds rolled in the heavens and thunder reverberated around me. It was fascinating and terrifying – the physical manifestation of my feelings. And I was suddenly tired. Not just a little bit sleepy, but absolutely wearied and worn out. I made for my library, thinking that sitting in my comfy old armchair and inhaling the scent of all the old books would be as soothing as anything. I came to a standstill just inside the door.

A man was sitting in my chair. The man who had rowed to my secret place in that little boat, who had found my location when no-one else could, who had dragged his boat onto my beach and waited for me in my haven. And now he was drinking tea from my mug and reading one of my books. He looked up as I came in and grinned.

"Hello Emily," said Asmodeus.

Chapter Thirty-one

Wow. In a sea of recent crap days this surely had to be the crappiest.

"I was just thinking about you," I told Asmodeus. My mind was spinning. How did he get in here? What was he doing here? What the hell was I going to do?

Asmodeus sat back in the chair, my chair, and contemplated me lazily. I had never in my life felt more like prey, waiting for the predator to strike. "You missed me?" he asked.

I shook my head. "I wouldn't say that. I mean, I guess I would've felt better if I'd stuck the knife right into your heart, or maybe even a major artery but I wouldn't say I missed you." I gulped. Where had that come from? Was I insane?

Asmodeus, however, seemed to find it amusing. He chuckled and took another drink from his mug, my mug. He regarded me over the rim. "Did you know?" he asked.

"That I hadn't killed you? I think the bellowing that you did kinda gave it away but after we ran? No, I didn't know." I moved a little further into the room and leaned my back against the book shelves.

He nodded. "I actually meant did you know that the Were knife was powerful enough to kill me but I suppose you've just answered that question too."

"I lifted the first thing that came to hand on the table. I guess it was luck, or maybe fate. Or perhaps God stepped in." I couldn't help smiling at that one.

Asmodeus smiled too. "I think we both know that's not an option. He doesn't care what happens to you, me, Sariel...none of us and definitely none of them." I assumed he meant humans. I said nothing. How could I defend a God that I hadn't even believed existed until recently? Asmodeus leaned forward in his seat and I instinctively pushed my back further into the case behind me. "He's a scientist you know."

"God's a scientist?" Well, that was a new one. "Never mind your philosophizing. How's mum?"

He made a dismissive motion with his hand. "She's fine. May never get over being dumped by her kids but, hey, life's a bitch, right? So anyway, back to God." I shrugged off his comments about Mum. She'd known what we were doing, she'd even told us to do it. The fact that I was still weighed down by the guilt of actually doing it was an easy point for him to score with. I let him keep talking. "He took this planet in this existence and breathed His spark of life onto it. Then He decided to make it even more interesting. He created beings, a male and a female and He created a special place for them, appointed some of us to watch over them and then waited to see what happened. He thought that they were fascinating, wonderful, amazing, He got so full of Himself, so drunk on the glory of His ability to create. And then He wanted His Angels to think that they were glorious too. He wanted them to bow down before them like they had to bow before Him. He wanted them to swear their lives for the humans, to fight for them on this world if they needed it. He knew, you see, knew that there were ancient beings on this planet, ancient beings that He forced out before He could take over. Ancient Demons."

I frowned. "Demons were here first."

Asmodeus nodded. "This was their planet and they won't rest until they get it back, until humanity is wiped from the face of it, or converted."

"Converted? Yeuk. That doesn't sound good."

He chuckled again. "Sometimes you seem so wise and then you say something like that and I remember that you're still a child."

I rolled my eyes. "So, why are you telling me all this? Is this part of the 'conversion' thingy?"

He shook his head and leaned back in his seat again. "No, I want you to understand the part that you play in this."

"Oh, dear," I scoffed. "What a pity but you seem to have me confused with someone-else. I don't have a 'part' in anything except the mess that you've made of my life." I stabbed a finger at him. "You messed up my mum's life and just when she was getting it together you showed up again and now look at us. The only 'part' I have here is a victim of you being an asshole."

He looked surprised. "I'm a Demon…"

I shook my head and folded my arms again. "That's secondary. There are plenty of other deadbeat dads out there who can't blame the fact that they have Demon DNA to excuse the mess they make of their kids' lives. I agree that all of you should burn in hell but that's it."

Asmodeus smiled thoughtfully. "So, if I wasn't a Demon….?"

"You'd still make a lousy dad."

He shook his head. "We're getting off the point…"

"Oh, yes, please, let's get back to the point." I drawled and rolled my eyes again.

"Emily!" Asmodeus shouted and the walls of my mind practically shook with the force of it. "You will listen to me!"

Ignoring the fact that my heart was now beating frantically and I was covered in goose bumps of fear, my mouth seemed to have its own agenda. "Yeah, whatever. Get on with it." I said. I tried to bite my tongue. *Shut up*, I told myself.

Asmodeus took a few deep breaths – probably to stop him from reaching out and throttling me. "When Lucifer refused to bow down to the humans that God had made, it started a kind of revolution in heaven. There were those who followed God blindly, accepting His will and His commands as the absolute authority and there were those who had more….rebellious natures. Lucifer became their spokesman. Great battles were fought and eventually God and His supporters triumphed. Lucifer and his supporters were banished from heaven."

"Blah, blah, blah. And they became Demons and built little Demon homes together and named the town Hell and so on and so forth. I know all this stuff." I made impatient twirling motions with my finger. "Are you done now?"

Asmodeus's face darkened with fury again but he held onto his temper with a control that I couldn't help but be impressed by. "The humans that God created disappointed Him," he continued, "They disobeyed Him and so He cast them out from the protection of their garden and onto the planet. He set Watchers in place to keep an eye on them but the Watchers were never supposed to interact with the humans. They were only to watch, never to reveal themselves. But they saw the beauty of the human women and they spoke to the humans to get closer to the women."

I sighed. "Again with the yadda, yadda, yadda. I know where you're going with this. Sariel was one of the Watchers, he got chucked out of heaven 'cause he screwed one of the humans. I know all this so you aren't telling me anything that's going to make me hate Sariel. Forget it. Go home."

Asmodeus grinned. "Is that what he told you?" I looked at him which I suppose was answer enough. Asmodeus threw back his head and laughed uproariously. He shook his head. "Oh, that's just so precious." His laughter trailed away and he focused his attention on me. "Sariel didn't fall because of lust, Emily. He fell because he shared the secrets of Heaven with the humans. You think all those ancient civilizations were smart enough to build all those incredible temples and cities on their own. You think the Atlanteans figured out how to use the power of the universe on their own? Or the Nazca lines were drawn without the help of beings who could actually look down from Heaven?" He paused and cocked his head to the side. "Perhaps you're one of the poor deluded individuals who think that aliens came by and helped out?" I gave him as withering a look as I could manage and he grinned. "I didn't think so. So I suppose what you have to figure out is why Sariel would lie to you about why he fell, especially when he needs you so badly."

I tutted at him. "Don't be ridiculous. Sariel doesn't need me; he's just helping me to get away from you, like he's helped loads of other people too."

Asmodeus made an exaggeratedly sad face. "Oh, poor Emily. Kept in the dark about absolutely everything." He shook his head and sipped at his drink again. "What are the Fallen most afraid of?"

"Nothing." I told him without hesitation, earning myself another chuckle.

He made an 'errrrrrrrr' sound. "Incorrect, Emily. Try again."

I shrugged. "Boredom."

"Not a bad try," said Asmodeus, " But errrrrrrr. Incorrect. The Fallen are afraid of turning." He sat back, clearly delighted with himself for imparting this precious knowledge.

"Turning?" I scoffed. "Turning into what? Butterflies? Fashion victims?"

Asmodeus leaned forward again, looking me in the eye. "Demons, Emily. Push them hard enough, torture them often enough, take away all the things that they form attachments to, break their hearts, blacken their souls and eventually they are 'converted'; they turn into Demons." He waited. I held his gaze calmly but my mind had already processed the information and found the truth in it. Sariel's 'changes'; the black eyes, the fiery rage, even the gravelly voice and the red walls around his mind. Those were all symptoms of a deeper sickness. "Sariel's time is running out. He's held on for a very long time, longer than any of the others we've caught but he's close to breaking now. I can feel it in him and I know you do too." He stood up slowly and carefully and came to stand in front of me. I let him. He wasn't going to hurt me. That wasn't the point of this little visit.

"You want to know what your 'part' is, Emily?" he asked in a voice that was full of quiet anticipation. This was the endgame. This was why he was here. And suddenly I was afraid. I didn't want to hear this. I didn't want to play his guessing games anymore.

"No," I told him. My voice was soft and I could hear the tremble in it.

Asmodeus licked his lips, his eyes were shining. "The Fallen believed that they would not be left here forever. They believed that one day they would be forgiven and presented with the means to return home. That their God would send a sign, a portent. A human, who would be marked by one of the Archangels and who would bring them home." He paused. "They've been waiting for a very long time, Emily. Sariel thinks that you're the sign. You want to know why he lied about how he fell?" I shook my head. "Ah, well, since I'm in the mood to spill the beans, I'm going to tell you anyway. Anyone with half a brain can see that you want him, your tongue practically hangs out of your mouth every time you're around him. He knows how you feel, he knows what you want. And it suits him to keep you like that until he gets the confirmation from the others. Confirmation that you're who he thinks you are. Until then he'll string you along, maybe hold your hand now and again, perhaps even give you the odd, hot, hungry kiss. Has he done that, Emily? Have you been kissed by a Fallen Angel? I bet it felt good. I bet it blew your tiny little half-human mind." He sniggered and I closed my eyes. "But the truth is, Emily, that you're just a tool to save him and the others. The truth is..." I felt his breath on my forehead and gasped. How had he managed to get so close? I willed my eyes to stay closed. "...he doesn't want you. He's repelled by you. You're too young, too naïve, too ugly for the likes of him, too..."

Something snapped in my head and my eyes popped open. I felt cold and hot at the same time. My mind emptied of everything but anger. Asmodeus stepped back, his face was expressionless. My arms rose from my sides and outside, the storm rose in intensity. Lightning flashed, the air sizzled and crackled with energy and my eyes blurred. I felt it then, a power so deep and so strong that it almost overbalanced me. It was waiting, wanted me to take it in, to use it. And, oh, I wanted to. I wanted to cut Asmodeus down where he stood, to make him suffer. I opened my mind to reach for the power, to let it fill me up and then I heard him very faintly. Sariel. He sounded hoarse, like he'd been shouting for hours. It was only through force of habit that I listened to him and it was only for a second, but it was enough.

Mind games, Emily, Sariel was yelling. *He's playing mind games with you. He wants you to do this. He wants you to surrender to him, to your blood. He wants...*

I tuned him out, forced him away and turned back to Asmodeus. He was practically rubbing his hands together, his smile was wide and his eyes were glittering; his cheeks flushed with happiness. And then he realized that I was staring at him calmly. The change was almost comical. His mouth dropped open in shock and his hands reached for me. "No," he began to shout. "Do it! Take it. It's yours. Use it. Become my daughter. Become..."

My brain and mouth, thankfully still operating on some level that the rest of me wasn't attuned to, saved me. "Get out of my head," I told him softly and pfft. Just like that Asmodeus was gone.

CHAPTER THIRTY-TWO

I woke up in near darkness, with a number of blurry pale faces staring down at me. "I think she's back," said a voice that I recognized as Aaron's. There was a muted purring sound all around and a weird unbalanced feeling.

"Oh, thank God." That was Annie, sounding scared but relieved.

"Does that mean she's safe?" Seth, his voice ragged with worry.

"For now." Jude, close by.

"Bene, everyone. Get back and give her some space. Here, Emily. Drink this," It was a woman's voice. I sat up and wiped tears from my eyes and face, accepting a small cup of water from none other than Isabella D'Anucci. I almost dropped the cup in shock. She smiled. "Is okay. You are safe now."

"But…" I said and was shocked at how growly my voice was. "You…" I sighed and took a deep breath before I tried again. "You and Asmodeus. You're his friends."

Isabella smiled sadly. "No. Not un amico. Never. But he is powerful and he knows who we are. Sometimes it is necessary to …" she spoke a few rapid words in Italian to someone behind me.

"Put on an act. Pretend." The voice translated. I looked over the seat. A boy of about nineteen was sitting there, leafing through a magazine. He smiled at me. "Glad you finally woke up."

I frowned and shifted so that I was sitting up more comfortably. I sipped the water and looked around. "Hey. When did we get on the plane?" I asked, surprised.

"While you were fighting the evil dragon," Seth said from beside me. He gave me an awkward hug and I laid my head on his shoulder.

"What did I do?" I asked softly. I was suddenly feeling really embarrassed.

Seth shrugged. "You fell asleep in the car. We figured you were just tired."

"And then Sariel kind of told Aaron. Somehow." Dylan leaned

138

over from the seat in front. "They seem to have some kind of Martian mind-meld thing going on." I grinned at him, although he actually looked serious.

"So then we couldn't wake you." Annie's head popped up beside Dylan's. "It was really scary. I thought you were dead." She gulped and Dylan put an arm around her shoulders. She leaned into him gratefully.

"So then you started mumbling about Asmodeus." Jude appeared beside Isabella. Her nose had been taped up but it was still swollen. She'd changed into a clean t-shirt as well. "Seth was going nuts. Shouting at us all to do something. He was so worried." She looked warmly over at Seth and something travelled between them for a second.

"I carried you onto the plane," said the boy behind me. He reached out a hand. "I'm Paul by the way. He smiled, revealing a set of fangs. I gasped and squashed myself closer to Seth. Paul blushed. "Er, yeah, sorry about that. I'm a half-breed too. Didn't get off as lightly as you guys though. Didn't mean to scare ya. I don't use them unless it's a special request." He grinned and his eyes danced with mischief. I shook his hand tentatively and then turned back to Isabella.

"So you came for us?" I asked. She nodded, still looking at me with concern. "And you know where this place in Italy is? The place that we're going to?" She nodded and looked around questioningly as if she was afraid to give out too much information. A thousand questions were buzzing around my head but I was also feeling wrung out and exhausted.

"You're tired?" Isabella asked gently.

I nodded and then sighed. "I'm afraid to sleep in case he comes back."

She made a face and sank into the chair across the aisle. "He won't try that again, mia cara. Your defenses are up now, you know what to expect."

"But they didn't keep him out before," I argued.

"No. And that's more than I have the words to explain. Sariel will have to do that." She smiled but I looked away at the mention of his name. Isabella reached out a hand and gently turned my face to hers again. "Merda! Look, Emily, whatever Asmodeus said it was to confuse you, to make you turn from your friends and to…" she frowned and, exasperated, said something to Paul. "My words are letting me down again," she said, exasperated. "There may be verità in what Asmodeus said, there may be lies. I don't know. But I know that you can trust Sariel." I said nothing and she sighed, leaning close to me. "He was preoccupato, so worried." She whispered. "He couldn't reach you, He thought he'd lost you."

I made a face but couldn't bring myself to start an argument with her. Of course he was worried about losing me. If Asmodeus was right then he needed me to be in one piece. Isabella watched me with a frown on her face but she obviously decided that this wasn't the time or place to talk about it.

"Try to get some rest, cara Emily. We'll talk more when you've had a chance to…think about things." She stood up gracefully and left me alone with my friends. I turned to find that they were all staring at me.

"Do you want to talk about it?" Annie asked softly.

I shook my head. "Not now. Maybe later. Like she said, I need to think about things. So, what's the sitch here? How does she know Sariel?" Everyone looked at each other with identical 'oh-crap' faces. I sighed. "C'mon guys. This seems to be my night for unearthing all the juicy secrets. Spill."

Seth put me out of my misery. "Isabella is apparently descended from Sariel," he said in a flat monotone.

I raised an eyebrow. "Pardon?"

Seth sighed. "Isabella is one of Sariel's descendants."

"Yes, I heard you the first time." I snapped. "But how?"

Dylan frowned at me. "What do you mean 'how'? Obviously at some point in the past, the very distant past if Isabella is to be believed, Sariel had a wife or partner, or girlfriend or something and she got pregnant and had children and they had children and…." He trailed off as Annie dropped her head and Seth covered his eyes. "What did I say? I was just explaining…."

"Yes, D. We know what you were explaining but we've all done

140

Biology in school. I don't think that was what Emily was asking," Annie dragged Dylan down into their seat again as I heard him protest.

"But then what was she asking? I don't get it?"

"Wait a minute!" I sat up straight as I realized something else. Annie and Dylan's heads popped back up above their seats. "Oh. My. God," I whispered, feeling my heart constrict in my chest as I looked at my friends. "What about your exams? Aren't you guys missing them?"

Annie's face lost some of her worried, frightened look and she shook her head. "Wow, your head really is messed up. Our exams are over, sweetie. Our timetable was crazy for the whole of the first fortnight but it meant that they were all over with quickly."

"Yeah," Dylan nodded his shaggy head glumly. "We basically had frees for the rest of the week, apart from the extra credit revision classes that we were taking for Mr. Dobbs and his year twelves."

I frowned. "The what now?"

"Oh, Mr. Dodds got us to take revision classes for his year twelves' – apparently he felt he wasn't 'reaching them'. Annie did her best interpretation of Mr. Dodds' sad, deep drawl and we all grinned. "It was ok, actually. They get revision with someone whose voice doesn't automatically send them to sleep as soon as they walk through the classroom door and we get extra credit on our end of school assessment reports."

"I was even allowed to oversee experiments," said Dylan enthusiastically.

I giggled and bumped fists with him., "Nice. Even after the whole Bunsen burner incident?"

Dylan nodded somberly. "Even after that."

Another loose end occurred to me. "What about your parents? They'll be frantic!"

Seth sighed and pulled me into a hug, "Would you listen to yourself? Worrying for the whole country now. Isabella sorted it all out. We're all going to Italy for a post exam holiday or something."

I raised an eyebrow at him and made a face at Annie and Dylan, "And your parents bought that?"

"She made it sound totally plausible, Em," Annie told me, "Made it sound like she was your Aunt or something, like we'd met before and stuff."

"Yeah, but still…some woman they've never seen before turns up and says she's taking their child on holiday and no-one freaks out?" I shook my head, suddenly feeling exhausted.

"It was her whole manner though," Dylan said thoughtfully, scratching his chin. "I mean you know what my mum's like and she thought Isabella was just lovely – made her tea and all." Annie and Dylan grinned at each other.

"Thought for a while we were going to have to bring your mum along," Annie said giggling.

"Yeah, it was a whole female bonding situation," Dylan admitted looking at me with his earnest little-boy-amazed face.

"Wait." Now I really was confused. "Your parents MET Isabella? When was this?"

Dylan's expression became 'step-away-from-the-crazy-lady'. "When we picked up our cases," he said, making it sound like a question and turning to Annie for guidance on how to proceed with the problem that was my lack of memory.

Annie rubbed his arm affectionately, "You were coming down from the whole Asmodeus is in my head thing, Em."

"Oh. Right. I see." I didn't see but I suddenly didn't have the energy to worry about it. Isabella sorted the problem, my brain told me, chillax you daft cow. I rubbed my throbbing temples and did my best to ignore the fact that my brain was calling me names.

"Right, that's enough now. Get some rest, Em." Seth waved Dylan and Annie away and folded me into his side, pillowing my head on his shoulder. I ignored the fact that Dylan was giving him frantic WTF? Eye signals over my head – wow, I was getting pretty good at the 'make like you're an ostrich' school of dealing with things – and closed my eyes, grateful to Seth for knowing what I needed just then. I tried to shut out the hum of the plane and the scattered rumble of low conversations around me, concentrating instead on Sariel whose presence was strong in my mind. I could almost feel him hovering and then pacing, waiting for me to process everything, wisely staying quiet and letting me be. Conversation died down, the engine noise faded into the background of my dreams and I slipped into dreamless sleep, lulled by Seth's steady breathing.

I woke before the others as the plane began to descend, unwrapped myself from Seth's embrace and peered out the window, getting my first glimpse of Italy.

CHAPTER THIRTY-THREE

The plane had landed at a small airfield in what appeared to be the middle of nowhere. The hangar and small adjoining office had a feeling of abandonment with layers of grime on the windows and weeds growing up through cracks in the cement. It was just before dawn, quiet and calm but with heat in the air already and light starting to creep across the horizon.

Two limos were waiting beside the office building, shiny and sleek in the midst of all the dust and dirt. Two tall, burly men stood beside each car watching us impassively as we clambered out of the small plane and stood blinking and yawning. Isabella took charge immediately, barking orders in rapid Italian as small amounts of luggage were transferred to the cars. She caught my eye as she passed and reached out to touch my arm. "Almost there, Emily. You are all safe here."

I nodded without comment and followed Seth, Annie and Dylan into one of the cars. It was comfortable and luxurious but I barely noticed. I felt tired, cross, on edge and in need of a soak in a hot bath for maybe a year. Annie opened her mouth to speak but closed it again as Paul hopped into the car, pulling the door closed behind him and settling himself next to me with a happy grin. "Hello again, principessa. Comfortable?" I sighed which he obviously took for an indication of darn thrilled I was to see him. The car began to move and he gestured towards the smoky windows. "So, you want me to point out some of the places of interest? That tree out there for example is a perfect example of an Italian...tree." He grinned and bounced in his seat like an excitable puppy. "And this road we're on is called the ...um...road to Isabella's house."

"Anyone got a stake?" I shouted. The partition between us and the driver came down. The passenger, who I supposed must be a kind of bodyguard, turned to face us. "Are you hungry?" he asked in heavily accented English.

"Pardon?" I asked.

"You are asking for a steak, yes?"

I shook my head. "No, I was thinking more of a stake. You know, yay big." I Demonstrated with my hands. "Made of wood or maybe silver? Wicked sharp point?" He lifted an eyebrow and so I pointed towards Paul. "Fang boy is really annoying." The guard looked in Paul's direction.

"I was just pointing out the attractions around here," Paul protested. The partition rose silently up again with the guard eyeballing us the whole time. "I think you upset him." Paul told me sadly.

I turned my attention away from him and closed my eyes. Sariel's presence in my head was so strong I was surprised I could still think for myself. A sudden thought occurred to me. *Trying to take me over, eh? Like Asmodeus and my mother.* He didn't answer but I felt his attention through our link. *Sorry, Sariel. I'm not going to be your puppet anymore.* His annoyance trembled between us and I put up every wall that my mind could muster. From now on I was blocking everyone and everything from my head. It was my brain, it was a bloody good one and no-one else was going to use it.

Needing another distraction I looked around the car. Annie and Dylan were chatting quietly, Seth was looking out of the window beside him and Paul was…staring at me.

"D'you mind?" I asked. "It's rude to stare."

Paul gave an embarrassed laugh. "Sorry. I just…well, you're not what I was expecting."

I snorted. "Yeah? You'd be amazed how often I get that. Expecting a big blonde in high heels and a short skirt?"

"Um…"

"Or maybe a Jude clone – all fierce and athletic?"

"Er…"

"Or maybe you just wanted a bloody little puppet like everyone else wants." Paul was gaping at me, his mouth open in astonishment. I was crying, I could feel little hot tears slide down my cheeks and automatically I reached for Sariel, wanting his comfort. He flooded our link with golden warmth. It was like being wrapped in a warm duvet or a big hug and I basked in it for just a moment before

145

realizing what I was doing and pushing him away again with a strangled cry of irritation. I put my head in my hands and cried, sobbing out all the hurt and anger and frustration that Asmodeus had made me feel. At some point Annie and Paul changed places and she pulled me into a hug, whispering that everything was going to be okay, that we would work things out and nothing was worth me getting so upset about.

I shook my head and turned myself around to look into her troubled eyes. "I don't know this time," I told her. "Asmodeus filled me in about some stuff and…well, I don't know how to deal with it." Annie looked around for support. Seth and Dylan were there instantly. Dylan took one of my hands and squeezed it, Seth leaned over and pushed some of my messy hair out of my eyes.

"That's what we're here for, remember?" Seth told me. "We've got your back.

"Yeah. That's what friends do, Emily." Said Dylan softly. "You can tell us. A problem shared is a problem halved. Well, technically quartered in this case."

I took a deep breath and nodded, giving them all a watery smile. "Thanks guys but I don't know if I should be getting you any deeper into this crap than you already are."

Annie sighed and sat back. "Emily, how many times do you have to be told? We're here to help. No matter what. Quit whining about how sorry you are and worrying about all the what ifs. Just lay it out and we'll deal with it, okay?"

Dylan grinned at her. "Wow. You're hot when you're angry."

Paul spoke up. "Look, I don't know you guys and you don't know me but I probably know more about what's going on here than you do. She's trying to protect you. There are things that are dangerous to know and once someone tells you them, there's no going back. "

Annie tutted. "If I wanted to hear what you think, I would ask."

I held up a hand. "No, wait. He's just trying to help." Paul gave me a grateful smile. "And he's right, he knows more at the minute than we do. So, question number one, where are we going?"

We all turned to Paul who looked momentarily stunned. "Um, we're going to Casa Cielo." He straightened up a little, warming up to being the centre of attention. "It's been around here in one shape or form for a really long time. It's like a meeting place, a haven for anyone passing through who needs a place to crash or hide out for a bit. And it's been in Sariel's family for ...a really long time."

"And Isabella's one of Sariel's descendants?" Dylan asked. Paul nodded. "This is amazing, We know people who have links to the beginning of everything. And it's all real. Wow, it's absolutely blowing my mind." He chewed on a knuckle.

"And you're loving it." I told him, grinning. I turned back to Paul. "So, what's this place like?"

Paul shrugged. "It's really just a big old Italian olive plantation. In fact it produces some of the most famous olive oil in the world. You've heard of Moraiolo?" We shook our heads. "Well, the point is that it's a pretty busy place. And it covers a lot of land. The main house, where the family live is on the side of the mountain with the plantation in the valley and the mill and processing plant are to the east."

"The mill?" asked Seth.

Paul nodded. "Yes, the company uses all the old methods to produce the oil, at least as far as possible, and one of those methods is to grind the olives into paste using mill stones."

"So are there many workers?" I asked, wondering how all the comings and goings of Angels and runaway Demons were kept from them.

"Yes but they live in the workers rooms near the plant. They work on a rotational basis – 4 weeks on and 4 weeks off - and Isabella arranges for them to be bused to and from the local towns."

"It sounds like a big operation." Dylan muttered.

"It is, but it's also a good cover." Paul grinned at us. "The house is amazing – all these secret passages and hidden rooms and then there are the caves."

"Caves?" I squeaked. I didn't have very happy memories of caves.

"There are caves running through the mountain behind the house," Paul told me. "They're like a maze. But they're escape routes and hiding places in case the house is compromised." We all stared at him and he laughed. "It's never happened so don't look so worried. Besides, I heard one of the guards talking and everyone should be here by the end of the week. With all that power around, no-one would dare try anything."

"What do you mean 'everyone'?" Seth asked, mirroring my own thoughts.

"The rest of the Fallen families, they're all coming." He looked excited. "It's been centuries since they all came together like this. It'll be incredible. Of course they couldn't reach some of them, some are still in hiding and some are..." He paused, grimacing.

"Converted." I finished for him.

The others looked at me in surprise but Paul nodded sadly. "I didn't know if you knew about that yet."

I sighed. "It was one of the things that daddy dearest thought I should know about." I met Annie's curious eyes. "I think I'm ready to tell you now." I said softly. Dylan gulped audibly and we all giggled. "Sorry," he said, his face serious. "It just felt like a gulpy kind of moment."

And it was. Taking a calming breath I haltingly began to tell everyone what I now knew about Angels and Demons.

CHAPTER THIRTY-FOUR

I woke up tired.

An anxious afternoon siesta of constantly blocking all access to my mind as well as stopping my thoughts from being broadcast had meant that I had slept but not rested. The fact that I was on the lookout for Asmodeus and his stupid little boat didn't help matters. I checked my watch. It was after three thirty but still hot. I'd showered as soon as we'd arrived and again before I lay down but I was sticky and stinky again already. I groaned and rolled over on the bed.

I had left the window of my room open and the light, gauzy curtains were fluttering in a light afternoon breeze which was beautifully cooling on my skin. I stretched my arms above my head and felt my lazy muscles protest.

Someone knocked at my door and, without thinking I said, "Come on in. It's open."

The door opened and then there was silence. Confused, I opened an eye and then gasped. Paul was standing in the doorway, his eyes almost popping out of his head.

I sat up fast, yanking my t-shirt down over my stomach again.

"Er….Isabella wondered if you wanted to come down for some food," he stuttered.

"Yep. Be right there." I told him, blushing furiously.

Thankfully Paul disappeared again and said nothing when I finally made my way into the kitchen about half an hour later. The place was already packed – the long cherry pine table was covered in heavenly smelling food and surrounded by people. Annie stood from her seat at the far end and called me over. She'd kept me a space.

After a quick round of hellos and how-are-yous, I helped myself to some warm crusty bread and dipped it in some of the flavored oils on the table. It was delicious, all the fresh flavors bursting on my tongue. Yum. I chewed happily, letting my gaze wonder around the room. There were all the guards and drivers in shirt sleeves, chatting and drinking cups of coffee, Isabella was running around wearing an apron and pouring glasses of cold lemonade and cups of hot, strong coffee. There were a lot of new faces. Some were looking at me in open curiosity; others were avoiding my eyes completely.

I concentrated on keeping up my barriers and filling my belly. There was pasta on the table too, in some fresh tomato-based sauce, piles of roasted vegetables and a lot of different breads. Seth was obviously in his element, a plate full of everything and Jude chatting animatedly to him. Annie and Dylan were deep in conversation with an elderly man who was sitting opposite. They seemed to be talking about the big bang theory. Trust them to find someone to talk science in a strange house in the middle of Italy.

"Miss Carson? I wonder if I could have a moment." I turned to find a man with intense blue eyes and a serious expression on his olive-skinned face beside me. Aaron was hovering just behind him in a state of agitation.

All conversation ceased and I sighed and put down the piece of bread that I'd been chewing on. Typical. Just when I was starting to relax.

I made a show of wiping my mouth on a napkin and giving my hands a quick clean before I turned to the man and held out my hand. "Emily Carson. Pleased to meet you Mr…?"

He shook my hand stiffly. "Roberto Angelus. At your service. I am the…organiser for the D'Annucci family."

Organiser? I waited for an explanation but it seemed that Mr. Angelus (seriously?) was done with the frivolities of introduction. "So. What do you want to talk to me about?" I asked.

He looked around the room. "Perhaps we could go to the library?" he suggested.

I leveled a glare at him. "Nope."

He blinked. "The drawing room?"

"What's wrong with here?" I asked, turning my attention back to my bread. There was a little frisson of astonishment around the room.

Mr. Angelus gave a little snort of derision. "I hardly think this is the place to be discussing…"

"Why not?" I wasn't in the mood for this snotty little man and his agenda. "I don't like secrets, Mr. Angelus. There've been quite enough of them around lately and I'm starting to get majorly pissed off. Is there anything you need to say to me that these other people shouldn't hear? Anyone in this room that you don't trust?"

"Certainly not!" he pouted.

"Great. So pull up a pew and let's get acquainted." I pointed to a free chair over by the French doors.

Mr. Angelus looked disgusted. Whether it was my attitude or the fact that he didn't care to get 'acquainted' I wasn't sure and didn't really care. Across the table the elderly man who'd been talking to Annie and Dylan gave me a grin. He reached a hand across and I shook it. "I am Gadrel, Miss Carson. Delighted to meet you."

I nodded. "You too. And just call me Emily. Okay?"

There were more introductions after that. A whole torrent of them. I had a momentary panic that I'd never remember all the names but it passed as the guards came forward and shook hands too, as did the servers who were in the kitchen with Isabella and a young boy of about 8 wearing a pair of shorts and a Man United t-shirt. His name was Antonio and his brown eyes watched me with something close to awe. "Can I see it?" he asked as we solemnly shook hands.

"See what?" I asked.

"The Were knife that you used to stab the evil Demon Lord, Asmodeus." He said it all so matter-of-factly that I was momentarily lost for words. A few chuckles sounded around us.

"I, er, gave it back," I told him.

He frowned. "You did? But how will you defend us when he comes for you?" I gulped and Isabella quickly shooed the boy away. He turned back at the door. "Can I talk to you again later?" He asked. I opened and closed my mouth a few times, still incapable of speech.

Thankfully Seth stepped in. "Hey, you have a football?" Antonio nodded. "Then bring it by later and we'll have a game."

Antonio's face brightened into a radiant smile. "Really? Great. Arrivederci!"

We all laughed and then I turned to Mr. Angelus. "Ok, pal. Spill."

CHAPTER THIRTY-FIVE

M r. Angelus, it turned out, was a kind of lawyer/p.a./ secretary/general dogsbody for the family. And he took his job extremely seriously. I suppose if I was working for a group of Fallen Angels, I'd probably want to get things right too. Our conversation consisted of him telling me the arrangements that Sariel had made for our stay in Casa Cielo and me listening with Annie, Dylan and Seth making occasional gasps, noises of approval and comments like 'Wow' and 'Really? Cool.'

The upshot was that Sariel had thought of everything – we would train with two of the guards every evening to keep us in shape (joy); all our needs and wishes would be catered for by the staff under Isabella's guidance – this was to include clothes, toiletries etc.etc. We would be instructed in the layout of the caves by the caretaker; we would have lessons in the morning to help us catch up and keep up with our school work so that when we returned to school we would be able to take our final exams at a later sitting.

I stopped Mr. Angelus. "Wait. He seriously thinks that we'll be back at school in time to take our exams?" Annie and Dylan were grinning happily at this news, Seth was frowning a little but I could see hope in his eyes. The idea that this might all be over in a couple of months and we could all go back to our normal lives was seductive but I didn't buy it.

Mr. Angelus smiled happily. "Yes, Miss Carson. That would appear to be his intention."

I pushed my chair back from the table and stood up, rubbing my eyes. I could feel the attention of the rest of the room. I looked down at Annie, at the smile on her face and I knew that this was one argument I wouldn't have in front of her. "Is that everything?" I asked wearily.

Mr. Angelus looked confused but he nodded. "Yes, Miss. Those are the Padrone's wishes. He will of course be here on Friday night should you wish to discuss things further. I'm sure he would be able to find an opening in his schedule to talk to you…"

I barely heard him. Sariel would be here in 4 days. Conflicting emotions filled my mind – fear, anger, excitement and above it all the need to see him again. I pushed it all down and swallowed the sudden lump in my throat. "So do we get to hit things now?"

Mr. Angelus closed his mouth with a snap. I wondered if maybe he'd been speaking, had I interrupted him? Well, it was a bit late to be worried about that now. He nodded stiffly and gestured to two of the guards who were lounging against the back wall. "Bruno and Don will show you to the courtyard." He began to load papers into his case with an air of a man who was trying to cover up his annoyance before he lost his temper. I sighed. He was just doing his job and I hadn't made it very easy for him, besides making enemies among the people who were trying to help us was not a good idea. I held out my hand and, after a moment of confusion, he shook it.

"Thank you, Sir." I told him. "I'm sorry if I was perhaps a little...um, terse. It's been a tough few days."

He cocked his head to the side and looked at me carefully, the first honest assessment he'd made of me since we'd met. "You are very welcome, Miss Carson. Madame D'Annucci has my number should you ever require my services or...advice." His smile was genuine and I relaxed a little.

The little gathering began to break up after that and Seth and I followed the two guards, Bruno and Don out into the courtyard to get our asses kicked.

The days fell into a comfortable routine; we had classes in the morning with a retired English teacher called Marvin who looked like Dumbledore crossed with a Bondi Beach surfer – white beard and garish Bermuda shorts; lunch was a crowded, noisy affair with a bunch of new people present every day; after that was the afternoon siesta in the air conditioned cool of our rooms followed by guided tours of the cave system in the company of Isabella's grounds man/caretaker dude who spoke in rapid Italian which had to be translated by Paul; work out and self-defense training with Bruno and Don and finally dinner in the cool of the evening, usually in the courtyard with lots of flickering candles and vino for the adults. We were kept busy – both in body and mind, although our ever-increasing circle of acquaintants was a constant reminder that Sariel would soon be there and I had no doubt that whenever he arrived something would happen. If anyone else knew what that something might be then they were keeping quiet about it.

On Thursday, just before siesta Paul poked his head around my bedroom door. "Want to play hooky?" he asked.

"Are you serious?" Okay, I admit it, he'd kind of grown on me in a 'cute but mad puppy' kind of way, with his goofy grin and spiky dark hair. I was even getting used to the fangs.

He shot me his grin. "Downstairs in ten. Bring a swimsuit."

I stood staring at the closed door for a minute after he left. Bring a swimsuit? I hadn't seen a pool, and we'd been pretty much everywhere in the past two days. Wait. Did I even have a swimsuit?

CHAPTER THIRTY-SIX

It turned out that I did have a swimsuit. Isabella had ordered clothes to be delivered to us on Tuesday morning – all in our sizes and mostly to our tastes, which was kind of creepy but I was too fed up wearing my stinky t-shirt-and-jeans combo by that point to care. My swimsuit was black with a kind of red panel down each side. It was functional rather than cute but that was fine by me. I grabbed a towel and headed downstairs.

Seth, Annie, Dylan, Jude, Paul and three others were waiting. Paul made rapid introductions – Dean, Adrian and Lisa were part of the families – it was starting to get a serious mafia vibe around here – Dean was from Canada, Lisa and Adrian were both from France, but from different branches of the Fallen family tree. We all followed Paul through the courtyard and up the path into the caves. The sun was incredible and I was feeling like a roast turkey within minutes. Dylan kept rubbing the back of his neck and finally put his towel over his head which made Annie giggle. Paul switched on a large torch as we stepped into the cave system and within maybe ten minutes the temperature had cooled enough to give me goose bumps. We seemed to be heading downwards into what the caretaker had told us was towards the first set of stores at the base of the mountain. We came to a fork in the path and Paul took the left. I tried to remember if we'd been here before but it was hard to tell – all the cave walls looked familiar to me.

After walking for maybe another five minutes Paul stopped and we dutifully halted behind him. He turned to face us, the torch dancing around the walls and sending shadows leaping all around like dancing Demons. I shivered. "Now, ladies and gentlemen," Paul announced. "The main event." He reached to his left and flicked a switch. Lights came on somewhere in front and, grinning happily, Paul headed in that direction. There were gasps of delight as one by one, we turned the corner and saw the cavern.

It was maybe the size of a school football field and the height of a bungalow with soft amber lights coming from beneath the water of a deep natural pool. The rocks ringing the pool were smooth and Paul dropped his towel onto one, kicked off his shoes and pulled off his t-shirt. He glanced back to give me a teasing grin and then jumped into the water with a whoop and a splash. He surfaced, shaking water from his eyes. "Come on in, the water's great."

One by one we followed self-consciously. Lisa was wearing a cream crochet bikini that clung to her curves and looked incredible against her tanned skin. Annie and I watched her execute a perfect dive in and smiled wryly at each other. Annie was wearing a pink suit dotted with large flowers in shades of blue and yellow. She looked cute in it, if slightly pale next to the others. We each slipped into the water and I gave a surprised giggle. Paul surfaced near me. "You never said it was warm." I accused. "How can it be warm?"

He shrugged. "Why worry about these things?" He splashed at me, laughing as I spluttered and coughed, I splashed back getting water all over Seth in the process. Seth retaliated, soaking Lisa in the process and just like that a water fight started. The cavern filled with gasps, splutters, yells and giggles and boy was it fun. I hadn't laughed as much in ages. We were all soaked and panting when Adrian finally called a halt and swam to the edge of the pool to rest, dragging Lisa with him.

Paul and I kept going for a while longer, neither of us wanting to be the one to back down but finally my legs were too tired to tread water anymore and I slipped away from him, grabbing one of the side rocks to give myself a rest. "Are you quitting, principessa?" Paul teased. I shot him a look but nodded, too busy catching my breath to speak. "C'mon, let me show you the hot tub." He took my hand and dragged me after him.

I let him pull me through the water, slipping onto my back and luxuriating in the feel of the water. I remembered the pool in Ipswich; going down all the slides with Annie and Dylan; firing water cannons at them. It seemed like a lifetime ago. Paul pointed towards a gap in the rocks and kept swimming. Letting go of his hand, I followed and, looking around realized that there were a number of alcoves like this one around the outside of the pool. The one we were swimming into led further back than the others, under a shadowy overhang. I was too busy being amazed by what was happening under the water to care about a few shadows. The water was a little shallower here and bubbles were rising to the surface. I sniffed the air, glad that I couldn't smell any noxious gases escaping from underground. Paul leaned up against the edge of the pool, stretching his arms out to help him balance. I swam in and looked down into the water. Beneath me the bubbles seemed to be coming from all directions. "What is this?" I asked, excited.

"A hot tub, like I said," Paul told me proudly.

"Manmade?" I asked him, wishing I had goggles so I could slip under water and check it out properly.

He shook his head. "Nope. All natural. You like?"

I laughed. "Yes, me like a lot. I must get Dylan and Annie to have a look at this." I turned to go looking for them but he pulled me back, a funny look on his face.

"So this was a good idea of mine then?" He asked, pulling me over to the edge beside him.

I nodded. "Yes, a great idea. Thank you." And I meant it. I had lightness to my heart that I hadn't felt for a long time.

He smiled. "Good. I hoped you'd like it." He reached out a finger and touched my lips. "I like to see you smile, Emily. You should do it more often."

I was going to tell him where to get off, that I smiled all the time thank you very much, and then I realized that he probably hadn't seen me smile much. I sighed. "Yeah. Hasn't really been a huge amount to smile about, y'know."

He nodded. "I remember how it felt when my mum brought me here."

"Your mum did?" I wracked my brain, trying to remember names and faces of everyone at the house. "Which one is she?"

Paul made a face. "She's not here. We were being chased and she figured if she stayed then she'd put me in danger. She just left me off and…never came back."

I looked at him. "So, where is she?" I asked, willing him to smile and tell me Vegas or Swansea or something.

He shook his head. "They caught up to her in Ireland." He

smiled sadly at me. "My father decided to make an example of her, to discourage any of the others from trying to get away too. They tortured and killed her in front of the rest of the House." He swallowed thickly and my heart went out to him. I leaned over and hugged him.

"I'm so sorry," I whispered. He nodded, his cheek against mine and sighed into my hair as he hugged me back. There was no intention in me for anything else to happen but I felt the change in him pretty quickly. His sadness turned into tension and his arms tightened around my waist as he turned his head and pressed his lips against mine. The shock of actually kissing someone, anyone, lit up my mind for a second and I felt the disturbance of it sail through the link I had with Sariel. Paul was deepening the kiss, one hand pulling me tighter against him and one slipping into my wet hair, but it was all happening at a distance because I was concentrating on the messages I was getting from Sariel. He was not a happy camper and the knowledge burned through me, igniting my mind and making me kiss Paul back with more enthusiasm than I might otherwise have done.

Sariel's anger flashed in my head and I knew he was having to bite his tongue not to say anything. I slid my hands up Paul's back, over his warm, wet skin and felt him gasp against my mouth. He broke away for a moment, his lips slipping down to my throat, his fangs grazing my neck. I shivered, remembering Lucas's bite and Paul took the shudder to be appreciation of his kissing technique. He found my lips again and this time he was a little rougher. I let Sariel feel it all and the intensity of his anger and jealousy inflamed my body. And then suddenly he was gone, he had blocked himself and I was left with Paul and his kisses.

It was like a cold bucket of water in my face.

I pulled away and leaned against the rock. Both Paul and I were breathing heavily but he was smiling happily. "Wow. You are seriously hot stuff, Emily Carson. No wonder there's so much fuss about you."

I gave him a lop-sided smile. "Yeah. Hot stuff. All us nerds have hidden depths."

Paul reached out for me again. "Really? I'd like to investigate your hidden depths," he whispered and I rolled my eyes.

"Seriously, Paul. That's your line?" I was trying to keep this light. Kissing him back had been insane, and I'd done it for all the wrong reasons. I knew that if I hadn't felt that rush of emotion from Sariel I'd have stopped him. Probably. I mean, Paul was cute and any action was better than nothing. Right? And according to Asmodeus, Sariel wasn't interested in me for anything other than being the means by which he could go home. And yet…I'd felt his anger, his jealousy. Hadn't I? I was tempted to reach for him again but I figured his barriers would still be in place so I turned to Paul instead and gave him a shy smile. His eyes took on an intense look and I knew that he was going to kiss me again. Crap. What should I do? "Hey guys? We need to make a move if we want to get back before siesta's over." Dean called from the far side of the pool. Paul looked up and I breathed a sigh of relief.

"Yeah, we're coming now," I called back and headed in Dean's direction. Paul caught my hand and stopped me long enough to plant another kiss on my cheek before splashing me and swimming off laughing. I swam after him, feeling confused and slightly freaked out. But I was smiling.

CHAPTER THIRTY-SEVEN

Our routine continued as usual on Friday although it was a tense day for me. Sariel would be here soon. I'd have to face him. We'd have to talk.

"How am I going to approach this?" I asked Annie as we walked upstairs for siesta. "I mean do I say 'Look, Sariel. I know what your little game is. Asmodeus told me everything. You lied to me and I don't trust you anymore.' I mean is that too blunt?"

Annie looked at me. "You are blunt, Emily. That's kind of your thing."

I stopped walking for a minute and put my hands on my hips. "I am not..." I quit talking. She was right. I could be kind of tactless. I sighed and nodded. "Ok. So maybe I'm Little Miss Harsh from time to time." Annie raised an eyebrow but wisely said nothing. "I still don't know how to sort this out without coming across ungrateful and stuff."

We'd come to the door of Annie's room and she leaned against it, studying me. "What part of what Asmodeus told you bothers you most, Emily?" I opened my mouth to answer but she held up a hand. "Once you figure that out then everything else will fall into place."

"I don't like any of what he told me!" I complained. "It was all pretty crappy and most of it was downright unbelievable."

She rolled her eyes. "This whole situation is pretty crappy, Em. And unbelievable. We're in Italy for crying out loud. Sharing a house with Fallen Angels and their descendants. That's a major trip right there. And your dad is a damn Demon. You don't get much more freaky than that."

"Or crappy," I pointed out.

"Or crappy," she agreed, "But you're missing my point."

I sighed and rubbed my hands over my face. "Ok, so hit me with it."

She shook her head. "Nope. This is like a Chem test. You remember the one with the sit down paper and the practical where you aced the paper and then stood gaping at the Bunsen burner

160

like a fish?" I nodded. Sit down papers were no problem for me – it was all just a matter of learning the principles and writing them down. The practical stuff was always more of a challenge. "Ok, so just like the chem practical I'll give you a clue and then you can go sort things out in your own head." I opened my mouth to argue but she was already talking again. "The principles of what Asmodeus told you were already in your head in their most basic forms, I think. He expanded on them, got down to the nitty gritty of their applications if you want. But there was something that he told you that hurt. And it was the one thing he could say that he knew would wound you enough to get you to the place where he wanted you to be." I frowned and then made a face. She was talking in riddles. Annie sighed and gave me a hug. She smiled at me. "There is no emotion stronger than teenage love, Emily. Nothing will ever feel so deep, passionate or compelling as the first time you surrender your heart to another person, completely and uncompromisingly. I'm there, sweetie, I know how this feels. What's the worst thing you can say to a teenage girl who's in love, Emily?" She opened her door and went into her room, leaving me standing in the hall more confused than ever.

I thought about what she'd said all afternoon – through siesta, cave walking, getting several shades of new bruising from Don and even at dinner when I realized that the population of our little home away from home had swelled again. The courtyard was full. Tables had been added practically every night since we'd been here but tonight there was no room for any more. Again introductions were made, faces came and went, I shook hands and ate chicken olives, feeling Annie's scrutiny from time to time.

As dinner ended, Paul came up behind me and leaned over to whisper in my ear. We hadn't talked about what had happened at the pool and he hadn't kissed me again – I don't know if I was pleased or depressed about that – but there was a tension between us now that hadn't been there before – an awareness of each other that felt weird and exciting all at once. His breath against my ear made me almost choke on a piece of garlic bread. "Come out with me tonight, principessa."

Once I'd finished choking I turned to look up at him. His smile flickered in the candlelight and his eyes looked like sparkling sapphires. There was a brief flash of fang which I managed to ignore. "Where can we go?"

His smile widened. "It's a surprise. Wear your dancing shoes."

I pointed the rest of my bread at him, "If this involves going into the caves at night..."

He laughed. "No caves, I promise. Will you come?" This was insane. It would more than likely involve sneaking out of the house. This was an important night. Sneaking out was what teenagers did - normal ones anyway. Sariel was coming tonight. "Come and have some fun, Emily. I want to see you smile again." He lifted an eyebrow, James Bond style.

"Okay," I told him, surprising myself as well as him. "When?" He whispered a time and drifted off leaving me slightly breathless. I turned around and Annie was watching me, a what-the-hell-are-you-doing look on her face. Uh, oh.

"Have you completely lost your mind?" She squeaked later. She was sitting on my bed while I pulled everything out of my wardrobe in an attempt to find the right outfit to wear on a night out that would involve sneaking, dancing, flirting and, hopefully, kissing. It was hopeless. I was no good at this kind of thing. And Annie was too freaked out to help. "Paul? You're going out with Paul? Tonight?" She fell back on the bed mumbling about insanity running in the family.

"Would you quit calling my mental health into question and help?" I complained from the bottom of the wardrobe where I was certain I'd seen some shoes with heels. "Ah, here they are. What do you think of these?" I pulled out a pair of strappy black open toed sandals with wicked looking heels.

"You'll fall on your ass in those. And how would you dance?" She shrieked. "As for sneaking out? The guards would hear you clip clopping down the drive for miles around."

I rolled my eyes. "Very helpful. Not."

Annie shook her head. "You know that fashion and I aren't exactly best buddies, Emily. You should ask Lisa."

"What?! I don't want the whole house to know that I'm going out."

"Well, Lisa is from Paris, right? So she's fashionable to a point that you and I could never hope to get to. If you want to look good for a date with Paul - have I mentioned that you're insane? - then call her in."

I chewed on my lip. "Will you stay?" I asked. She nodded and I ran down the hall to find Lisa.

CHAPTER THIRTY-EIGHT

Lisa eyed my choice of red dress and strappy black sandals with an expression of astonishment. "You are wanting to go on zee date? In zeese?" I nodded and she made a face. "Are you inzane?" Annie smiled happily and folded her arms, giving me a told-you-so look. "Come to my room. I ave a very sexy outfit for you." Annie's smile was replaced by a scowl which made me grin. I pulled her after me to Lisa's room.

To say that Lisa had a vast number of clothes would be an understatement. Mind you if you had a killer bod like hers and a supermodel face to go with it then I guess you might enjoy clothes. She studied me critically for a few moments and then dived into one of her suitcases and pulled out several tops in varying shades of plum. She held them up against me one after the other, mumbling in French, and then she opened her wardrobe and began pulling clothes out of that too. Annie's eyes were almost popping out of her head.

Fifteen minutes later I was dressed in a long swirly black skirt made of layers of chiffon and silk. It swished around my ankles and revealed a length of tanned leg through the split in the side which extended above my knee. On top I wore a kind of black gypsy top with lace around the edges and little black beads which gave it enough sparkle to be dressy without being cheesy. The top covered my boobs but showed off my belly which was toned by work outs, lots of walking in the caves and eating healthy food. It still made me feel self-conscious. I wasn't used to showing a lot of skin – especially my belly – but Lisa thought it looked amazing and Annie had actually agreed with her. I wore a pair of strappy shoes with wedge heels that made my legs look as though they went on forever. And the heels were soft so there would be no clip clopping.

I looked in Lisa's mirror and was happily stunned. "Ok. So now I just need to give my hair a quick brush and I'll be off," I said grinning.

"What?!" Lisa looked horrified. Annie giggled into her hand.

"You are going to go out without make oop and air styling?"

"Um…yes?" I said.

"No." Lisa said, shaking her head emphatically. "Wait ere please." She took off and reappeared a few minutes later with Jude, looking confused, and a large canvas bag. "You can zee what I mean?" Lisa asked as Jude stared at me.

Jude nodded. "Yeah, fab outfit spoiled by that ridiculous mop of hair and a pale, boring face." She smiled sweetly at me as I folded my arms.

"She is NOT putting make-up on my face." I told Lisa.

"Why not? She is good, no?"

"No. She doesn't like me so I'll end up looking like a clown." I turned to Annie. "Back me up here, Annie."

Annie shrugged. "Well, considering she worked in a beautician's for a while, maybe you should let her have a go."

I turned to Jude. "You were a beautician?"

She shook her head. "No, my older sister was. I worked there as a general piker upper of stuff for pocket money when I was younger. They taught me some bits and bobs." She smiled at me. "I promise I won't make you look ridiculous." I sighed and sat down as Lisa and Jude began plugging in straightening irons and unloading what seemed to be a ton of make-up from the bag. "So is this for the whole meeting-up-with-Sariel thing?" Jude asked. "I hear they'll be arriving in about three hours."

Annie made a little murmur that I didn't catch. I shook my head. "No, I'm going out on a date."

Jude had begun to brush the tangles out of my hair. She paused. "You got a date? Around here?" I nodded. "Who?"

"Paul," Annie told her, beating me to it. "She's sneaking out tonight with Paul."

"And you don't think that sneaking out when there's a shed full of Demons after you is maybe a bad idea?" Jude continued, yanking the brush through my hair with slightly more vigor than I deemed absolutely necessary.

I frowned and resisted the urge to roll my eyes and pout like a six year-old. Trust Jude to try and burst my happy vibe. "We're in Italy, miles away from the action and anyway, Paul'll look after me." I smiled and nodded at myself in the mirror, content with my reasoning.

"And do you think Sariel would approve?" Annie said softly, taking care not to meet my eyes.

Like Sariel gives a damn…" I muttered, "And like I would care what he thinks anyway." So much for not acting like a six year old. I picked imaginary lint off my dress, feeling the weight of the glances that were being exchanged over my head. I looked back into the mirror, leveling my very best 'don't-mess-with-me' glare at Annie, "I'm going out tonight with Paul, whether Sariel or anyone else for that matter, approves or not."

There was a moment of strained silence while Annie and I locked glares and then her eyes slid away as Jude said, "Oookaaay. Better get on with getting you ready then."

I checked my watch. "I'm meeting him at the back of the house in twenty minutes."

It was all hands on deck after that. Annie and Lisa finished my hair under instruction from Jude while she did my make-up and I sat as patiently as I could, practicing sucking my belly in so that I wouldn't look like a total heifer in Lisa's outfit and checking my watch every thirty seconds. Finally I was done and Lisa stood me in front of the mirror.

"Wow." Annie said. "Paul's going to freak when he sees you. Did I mention you're mad? This is wasted on him. You should be…" Jude silenced her with a nudge that I was too busy admiring myself to take much notice of. My hair shimmered down my back and curled gently in luscious waves onto my shoulders. My make-up was beautiful – smoky eyes, delicate neutral lips – and minimal so I didn't look like a clown after all. I looked amazing. Very not-me like. Impulsively I gave Jude, Lisa and Annie a hug.

"Thanks guys. I can't believe how good you made me look. Wow. This is going to be an amazing date, right?" They all nodded mutely. I checked my watch again. "Damn. Gotta go for my date. See you later. Did I mention that I'm sneaking out for a date?" I headed out, excited and feeling like Cinderella, to meet Paul.

CHAPTER THIRTY-NINE

Okay, maybe it was just because I didn't usually do this sort of thing but sneaking out with Paul was great fun. From the second I met him at the back door of the house and saw his grin widen as he checked out my outfit, while we dodged the guards along the edge of the gardens, my hand in his as he led me to the lane that led to the workers' accommodations and the car he'd stashed there earlier, driving along the road from the house with the lights off, singing along to Sheryl Crow and Limp Bizkit on the crackly radio, laughing like crazy at nothing in particular; the whole time my heart was thudding in my chest and a feeling of euphoria made my head spin. This is what I'd been missing and I wanted more.

The nearest town was almost thirty miles away but the time flew and if I wondered about his driving licence or where the car had come from, I said nothing in case I broke the spell. We finally pulled into the car park of a hotel/bar/restaurant type place and Paul led me to steps and I felt the bass beat of the music from below in my feet as we descended the steps and he stopped to grin at me before opening the door.

The basement was filled to capacity and the music was so loud that I could feel the thud in my chest. It was dark, the only light was coming from behind the DJ at the back of the room and from a small bar to the side. This was only my third time in a club – the first had been owned by the school bitch's dad, the second by Demons; I sincerely hoped this one was normal.

And so we started to dance. And dance. And dance. And dance. We had a break to get a drink and then we danced some more and Paul introduced me to some of the locals – he seemed to know quite a few of them, especially the girls who gave me a thorough look over as they were introduced. And so what if they whispered something into his ear afterwards, I wasn't bothered. I was having a good time and we were just friends. Right?

My feet were starting to hurt in my borrowed shoes and I was beginning to feel a little disoriented in the dark room and the press of bodies but I kept telling myself that this was fun; this was what normal seventeen year old girls did. This was what I should be doing on a Friday night – not waiting for gorgeous but complicated Fallen Angels who only put up with my company so that they could use me. I threw myself back into the dancing again, enjoying Paul's attention as I twirled and sashayed in front of him. His eyes were on me every time I looked at him and his expression was intense again. Now and again his hand would brush my waist or my shoulder and a little zing of anticipation would race through me. He's going to kiss me again, I thought and my head spun a little more.

And then I caught sight of a familiar face and I almost passed out. Sariel was here. No, wait. He was gone again. I turned around, confused. Paul leaned close and asked if I was ok. I nodded woodenly and went back to dancing, trying not to look as spooked as I felt. Had I seen him? Was he really here? Or was my mind playing tricks? Someone bumped into me from behind and muttered either a curse or an apology, I was sent slamming into Paul who grabbed my arms and laughed down at me. "Maybe we should've made that last one a water, huh?" He grinned. "Want to sit down?" I nodded and he led me through the crush and outside where we leaned against the wall at the top of the steps.

A lot of revelers had made it out here; some just for air, some for cigarettes, some to chat and more than a few to make out. Paul handed me a bottle of something cold and I gulped it down greedily before checking the label and realizing that it was beer. Oops.

"Maybe I should just stick to water," I told him.

He shrugged. "Whatever you say, principessa. Would you like me to get you some now?" I nodded gratefully and he headed back downstairs.

I leaned my head back against the wall and closed my eyes which was a huge mistake. My head whirled and looped and my stomach immediately did a few little queasy rolls. I snapped my eyes open again in a hurry but the world just would not stop spinning. Oh, this was not good. This was not good at all. I glanced around but no-one seemed to be taking much notice – I suppose I was just another stupid drunk girl on a Friday night.

Paul reappeared and pressed a bottle into my hand. The lid was already off and I squinted at the label before taking a drink. "What's the matter?" Paul asked in a mock-hurt voice. "Don't you trust me?"

I managed a smile. "Yes, of course. Just a reflex action." I staggered a little and Paul put an arm around my waist, steadying me against him. He chuckled.

"Well, you look as though it's time to head back."

I nodded. "Yeah. Sorry. I don't get out much." I told him by way of apology and explanation.

We walked back to the car and I was very grateful for the support of his arm. He opened my door first and helped me onto the seat. "Wow, I mumbled. You're such a gentleman." Paul gave me a wry grin.

"I wasn't intending to be, principessa. And I guess a proper gentleman wouldn't have got you drunk, huh?"

He wasn't intending to be? What did that mean? My brain mulled that one over as I told him, "It's not your fault that I make a lousy teenager." I blinked up at him, feeling my fuzzy brain respond lethargically to a concern that I was sure I should be panicking about but which seemed far, far away on the other side of a good night's sleep. "Wait. Are you going to drive?" I looked at the driver's seat and back at Paul. "You had the same amount to drink as I did. We might crash and that wouldn't be good." I waggled a finger at him, fascinating myself as it wobbled to and fro in front of my eyes.

Paul chuckled and made a lunge for my finger, his fangs snapping the air a few millimeters away from it which, for some reason, I found hysterically funny instead of incredibly scary. "Relax, principessa. Vamp genes come in handy sometimes – it would take twenty times what we drank tonight to make me even a little tipsy."

He leaned forward a little more, his twinkling eyes suddenly becoming serious and as my brain began to do a little happy dance and shriek 'He's gonna kiss me! He's gonna kiss me!' my mouth opened and I said, "I bet all your exes in there didn't get drunk the first time you took them out." Way to spoil the moment. Stupid mouth.

Paul grinned happily. "If I didn't know better I'd say you were jealous."

I shook my head, wincing as little mini-earthquakes popped off inside my skull. "Nope. Not jealous at all. We're just friends." Dammit. Shut up, Emily!

"We are? Well, that's disappointing." He made a face and then smiled. "So tell me, do friends do this?" He leaned right in and kissed me hard on the lips. So hard in fact that he crushed my top lip against my teeth. Some part of my brain registered annoyance, another was disgusted but the part that really, really, really wanted to be a normal teenager was celebrating with a 'Paul kissed me' party. Is this what it felt like when a guy got carried away? Cool.

And then he wasn't there anymore.

I giggled and looked around. "Where'd you go?" I called and was alarmed to hear the slur in my voice. I looked at the driver's side in case he'd decided to get into the car. Nope. I turned to look behind me in case he was walking around to the driver's door. Nope. I peered through the windscreen in case he'd, for whatever reason, decided to go back into the club. As far as I could see he wasn't walking back that way either. Hmmm. That was weird. Is it normal for a guy to kiss a girl and then evaporate? Maybe half-Vampire types did. Or maybe my beer breath had been so bad that I'd managed to incinerate him. Great. The first guy to show any major interest and I'd...Oh. Mega. Crap.

A shadow had appeared at the open door of the car and I suddenly knew where Paul had disappeared to. I looked up into Sariel's face and smiled weakly. "Hi."

Sariel looked murderous. He opened the back door of the car and shoved Paul inside and then slammed my door and headed around to the driver's side. I swiveled in my seat to get a look at Paul. "You okay?" He nodded and grinned but carefully schooled his face into an expression of meek apology as Sariel climbed into the driver's seat and closed the door. He clipped on his seat belt, leaning across me to sort mine out too. I inhaled and sighed happily. He smelled exactly the way I remembered him and I wondered if he still tasted like sunshine and honey and all kinds of manly spices. Yum.

Sariel glanced in my direction and angrily put his foot on the accelerator. We skidded out of the car park and shot off into the dark. "Do you have any idea what time it is?" he asked finally.

I shook my head and held up my bare wrist. "We decided my watch didn't go with the outfit," I told him before hiccupping loudly.

Sariel's face darkened even more and he eyeballed Paul in the rear view mirror. "You are in all kinds of trouble, boy. Taking Don's car, kidnapping Emily, taking an underage girl to a club. Plying her with alcohol…"

Paul and I began speaking at once.

"I wasn't kidnapped…"

"I didn't know she couldn't hold her drink…"

I turned to look at Paul, giving him a sad shake of my head. "That was way harsh. I was standing up for you."

He sighed and leaned over to brush my hair away from my face. "I'm sorry. I just…"

"Keep your hands off her," Sariel roared making Paul and I gasp. I squinted at Sariel and sure enough his eyes had darkened considerably.

You need to calm down before you go all grrrr, I told him.

He looked over at me, an eyebrow raised in astonishment. *All 'grrrr'?*

Yeah, y'know. I made what I thought was a snarling face and made my fingers into claws. Sariel blinked .

I'm not going …grrrr…I'm just angry with him. He was trying to get you drunk so he could take advantage of you.

He was? Wow. I was ridiculously pleased for a moment and then I shook my head. *Wait, no, that can't be right. He was going to drive me home.*

Sariel glanced into the rearview again. *I read his mind, Emily.*

He was planning on doing some very naughty things to you tonight.

"And you stopped him?!" I said aloud.

Sariel rolled his eyes as Paul spoke up from the back seat. "Pardon?"

"Nothing. I wasn't talking to you." I told him and turned back to Sariel who was gripping the steering wheel as though he was going to rip it from the car. *What are you? My own personal fun ruiner?*

Sariel grimaced. *I just don't want you doing something you'll regret when you sober up.*

Like what? It may come as a surprise to you but there are actually people in the universe who find me attractive and don't just snog me to keep me sweet or put their wet dog scent on me.

Sariel looked at me sharply. "Keep you sweet? What the hell are you talking about?"

"You thought I was some silly little sixteen year-old with a stupid crush, didn't you?" I folded my arms and faced away from him. "I knew the score anyway, Sariel. I can deal y'know? I just wish you'd been honest with me instead of…instead of…"

"Instead of what?" asked Paul from the back seat. Sariel and I ignored him. "Fine. I'll just sit here and listen to you two talk in riddles then, shall I?"

"So long as it means you're keeping your mouth shut," Sariel snapped.

"Hey! Don't speak to him like that," I shouted and slapped Sariel's arm. "At least he's honest about what he wants."

Sariel glowered. "Name me all the times I lied to you, Emily. Name them."

I shook my head. "No. Why should I? You know what you did. Asmodeus said…"

Oh, so you're listening to Asmodeus now? Well, that's just wonderful. Maybe I should just let you go live with him. Want me to list all the times that Asmodeus has lied to you? All the times he's hurt you and the people you care about?

"No." I said.

No, of course not. Why do you suddenly want me to step into the

172

role of the bad guy? What happened to change what we...what you and I...what we have been through?

"HE told me everything, Sariel. All the stuff that YOU kept from me. When were you going to explain that the only reason you were protecting me was because I might be some kind of gizmo that'll help send you all back up there? That you didn't fall out with God because you fell in love with a human? I mean, seriously, what was that? Some bullshit story you made up to keep the silly little half breed from getting too attached?"

"Don't call yourself that." Sariel's voice was gruff. He kept his eyes on the road.

"That's what I am. The little half breed blessed by an Archangel. Oh, lucky me!" I was crying, the tears rapidly turning into a flood. "I notice you aren't denying anything. Well that's just peachy."

"Emily..." Sariel reached over to take my hand.

"Don't touch me, Sariel. " I flinched away from him. "Don't even speak to me. Again. Ever."

I huddled up against the window, as far away as I could physically get from Sariel without climbing onto the roof and I cried softly the rest of the way home, telling myself that I didn't want him to pull over and take me in his arms and kiss me and tell me that everything was going to be ok. I didn't want that at all. I never wanted to hear him speak again, never wanted to have him in my head, never wanted to feel the hot velvet of his lips on mine ever again...nope. Never. He hadn't denied anything so Asmodeus had been right and I'd make sure Seth and I get the hell outta there as soon as we could.

At the house, I was out the passenger door and staggering into my room before either Paul or Sariel could stop me. I didn't want to see or talk to either of them and it wasn't until I had changed, replayed the night in my mind several thousand times and was finally lying in my room in the calm and quiet waiting to fall asleep that I began to feel them - presences at the edge of my consciousness, minds almost linking to my own - that I remembered. The other Angels had arrived.

Chapter Forty

Isabella brought a tray of breakfast to my room in the morning. She opened the curtains blasting the room with golden sunlight and I peeled my sweaty, mascara streaked face from my pillow.

"What time is it?" I asked, groaning when I felt my first morning-after-the-night-before headache and the bitter alcohol taste still on my tongue.

"Almost eleven," Isabella busied herself picking my discarded clothes off the floor.

"Eleven?!" I slumped back against the pillows. "I missed most of morning lessons."

"Lessons were cancelled this morning. We decided to give you all a day off so you can rest and…recuperate." I forced myself to meet her eyes, waiting for the lecture about drinking and boys and sneaking out that I was certain my mother would have enjoyed giving. Instead Isabella looked at me for a few seconds and then gave me a sad smile. "Sariel has decided not to postpone things any longer; he will be introducing you to the others after dinner tonight."

I nodded and turned my attention to the window until she took the hint and left my room, closing the door quietly behind her. So, I thought, now that I've rumbled onto his little set up he just wants to get everything over with. Don't blame him; I'm about done with this whole charade too.

I ate my platter of fruit, yoghurt and toast slowly, sipping some orange juice and blocking all the others in the house from my mind. I could feel them but it was hard to tell how many there were – it felt like a lot.

Annie came up to see me just before lunch, she was bubbling over with excitement, dying to hear what had happened the night before, and then she saw my face and her smile froze. "Oh, God. What happened? You look like crap," She plonked herself on the end of my bed and gave me a critical once over. "Didn't anyone ever tell you never to go to bed in full makeup. You have serious panda eye problems and half your eye shadow is on your cheek. What happened?"

I sighed. "I had a great night until I drank a bit too much …" Annie gasped, "…and then Sariel showed up as Paul was kissing me…" she gasped again, her mouth dropping open, "…and so I told him I hated him for lying to me and he drove us home." I shoved the last crust of my now-cold toast into my mouth and glared, daring Annie to ask more questions. She did of course. One after the other. You were drinking? Yes. Paul kissed you? Yes. What was it like? Great. Is he a better kisser than Sariel? Pass. How do you know that Sariel lied in the first place? Asmodeus said so. Did he deny it? No. Did you give him a chance to? "Well of course I…" I paused. Had I given him a chance? "Well, I'm pretty sure I…" Or had I just accused him of everything and then told him I believed Asmodeus and then told him to shove off? Hmmm.

Annie sat back. "You're an idiot," she told me.

"What?!" I pushed the tray off my lap and got to my feet. "What do you mean I'm an idiot? He lied, I caught him out and now he wants to get the whole show-and-tell thing over with his pals so he can get rid of me and shimmy back up the Angelic ladder again to his penthouse apartment beyond the pearly gates."

Annie raised an eyebrow. "Wow. Asmowhatsit really did a number on your brain, Emily. Did you even think about what I said?"

"Of course I did. I thought about it for ages. And I came up with absolutely nothing. Do you know why?"

She made a face. "Enlighten me oh-she-who-knows-all," she drawled .

"Because there's nothing deep and meaningful to figure out. Sariel lied. End of."

"End of? You're serious?" Annie had stood up and she faced me with her hands on her hips. "One little conversation with Asmodeus and you're chucking Sariel on the Demonic slag heap with all the rest of the liars and losers. Who was it who protected you for the past few months? Who was it who got tortured for you? Who was it who …"

"Yes, yes, yes." I stopped her. "All very noble of him, wasn't it?

He protected me because he wanted to get me here. In front of his buddies. So they could judge whether or not I'm some bridge back home. That was all he was interested in."

"Oh, really?" Annie sneered and folder her arms.

"Yes, really."

"And the times he kissed you...?"

"He was just leading me on to keep me sweet 'cause he knew that I..." I stopped, blushing furiously.

"You what?"

"I wanted him to." I finished lamely.

"So, getting back to what I was trying the make you understand the other day..." Annie sat back down again, her eyes were flashing dangerously. "What was the thing that Asmodeus told you that finally drove the knife in?"

"What knife?" I turned away from her. "Just 'cause it was Asmodeus doesn't mean a knife was involved."

"Oh, no you don't missy." Annie caught my arm and swung me back round to face her. "You will listen to me for once. Figure this out, Emily. Use that super brain for something more than bloody maths. Let's go through this at a pace that you will be able to cope with, shall we? Asmodeus told you stuff, yeah great. Now I'm trying to get you to see past all the stuff he came clean about and figure out why."

"Because he thought that I should know?" I asked in a small voice, knowing even as I said the words that it was complete rubbish.

"Try again."

I sighed. "I know what you're getting at. I've thought of it already."

"Then say it out loud so that I can hear it." Wow. She sounded really pissed off.

"He probably told me all of it to discredit Sariel." I mumbled.

"Ha-le-lu-jah," Annie sang. "And - now this is the important bit, concentrate, -what thing did he tell you that hurt you the most?" I bit my lip. Annie sighed and hung her head for a moment. "Okay, was it about the whole Angels-want-to-return-to-heaven

176

thing?" I shook my head. "Was it that the Watcher Angels showed the humans how to do stuff like build pyramids and make eye shadow?" I rolled my eyes. "Was it that Sariel is close to turning Demon?" I winced but shook my head again. Annie pulled me down to sit on the bed beside her. She took my hands in hers and sighed. "Or was it that he didn't ever love you the way you love him?"

I blinked at her. "But I don't..." She held up a hand. I swallowed. "I guess that did hurt, yeah."

"And why do you think that you were so quick to believe that?" Annie was speaking softly now, her eyes were sad and full of concern.

I shook my head. "I don't know."

"Yes you do. You think that you're too young for him; that you're not pretty enough; not worldly enough; too nerdy; a half-Demon instead of a half-Angel or a half unicorn or a half-fairy-tale princess or whatever it is you think floats his boat. To keep it short, sweet and to the point – you never thought you were good enough anyway. All Asmodeus had to do was say out loud the things you were already thinking. It's the oldest trick in the bully's handbook and that's what he is, a big, ugly, Demonic bully."

I gaped at her. "You make it sound so simple."

Annie sighed. "And it's not?" I shook my head and she pulled me into a hug. "Well, I've done my best to make you see sense but I suppose you think that Paul is a safer bet, eh? The playboy with the fangs who got you drunk on your first date is obviously Mister Right." I said nothing. "Ok. Enough of this. I promised D we'd meet him for lunch. You coming?"

I shook my head. "Not yet. I need to shower and, well, get over my um, late night I guess. Apparently I'm going to be centre stage later so I'd best be looking Angelic."

"Oh, that reminds me." Annie, ignoring my sarcasm, reached into the pocket of her jeans and pulled out two small, white tablets. "Paracetamol from Isabella. She thought you might have a headache." I grinned and she got up to leave, pausing at the door to look back. "Paul got extra work around the Casa and is grounded for two weeks as punishment. I saw him chatting to some of the others this morning. They all seemed delighted by the tale of your exploits."

"What was he telling them?" I demanded, feeling horribly let down again.

"Just that you guys had a great time, that you got pissed and, if Sariel hadn't shown up, you'd have been waking up in his room this morning." I closed my eyes and sank down onto the bed again. I really could pick them, couldn't I? When I looked up again, Annie had gone.

Chapter Forty-one

It was late in the evening when I finally left my room to come down for dinner. I had taken a long bath after siesta, dried and tamed my hair with Lisa's straighteners; changed into a pair of flat leather sandals, a demure navy shirt and a pair of dark pleated Capri pants. I left my hair down, applied a small amount of make-up and then, stomach turning with nerves, sat staring at myself in the mirror until it was time to head down the stairs.

The house was filled to capacity – there were people everywhere; chatting, laughing, drinking or selecting food from a long buffet table set out in the courtyard. - the atmosphere was like a family party. I was standing just inside the patio doors leading from the living room, soaking it all up and trying to get my bearings or spot a familiar face when an arm encircled my shoulder. "Wondered when you'd make an appearance."

"Hi, Paul," I shrugged his arm off. "Where are the others?"

"On the far side of the courtyard. Dylan is in full nerd mode." He followed me as I excused myself past huddles of bodies. "So, how's the head?" He whispered as we paused to let a waiter by - I couldn't see what was on the huge plate that he was carrying but it smelled incredible and my stomach rumbled in appreciation.

"I'm fine," I scowled. "No thanks to you."

"Hey!" Paul had the audacity to sound hurt. "How was I to know that you couldn't hold your liquor?"

"You used that excuse already, remember?" I was honestly trying to be civil but Annie's revelations about what he'd been telling the others had made me mad.

"Awww, c'mon, principessa. Be nice." Paul leaned close to my hair. "You know how much I like you, Emily. Stop breaking my heart." I melted a little in spite of myself. Or at least I did until he leaned forward and slipped an arm around my waist, grinning across the room at a group of young males who I vaguely remembered from the work out sessions. They raised their glasses to him and I angrily unwound his arm.

"I'm not breaking your heart, Paul. I'm just cross with you."

"For what? Taking you out and showing you a good time?" He sounded astonished now.

I shook my head. "No. For kissing and telling. Actually for kissing and lying." I left him standing for a moment, winding through the crowd and feeling my heart lift a little when I finally caught sight of Seth. He waved and then looked behind me and scowled. I followed his glare. Paul had caught up.

"I didn't lie." He hissed.

"Yes you did. You said I would've ended up in your bed if Sariel hadn't come along. That's a lie." I pushed on. Annie appeared carrying a plate piled high with about 2000 calories worth of creamy pasta. Dylan wasn't far behind, he was talking at the speed of a freight-train and waving a broccoli floret at Jude who was rolling her eyes.

"It's not a lie. You were enjoying yourself." Paul was still arguing.

"Name one person who doesn't enjoy dancing!" I shook my head.

Paul caught my arm and stopped me. "I wasn't talking about the dancing. I was talking about the....other stuff. At the car and before that in the pool. You enjoyed it when I was kissing you. You wanted more. That's no lie. If HE hadn't turned up, we'd have ended up spending the night together. There's no point in denying it, principessa. I know you wanted to."

I couldn't help it. I snorted with laughter. "You SO need to get over yourself," I told him and went over to stand beside Seth.

"Is fang boy annoying you?" Seth asked, eyeballing Paul.

"No, he's harmless. Leave it," I told him. "What's for dinner?"

Seth hadn't finished. "If he is upsetting you, just say, Emily. I'll sort it. Sariel said..."

"You'll sort it? Who are you? Stallone? And Sariel said what exactly?" I was in danger of fighting with my brother. Things were going back to normal already.

"Sit with us," Dylan called. "Before that weird French girl comes over." He whispered.

I grinned. "Are you talking about Lisa? She's not weird."

Dylan made a face. "Yes, she bloody well is. She wanted to know if I permed my hair and when I said I didn't she said she could straighten it for me. She's a nutter, I tell you. I mean, why the hell would I do this to my own hair?" Annie and I laughed.

"So, did he tell you yet?" Annie whispered.

"Who? Tell me what?" I leaned forward. "Is this scandal?"

Annie nodded happily. "I don't know if I should tell you. I think he wants to do it himself."

"Tell me, tell me, tell me, tell me," I sing-songed.

Annie flapped her hand to shush me. "Fine. You can take the heat if I wasn't meant to say anything okay?" I nodded. "So Seth and Jude are like, an item." She leaned back, eyes wide in a wow-what-do-you-think-of-that? pose.

I looked at her. "I knew that." I dead-panned.

"What?! Since when?!" Annie looked scandalized.

I was getting ready to tell her about my amazing ability to sense that Seth fancied someone, when all the chatter quieted around us and all eyes turned towards the centre of the courtyard. A man was standing in front of the buffet table, holding up a glass of red wine. He was tall, elegant and one of the most other-worldly looking people I'd ever seen, kind of like the elves in 'Lord of the Rings'. He raised his glass in a silent toast, his eyes roaming around the room. Everyone copied him, even Annie and Dylan. It was like a wave of wine and smoothie drinking – Dylan, along with everyone else under eighteen, was slurping what looked like a strawberry and banana smoothie with a straw. I looked around, feeling awkward and left out – I didn't have anything to drink for a start and it was all kind of creepy. Elf-man nodded once and then left the room. Some people broke away from their groups to follow him and I felt a touch on my arm.

Isabella smiled. "It's time, Emily. Come with me." I glanced back at Seth who was giving Jude a light peck on the cheek and handing his glass and plate to one of the waiters. I sighed with relief. Seth was coming. I wouldn't have to meet the Angels alone.

CHAPTER FORTY-TWO

Seth and I followed Isabella and the others out into the late evening air. I found myself searching for Sariel without meaning to and told myself not to be such an idiot; not that it mattered – I couldn't see him anywhere. No-one was speaking, just walking silently in a hap-hazard single-file. I couldn't help thinking about horror movies where the main characters are pre-programmed to walk silently to their doom by a knife/gun/bomb/whatever-wielding maniac. I slipped my hand into Seth's and felt a reassuring squeeze. Much as I was dying to ask about the whole Jude thing, I figured that now wouldn't be a good time, although I was nervous and really wanted something else to think about.

We were on a rocky path that led from the side of the house and down into the valley through the beautifully kept lines of olive trees. It was a beautiful evening, warm and still; our footfalls seemed to echo all around, mingling with the now distant hum of conversation and occasional laughter from the house behind us. Birds were chattering somewhere close, insects buzzing and flittering through the trees; the air around us thrummed with the strong scent of freshly turned earth and the heavy tang of olives. Somewhere to the east was the faint sound of chattering in lyrical Italian – the workers, I thought, finishing their shift and heading to their accommodations for the night.

We walked on, the sky darkened around us and the sounds of civilization got further away.

"Where are we?" I whispered to Seth.

He shrugged. "Still on Isabella's property but far to the west, away from the plant …and everything else."

"Is there even anything out in this direction? Any buildings I mean?" I stumbled and Seth caught my arm, keeping me upright. It was getting hard to see the path.

"Not that I know of. Is that a light?" Seth was squinting ahead of us through the trees. I stretched on my tip-toes, trying to see. Yes, there was a glow up ahead.

Isabella turned to face us. "It's not so far now, ragazzi." She smiled encouragingly and then frowned at the expressions on our faces. "Why so serious? This is a big night, si?"

"Si," Seth told her with a shaky smile. "A very big night. Which is why we're so worried."

Isabella made a 'pah' noise and flapped her hands. "These people are not so scary. They just want to meet you."

"It's a bit like meeting a hundred mafia dons, in the middle of the night and in the middle of nowhere," I told her earning a bray of laughter from our hostess.

"You have an interesting way of looking at the world, mia cara. I like it."

"Yeah, I'm thinking of changing my career choice from university lecturer to stand-up comic," I mumbled. Seth gave me an angry nudge and a glare. I sighed and put my head down, feeling Isabella's watchful gaze for a few more minutes until we came to the edge of the maze of trees and saw that the glow in the distance was a campfire.

"Angels have cookouts?" I whispered to Seth. "Or maybe there's a stake in the middle of that inferno where they'll burn us if we don't match up to their expectations. Or maybe they're a bunch of pyromaniacs. Or maybe…"

Seth squeezed my arm. "Verbal diarrhea, Emily," he cautioned. "A sure sign of nerves."

"What are you trying to say?" I asked miserably as I saw figures move in front of the fire, a lot of figures.

"I'm saying shut up," Seth told me with a smile to soften his words. "Don't let your big mouth get us into more crap." I poked him in the ribs. Big mouth? Me?

The big Angelic, pyromaniac cookout was a somber affair. At least until Seth and I entered the circle and then people began talking all at once. I looked around nervously. There were maybe 150 people around the fire – some were standing, some lounged, some sat cross-legged on the tightly-packed earth; most sat in clusters, chatting animatedly and glancing in our direction. There was a notable exception.

Sariel stood on his own, leaning against the side of a battered old truck, with his head down as though he was studying the stitching detail on his work boots. He was wearing a pair of grimy blue jeans and a dusty gray shirt with rolled-up sleeves. He looked all mussed up and utterly gorgeous. I looked quickly away and then looked back. There was an obvious gap around him, like people had purposely not stood beside him. I frowned. What the hell?

Isabella led us over to a gap in the circle and motioned for us to sit down. We sat and endured the stares and whispered comments for another ten minutes. "What are we waiting for?" I hissed to Seth who shook his head and swallowed. He was obviously feeling as awkward as I did. Annoyed on his behalf as much as my own, I began meeting the eyes of some of our 'admirers'. It was weird. There were old men, young men, short men, tall men; men with beards, men with moustaches, clean-shaven, designer stubble; all colours and nationalities. But the eyes? The eyes were all like Sariel's – startling silver-blue, shining like beacons in the flickering fire light. I think that was when it hit me – Seth and I were sitting around a large campfire with the actual Angels who had once been in Heaven. They had once been in HEAVEN. Wow. I might actually have passed out there and then but the woman chose that moment to make her entrance.

She walked in from the direction of the processing plant on legs that were encased in black leather and seemed to go on for miles. Her tiny waist was accentuated by a looping silver belt and the scrap of material she was wearing as a shirt did absolutely nothing to hide about an acre of her smooth, tanned skin. She tossed her long, shiny black hair and looked in annoyance at Sariel standing on his own, made a point of walking over to him and pressing a kiss to his cheek, before striding over and sitting down beside me.

I had just decided that I hated her when she turned her glare from her fellow Angels, grinned happily at me and stuck out a hand. "You must be Emily. Sorry I'm late. I'm Uriel. Sariel's told me all about you."

CHAPTER FORTY-THREE

I managed, with difficulty, not to say the first thing that came into my head, which would've been a snarky 'Yeah? Well he never mentioned you!' Instead I smiled sweetly and shook her hand, keeping my mouth shut.

Across the way from us the tall man who had spoken in the courtyard stood up and raised his hand for silence. Everyone shut up immediately and I resisted the urge to giggle or shout 'Demon!' and watch everyone panic. Beside me, Uriel leaned back on her elbows and laid her long legs out in front of her, crossing them daintily at the ankles.

"Now that we are all present," the man began, looking pointedly at Uriel who waved at him happily, "Or at least those of us who are able to be, I believe we should get started." He looked over at Seth and me and then frowned. "Where is the other potential?" Say what?

There were murmurs around the circle and a tall, aristocratic looking man in a well cut and no doubt expensive charcoal grey suit stepped forward with a small smile on his lips. "Lamma esse. Forgive me, brothers and sisters. I thought it would be rude of me to have him sit in your exalted company before he was requested." The man's hawk eyes rested on Seth and me for a moment before he glanced at Sariel. "Obviously our brother, Sariel, had no such qualms," he muttered under his breath but I had no doubt that everyone heard him anyway. He motioned to someone and a boy slipped into the circle.

Seth turned to me in surprise. "Is that…?"

I nodded. It was Adrian. The boy from France, who we all had taken to be Lisa's boyfriend. He stood looking around the strange gathering in the middle of nowhere with eyes as big as saucers. He caught sight of Seth and me and visibly relaxed, giving us a little wave. We waved back in sync. Beside me Uriel leaned forward a little and narrowed her eyes. "Is that Pierre?" She asked, her voice full of astonishment. Several others peered more closely at Adrian and the murmuring began again.

Adrian's Angel made an exasperated 'tuh' noise. "Don't be ridiculous. How could it be Pierre? It's been over a century since we tested him. He is returned to dust."

"Well, that looks mighty like him," Uriel persisted. She paused and frowned. "You're not still hounding the family are you? This boy is an ancestor of the first you brought. I can tell – the shape of the jaw, the high cheekbones, the sturdy build, the green eyes…all family traits."

"Is this true?" The man who was obviously the leader asked in a voice of such cold amusement that I wanted to hide behind Seth.

Adrian's Angel, looking flustered, pointed at Sariel. "And you think it is any more likely that his little whore has been gifted?" I frowned. Was he referring to me? Angrily he stalked around the edge of the circle, parading Adrian in front of him. "This boy is an ancestor of Joan of Arc, an heir to a legacy of God which is uncorrupted through the ages, the line is pure and the links to the church are strong and without question. These heathens," he pointed to Seth and me, "… are not only born to a woman of ill virtue but also tainted by Demon blood." Did he really just call my mother a 'woman of ill virtue'? "And not just any blood, they carry the line of the Lord Asmodeus. We could have spies in our midst, spies that he brought to us. We know how close he is to falling into darkness, who's to say that he hasn't already given himself over to it and is now working to destroy us from the inside? Can you answer me honestly that you trust our brother when he bares the symptoms of the sickness for all of us to see? Can you?"

Uriel opened her mouth to speak but I had already heard enough. I hopped up, strode forward towards Adrian and his benefactor and stuck out my hand. Both of them looked at it with matching expressions of shock and fear on their faces. "Hi." I said as loudly and clearly as I could. "My name is Emily Carson. I figured since you're going all out to make me sound like some demented-Demonic-half-breed-female-James Bond-type that we should get formally acquainted. Where I come from, which is planet Earth by the way, people tend to be civil enough to at least introduce themselves before they start dissing another person." From behind me I heard Uriel chuckle happily. I looked down at my hand, which was so far unshaken, and cleared my throat. "Will we try this again? Hi. I'm Emily Carson." I waited.

Adrian shook my hand, grinning. "Allo, Emily. I am Adrian de la Croix."

"Pleased to meet you Adrian," I told him with a smile and then I turned my attention back to the man at his shoulder. He was eyeing me with annoyance and distaste. "Do you need help with this?" I asked. His eyes narrowed. "This is the part where you shake my hand and tell me your name," I stage whispered. Another chuckle from Uriel, joined by a few others this time. The Angel looked around the circle defiantly and then sighed.

He reached out and pumped my hand once, letting go of it immediately and wiping his hand on the trousers of his expensive suit. "My name is Armaros."

I grinned and bumped his shoulder with my fist. "There ya go, Armaros. That wasn't so tough was it?" I folded my arms and gave him my best glare. "Now that the easy stuff's over you can apologise to my friend." I nodded in Sariel's direction. Uriel whooped with laughter.

"Apologise for what?" Armaros sneered. "For telling the truth? He is a heartbeat away from slipping into darkness. That is the truth."

I wiggled my head from side to side. "Maybe. Maybe not. Speaking as someone who relies on him for protection and has been with him on a daily basis for over a year, I think your assessment is a tad overly-dramatic but I guess you have a crowd to win over, right? So we'll let that go for the minute. No, what I was talking about is the fact that you were accusing him of bringing my brother and me here to spy for Asmodeus. You basically accused him of putting you all in harm's way which is complete crap. So apologise."

Armaros pushed Adrian behind him and squared up to me. "Are you calling me a liar?"

I didn't even flinch. "Yep."

To be honest I'm not sure where we would've gone next but the leader stepped in between us and gave us both equal glares of annoyance. "Perhaps we could get on with this and you two can work out your differences at a later date?" He suggested. "Armaros, take your potential and sit down. Sariel? Control your woman." He walked off and Armaros swung away, pulling Adrian behind him. Adrian shot me a 'what're-you-gonna-do?' look and I grinned at him.

"Come stand by me before you think about starting any more fights," Sariel whispered into my ear a second later sending a pulse of adrenaline through my heart. His hand slipped into mine and I allowed him to lead me back to his spot by the truck. We leaned against it and I was glad to have something to prop me up. First the head dude called me Sariel's woman and then the butterfly touch of Sariel's breath had awakened all my senses so now his hand in mine was the centre of my universe – I was aware of every tiny movement of his fingers, every slight rub of his skin against mine. I gulped, blocking my thoughts harder than ever. Sariel let go of my hand and I folded my arms, reminding myself that we weren't speaking and that nothing meant anything and that men were all bad news and that I should be concentrating on what the leader was saying.

"For the benefit of those with us who do not know me, my name is Samyaza. I am the leader of the Watchers, which is what we were before...before we fell. Perhaps a little history lesson is in order?" I saw Uriel say something to Seth and then she hopped lithely to her feet and walked over to stand beside me. Samyaza was still talking but I was zoning out. He was covering old ground – they were Angels, Eden was built, Adam and Eve, Lucifer, the snake, Angels kicked out, yadda, yadda, yadda.

"Nice take down." Uriel whispered.

"Thanks. Is this where you tell me I shouldn't have done it? Sorry but I don't take too kindly to people calling my friends names."

She grinned. "I wasn't going to say that. These guys need a little shake up now and again. They used to be warriors, leaders of armies. Killing Demons was all in a day's work for them. And now?" She made a face. "They've been here too long. They're content to sit in the shadows and wait for Him to decide that our punishment has ended. Meanwhile humanity is losing the fight for their souls."

I looked at her. For the first time since she'd arrived, her face was shadowed, angry or perhaps sad. I could easily imagine her as some kind of Amazonian warrior, she'd use a sword like Jude of course or maybe she'd have gun belts like Lara Croft. "So, if you were in charge?" I asked.

She laughed softly. "If I was in charge we probably wouldn't have survived for as long as we have. Sam knows what he's doing – he's keeping as many of us from embracing the darkness as he can." She lowered her head. "I still think that we should fight them."

I looked between her and Sariel, a realization forming. "So you're part of the Brotherhood too? Except it's not just a load of safe houses and hidey holes is it? It's a resistance. You're resistance fighters." Uriel's gaze flicked over my head to Sariel and I knew they were communicating. "Out loud if you don't mind," I told her.

She grinned. "He said that you were smart. I was just telling him that he was right." Her eyes sharpened. "So, once we get all this out of the way, will you and your friends be joining the resistance?"

I opened and closed my mouth. "I hadn't really thought much beyond this," I admitted. "I mean, I guess I expected to be told what to do next."

Uriel shook her head. "They'll take a few centuries to come to a consensus and decide whether they believe you're the real deal or not. And then they'll decide to wait and see what happens. In the meantime you'll age and die and the message, whatever it is, will be lost for another eternity." She shook her head. "It's always the same."

I looked around and a question came to mind. "Why do some of them look so old when you are all immortal and ageless?"

Uriel nodded. "Some of them have human wives and families.

They choose to age with their spouse until the end of what would be a natural lifespan."

"And then what? They lie in a coffin and play dead?" I was appalled.

Uriel giggled. "Seriously, can you see any of these guys getting buried? No, they change their outward appearance back to their ageless selves and begin again elsewhere. Or at least some do. For others, losing a life partner is too traumatic." She glanced at Sariel again and then back at me, raising an eyebrow and widening her eyes. I frowned. "Some of them find the idea of loving someone mortal again only to lose them to age is beyond what they can deal with. No matter how much they might feel for someone." Her eyebrows rose again, even higher than before and her eyes widened so much I was afraid they were in danger of popping out. Ok. Uriel was freaking me out.

I tried to think of an intelligent reaction to all that. Unfortunately when I opened my mouth, all my brain was capable of producing was, "Huh?" Uriel blew out her cheeks and whispered something in a mixture of languages. "Can we stick with English?" I asked.

"I said," She whispered, "that you were so quick to figure out about the resistance so how can you be so slow to realise that he..."

"Uriel!" Sariel snapped. "Enough. They're starting."

Uriel scowled and leaned back. I looked between her and Sariel wondering what the hell was going on and then my attention was caught by Armaros and leading Adrian forward again. Now what?

Chapter Forty-four

Adrian looked nervous as he stood in front of everyone again and I couldn't help feeling sorry for him. Armaros gave a little speech again (boy, was that guy ever in love with the sound of his own voice!) reiterating the fact that Adrian was a good boy from a good family whose ancestors included Joan of Arc and who had connections to God going back for centuries. Most people in his audience got pretty bored – there was a lot of mumbling and shuffling and even walking from one side of the circle to another. Uriel even got up at one point and put more fuel on the fire which made a crazy racquet.

Finally Adrian was waved forward to stand in front of Armaros and the show began. Armaros produced some cards from his pocket, told Adrian to close his eyes and then handed the cards to one of the Angels behind them. Everyone was leaning forward for a better view, the mumbling had stopped and there was a hush over the whole area – like we were all holding our breath for the finale. The Angel who had taken the cards chose one and put it in his pocket, Armaros then turned Adrian around and told the Angel to 'think' the card to Adrian. We waited. Adrian scrunched his face up in concentration, leaned forward a little and finally exclaimed "King of diamonds!"

The Angel produced the king of diamonds from his pocket and everyone clapped happily. I looked at Uriel, trying very hard to keep the sarcasm out of my voice. "That was really...good." I told her.

Uriel raised an eyebrow. "Please. Derren Brown does it better. And he's cuter."

I couldn't argue with any of that so I turned my attention back to Adrian who was now attempting to draw a shape that was being 'thought' at him by a vaguely embarrassed-looking Samyaza. Again he got it right. Armaros was almost purple with excitement. "Can you see?" He was asking, "Can you see what a gift this boy has been given."

I leaned over to look at Seth and had to bite my lip. The

expression on my twin's face was a cross between bemusement and boredom. Realising that I was looking at him he leaned forward, grinned and made a twirling motion at his temple with one of his fingers. I nodded, giggling. This was a lot more fun than I'd expected.

Adrian was now sitting cross-legged on the ground. He had closed his eyes and folded his hands together in front of him. Armaros gestured to Samyaza who handed him a long, gleaming sword. The sense of anticipation in the circle of Angels rose a notch as Armaros began to circle Adrian, skimming the sword across the ground so that it made a low hissing sound. Adrian stayed motionless, his shoulders rising and falling with each breath he took. Armaros lifted the sword above his head with a graceful swing, gripping it with both hands. He kept circling. Adrian kept breathing. My heart was thudding hard all of a sudden. Armaros looked menacing now, dangerous. I could see a few beads of sweat on Adrian's brow and a slight shake to his hands. The eyes of the other Angels glittered in the firelight. They looked enthralled and excited.

It happened so fast that I wasn't sure I'd actually seen it at first. Armaros brought the sword down towards Adrian's head and, just as I drew in a breath to scream, certain that the blade would lodge in his skull, Adrian's hands came up and caught the blade between his palms. Applause erupted and I buried my head in Sariel's shoulder for a moment.

I glanced at his face – as always he looked impassive although a small smile curved the corner of his lips. He was either impressed or amused by Armaros and Adrian's theatrics. I couldn't tell, although the urge to merge my mind with his and find out was more than tempting.

Beside us Uriel sighed and I forced myself away from Sariel. She was shaking her head. "Smoke and mirrors," she muttered, "Cheap parlour tricks."

Armaros swung around to face her. "You have something to say, sister?" he sneered.

Uriel nodded. "You think that a boy magician is what we

need?"

Armaros' eyes narrowed and his gaze flicked from Uriel to Samyaza and back again. He raised his voice. "You don't believe that this boy has been blessed with these talents?"

Uriel smiled dangerously. "I don't believe that an Archangel gifted him with them. Otherwise we'd have an army of amateur magicians running around boring the Demons to death with card tricks." There was muted laughter around us and several nods of agreement.

Armaros frowned and looked around. "I believe in this young man." He said loudly, pulling Adrian in front of him and parading him around the circle. Adrian looked slightly confused now, but relieved that his trials were over. Armaros stopped in front of me. "Perhaps before we judge we should see what Sariel's little Delilah can do."

I grinned at him. "Bring it on, little man," I whispered and Uriel laughed as Sariel took my hand and led me into the centre of the circle.

CHAPTER FORTY-FIVE

S tanding in the centre of a circle of Angels is nothing short of terrifying. I could feel the weight of their eyes on me as I followed Sariel to a spot in front of Samyaza who was calming everyone down and getting people to sit down again – kind of like a teacher in a classroom of sixteen year-olds. Finally, when he was satisfied that we had as much attention as we were going to get, he nodded to Sariel.

Unlike Armaros, Sariel wasn't a fan of big speeches and fancy words. Instead he turned to me and took both my hands in his, smiling gently. Oh, Lord, that smile! It was so familiar and yet it had been so long since we'd been together that it felt as though I was seeing it for the first time again. He was beautiful. There was no other description that would do him justice – well, maybe 'gorgeous,' 'hot' and 'swoonsome' could be useful too.

Sariel took a deep breath and studied me carefully. "I need to ask a favour, Emily," he said softly. "I need to ask you to open your mind to me again." I bit my lip and he sighed. "I know that you are finding it hard to trust me and I don't blame you. There are many things that I should have explained to you, things that I thought you wouldn't understand or weren't ready to hear but I forgot who I was dealing with." He grinned at me again and I felt myself smile back. "I was wrong and I'm sorry." His grip on my hands tightened for a second. "I believe that your gift, your ability was given to you by the Archangel Michael," There was a soft gasp around the circle as he said this and I realized that they were all listening intently to our conversation. I blushed but Sariel kept talking and never took his eyes from mine. "I believe that he gave you this gift so that we would recognise you as a portent, a messenger, who will show us the path back home, or at least set us on it. I may be wrong," he shrugged, "I don't think so but that's why we're here – I need my brothers and sisters to see what you can do and to decide if I'm right or wrong." He swallowed loudly. "They don't altogether trust me, Emily. You know why." I nodded and there was a murmur from somewhere. I ignored it. "I may be too far along that path to be saved but the others aren't." I frowned and opened my mouth to protest but he shook his head. "No, it's okay. I can accept it. I pushed myself to the limits of my endurance and I know that if I have to endure more of their torture, I will probably not survive it. You saved me the last time and I will never forget that. Will you trust me now?"

I nodded and then frowned. "I have a question," I told him carefully.

"Ask it. Ask anything."

"If I do this will they be able to read my mind too?"

Sariel made a face. "Perhaps. I honestly don't know." I shifted my weight from one foot to another and looked around the circle. The idea of all these strangers gaining access to my mind was frightening. I didn't think I wanted someone like Armaros rummaging around in there. "Are you afraid?" Sariel asked, studying my face. I nodded reluctantly.

Uriel stepped forward. "I could block for you, allow access one at a time." She told me. I thought about it but shook my head.

"It would take too long. And I would look like a weak idiot if I could only deal with one of you in my head at a time."

"Will it hurt her?" Seth spoke up behind me.

Sariel shook his head. "I wouldn't allow it. If I sense any distress I will shield her completely. I won't allow any harm to come to her, Seth."

Seth reached out and squeezed my arm. It was a comforting little squeeze but it was also an 'it's-up-to-you-sis-whatever-happens-I've-got-your-back' squeeze.

I took a deep breath, closed my eyes and nodded. When I opened my eyes again I also opened my mind.

Sariel flowed back in and the relief was astonishing. I had become so used to blocking him from my mind that I had forgotten how much I missed him being there. His presence lit up everything, filling my whole body with light and energy. I drank it all in, feeling the tense knots in my shoulders loosen and the agony of keeping my shields up for so long disappear. Sariel bent forward and pressed his forehead to mine. *Amata y'essa nomarre,* he whispered. To hear his voice in my head again was almost more than I could bear. I could feel tears on my cheeks but I was laughing aloud.

What did you say? Is that more Italian? I asked, and the fact that I was speaking to him like this again made me laugh even more. I must've looked like some kind of leaky lunatic to everyone else.

It's the language of heaven and I said that I have missed you so much, my love.

Your 'love'? Oh, well that was it. I cried like a baby. Asmodeus was forgotten. The circle of Angels around us were forgotten. I shook my hands free of Sariel's and leapt into his arms instead. He hugged me tight, burying his face in my hair and then planting little kisses along my cheek.

Someone coughed loudly next to us and I jumped back a little, blinking in surprise.

"Perhaps if we could all see what is so thrilling, we would all be crying and hugging one another?" Samyaza asked.

I frowned at him. "But I…"

Sariel shook his head at me. "Uriel and I were shielding you from the others." *That was a personal moment*, he finished with a smile. I turned to thank Uriel but she was sobbing into a tissue.

"Too cute, you guys are just too cute," she blubbed. Wow, Uriel the Amazonian resistance fighter was a softie at heart.

Sariel's face turned serious. *Are you ready?* I nodded and turned to face Samyaza and the others. The moment of truth had finally arrived.

Sariel let down the entire shield that he had protecting my mind and their consciousness streamed in. For a moment I panicked. There was no way I could contain this. My head would burst like a ripe tomato, or my brain would liquefy and I'd spend the rest of my days tied to a bed in a psych ward or my whole body would explode and bits of me would be roasting in the hot Italian sun this time tomorrow. I was hyperventilating. Thoughts rushed through my mind, thoughts that weren't mine, 'hello's and 'can you hear me' and 'I can teach you about the birth of mathematics'. I gulped in air but my lungs weren't working.

Sariel pulled me in front of him, took my hands in his again and spoke calmly and gently. *It's ok, Emily. You're not going to die, you're not going to explode and your head is much harder than a ripe tomato. Breathe slowly and relax.*

I was about to go into complete meltdown when I heard Uriel. Her voice was clear and strong, drowning out the others buzzing around my brain. *Leave her now. You will have other chances. Don't forget that she's human.* The buzzing slowed and then ceased. All that was left were Sariel, Uriel and Armaros. *Do you need a map to find the way out?* Uriel asked him, annoyance dripping from every word.

How have you done this? Armaros asked. *This is…impossible. What trickery have you resorted to?*

Trickery? There is no trickery here, Sariel told him.

You can feel it though can't you? Armaros growled. *There's darkness here. She would only have to reach for it once and it would consume her. Did he tempt you with it, little half breed? Did Sariel show you the way to harness the shadows?*

I turned to face him. His eyes were blue flames, flickering in the firelight and fixed on my face. "No," I said aloud. "But Asmodeus did." There was a collective gasp.

"And did you touch it?" Samyaza asked quietly. "The dark power? Did you?"

I shook my head. "Almost. It was…hard not to but I heard Sariel calling me and I stopped just in time."

"How did it feel?" asked one of the others? He sounded much too eager and I couldn't help stepping away from him. "It felt…horrible…" I told him, "…and beautiful." I dipped my head, suddenly ashamed but there was no point in lying to them, they could take a trip through my mind and find the truth if they wanted. Sariel put an arm around my shoulders and Seth slipped his hand into mine.

"And what of the other half breed?" asked Samyaza. "Does he have this gift?"

Seth shook his head and grinned his usual cocky grin. "Nope,

I was just blessed with good looks," he quipped. Uriel hiccupped a laugh and punched him playfully on the shoulder.

Sariel chuckled and then turned back to Samyaza. "I will take Seth and Emily back to the house. I assume you will wish to deliberate?"

Samyaza nodded glancing around to some of the others for confirmation. "Perhaps we would be better to sleep on it?" suggested one leathery skinned, white haired man. "You know, back at the house. Convene again tomorrow night?"

Samyaza sighed and it went to a vote. Uriel rolled her eyes as the majority voted to go back to the house and get some rest. She leaned close to me. "I told you, they've been down here too long. They're too comfortable. This is monumental. Our long-awaited gift from Heaven could be among us and what do they want to do? Sleep. Ridiculous." She wandered off after the others, shaking her head.

Seth blew out his cheeks. "Well, that was entertaining. What're you gonna do for an encore?"

I realized that Seth must be completely bored – he couldn't 'hear' what had been going on inside my head. All he would have seen was Sariel and I embracing and then everyone standing around silently while I gasped for breath and finally a short conversation with Armaros that must have made absolutely no sense whatsoever. I began to giggle. And the giggles turned into laughter. Before long I had to sit down and hold my sides.

Seth sat down beside me. "Is *this* the encore? It looks like fun but I don't know what the joke is."

"You..." I managed to splutter.

"ME? I'm the joke?" Seth frowned. "I don't get it." I laughed even harder.

Sariel was laughing too. He knelt down beside us. "Perhaps this will help," he said and put one hand on my shoulder and the other on Seth's. And just like that Seth's mind bloomed in mine. His mouth formed an 'O' of astonishment and then his face slipped into a smile of wonder. *This is....What the...? I'm in your head. Holy... This is amazing. How am I...?* His thoughts zipped around like bullets as he tried to make sense of it all.

I leaned against Sariel. *Thank you*, I told him.

Sariel was watching Seth with a curious expression on his face. He turned to smile at me. *You're welcome.*

"You're talking. I heard you." Seth pointed at us and then peered at our faces. "Your lips didn't move at all."

They don't need to, I told him. *This is what I was talking about.*

"This is wild." Seth whooped, pushing his hair back from his eyes. *Wild, insane, crazy, brilliant*, his thoughts whooshed by leaving kaleidoscopes of excited colour behind.

Perhaps we should be heading back, Sariel cautioned. *You will both need your rest if they are to make their decision tomorrow night.*

Yeah, yeah, bed sounds good right now, Seth thought. *Wonder if I can sneak Jude into my room again...* He looked up at us and his eyes widened. *Did you just hear that?* Sariel and I nodded, grinning. *Um...we talk a lot. She's good company*, he spluttered. A picture flashed into my mind from Seth's and in it he and Jude were doing a lot more than talking.

"Ewwww!" I screeched and pushed Sariel away, breaking the connection. "Too much information, Seth." Seth's face was the colour of cranberry juice and he was looking at me with embarrassment and concern. "It's ok," I told him with a grin. I ruffled his hair. "I know all about it."

"Who...?" He managed.

"Annie, you know she's a sucker for romance. Especially since her and Dylan are all lovey-dovey."

"Ah...," Seth folded his arms, unfolded them, looked at the heavens and then back at me. "Is this something we need to talk about?" He looked so worried and little-boy-like that I giggled.

"Maybe. But not tonight."

Seth drew a hand across his brow and made an exaggerated 'whew' noise but he smiled all the way back to the casa. I had at least made my brother happy so I figured it had been a successful night's work.

CHAPTER FORTY-SIX

I'd honestly thought that I was tired. I'd even had to smother a few yawns on the walk back up through the fragrant darkness of the olive plantation. Sariel and Seth had talked about a variety of subjects as we walked – olives, Angels, Uriel (knew she'd come into the conversation somewhere), mum (with Asmodeus but unharmed as far as Sariel's contacts could tell), the Weres (no news really. Adam was still blond and gorgeous in a 'ooh-what-lovely-teeth-you've-got' kind of way.).

I was glad that they were so chatty – it meant that I could concentrate on the fact that Sariel was holding my hand (yay), that his leg would bump against my hip from time to time (double yay), that he looked incredibly hot in dusty jeans (yum), that I felt totally and utterly happy and content for the first time in ages. I felt like everything was going to work out – the other Angels would make whatever decision they had to make, we'd go and rescue mum, kick Asmodeus's skinny Demonic ass and live happily ever after in a semi down the road from Dylan and Annie or something. Seth and Jude would have to get their own place obviously, but Sariel could move in with me and mum. It would be a kind of weird but funky happy families type thing. I was all about the positives as we walked. The negative stuff kept trying to make a dent in my rosy future fantasy but I was having none of it.

Seth said goodnight as we walked slowly back in through the courtyard, hugging me tightly and bumping fists with Sariel before he left – no doubt in a hurry to sneak into Jude's room or something. Ooh, nasty mental image!

Sariel and I stopped at the bottom of the stairs that led to my room and I finally had first-hand experience of what people meant when they say that 'the atmosphere was tense'. I don't know what I was expecting. I suppose in my fantasy Sariel would scoop me into his arms, carry me to his room (where was his room anyway?) and, well….let's just say I was expecting more than a chaste peck on the cheek and a 'Don't forget to block while you're in the house.'

And what happened? Sariel gave me a chaste peck on the cheek and whispered "Don't forget to block while you're in the house." And then, with a final squeeze of my hand, he was gone and I walked up the stairs alone, falling onto my bed with a huffy groan and fully expecting to fall straight to sleep.

Yeah, right.

Two hours later and I was still tossing and turning. It was Sariel's fault. I kept thinking about how he'd kissed me in front of everyone, how he'd trailed those sweet but totally bone-melting kisses along my cheek, how his hand had felt in mine, how he'd probably had to have a shower before he went to bed, how he was probably so tired after a full day working on the plantation and then such a late night that he'd probably just gone to bed naked after his shower.

I sat up in bed. This was getting ridiculous. I was turning into a perv. Maybe if I had a shower? Cold showers were supposed to work when you were thinking about guys being naked, right? Or maybe a mug of hot milk to help me sleep? Or maybe I should just head out there, find Sariel's room and jump on him.

"Grrrrr." I got out of bed and wandered into the bathroom without any real plan. "Shower then?" I asked myself. I looked at myself in the mirror – my face was flushed, my hair was tousled and my eyes were dark and sultry with sleep. I turned away from the mirror and my feet led me towards the door. "Okay then, milk it is." I whispered and opened the door.

Sariel blinked at me. His hand was raised to knock. We looked at each other, eyes wide. "Um…I was just…." I stuttered.

Sariel nodded and grinned. *You think SO loudly, m'amata.* He pulled me into his arms and this time his kiss was hard and needy and wonderful. I melted against him, allowing my hands to wander across his back and his shoulders as he crushed me against his chest. He made a low moaning sound deep in his throat that made me shiver with excitement. My body was suddenly all heat, liquefied limbs and tingling nerve-endings. I felt alive, aflame and more than ready to be treated like a grown up.

Tell me to stop and I will, Sariel told me, pulling back a little to look at me. The colour of his eyes was so close to silver that they glittered in the twilight shadows of my room. In answer I stretched out a leg and kicked my door shut behind him.

This is what I want, I told him.

With a sigh of contentment, Sariel scooped me up into his arms and carried me to bed.

Chapter Forty-seven

I'm sure there's probably an official way to deal with the-morning-after-the-night-before type of situations. Especially if, like me, you are completely unused to waking up with a gorgeous half-naked man in bed beside you.

I mean, do you bolt for the bathroom; shower, dress and be all squeaky clean and clothed by the time he wakes up? Do you sneak out as quietly as possible, hoping he'll be awake, washed, dressed etc. by the time you get back from breakfast? Do you wait 'till he wakes up and talk about what happened last night? Do you never mention it again? Do you 'phone a friend' and ask their advice? Wow. There really are some questions that textbooks don't give you the answers to.

Okay, so I was too busy admiring Sariel's tattoo to really think any of my options through anyway.

He was lying on his front with the sheet just above his waist and I was entranced by the realistic looking feathers of his Angel-wings tattoo. It was incredible. The feathers were dove-grey with little touches of silver and dark violet which seemed to flash and shiver in the breeze from my bedroom window. His tattoo artist friend, Danny, had created these wings for him – to replace the originals? Maybe. I wondered if Sariel's real wings had looked anything like these.

They were…similar. Much larger of course, but the colours were the same. I jumped guiltily, my hand about an inch away from touching his skin. Sariel turned his head around and leaned on his folded arms, looking at me. He smiled lazily and I swallowed. That smile. What I wouldn't do for that gorgeous smile.

Sariel's eye narrowed a little and the smile slipped away. *Are you ok?* He asked gently. I nodded. He sighed and pushed himself up onto his elbows. The sheet slipped a little lower down his back although I tried very hard not to notice. I was sure that sophisticated been-in-this-situation-before kind of girls wouldn't be craning their necks to get a look at a guy's butt.

Are you sorry that we…

"NO! Oh, dear me no. Not at all. I'm just…." I searched for the right word as Sariel's head tilted to the side and a devilish grin twitched the sides of his lips.

"You're what?" He asked, apparently enjoying the blush that I could feel spreading over my face.

I decided to be honest. He could probably feel what I was feeling anyway. *I'm not having second thoughts about last night, Sariel. You know I was…ready for that. I just don't know what to say or do now. I mean, it's not like I have any experience at this.* I grinned sheepishly at him, feeling my face heat up even more.

Sariel's eyes softened. He rolled onto his side, facing me and reached out to snake an arm around my waist and pull me closer. Our faces were inches apart. *There are no hard and fast rules for relationships, Emily. You do what works for you. Okay? This isn't a test so there are no right and wrong answers. You say what comes into your head and do whatever feels right to you.*

Okay, I told him with a grin and leaned a little closer to kiss him, letting my hand skim over his shoulder to cup the side of his face.

He sighed happily. *If you keep that up then we'll be late for breakfast,* he warned.

I giggled and snuggled closer. *So?* I let my hand slide down across the tattoos on his chest. He sucked in a ragged breath.

So, the others will be looking for us.

So? Let them look. I trailed a row of little kisses across the line of his jaw and nibbled on his ear. His hand gripped my waist a little tighter.

So, they are making their decision about you today. They'll want to talk to you about…things. Ask questions about…stuff.

I'm sure you have a point…? My lips trailed down his neck and gave him a little nip in the hollow of his throat.

Um…yeah…I did…have a…um…yeah, the point. They're doing something about something and we should…do something. My God, woman. I thought you were sweet and innocent.

I smiled against his mouth. *I was and then I met this Fallen Angel…*

Sariel growled in mock anger and tipped me onto my back. I squealed with delight as he tickled me mercilessly until I could hardly breathe and was begging him to stop. We lay side by side giggling until he looked at me suddenly with a deadly serious expression. *I love you Emily Carson.* The words were loud and strong inside my head.

I sat up, leaning back on my elbows. My heart was beating so loud that I was sure the whole universe could hear it. "Could you just say that again? Out loud?" My voice was calm and steady, completely at odds with the mix of amazement and ready to bust happiness inside.

Sariel smiled. He leaned over and kissed my cheek. "I said that I love you Emily Carson."

"Am I dreaming?" I asked him, feeling suddenly shy and mush-like. He shook his head and I hugged him, almost squeezing the breath from him. "I love you too, Sariel." I told him feeling tears sting my eyes.

I wonder if the human brain was specially designed to record moments of importance with complete clarity so that, during the rough days, a word or smell or sound will take you back to the perfect moments and give you the energy and will to keep going. In that moment I could smell the heat of an Italian morning, the scent of the cotton sheets and the spicy, intoxicating, unmistakable essence of the man in my arms. His skin was hot against mine, his breath sweet and warm as he kissed me and tears of happiness slipped slowly down my face.

CHAPTER FORTY-EIGHT

B reakfast was the usual mix of chaos and laughter. Everyone seemed to be in good spirits with Dylan and Seth trying to out-do each other in the lame jokes department.

"Why did the chicken cross the road?" asked Dylan.

"To get to the other side," Seth answered and rolled his eyes. "Come on, D. That one's so ancient, Sariel probably invented it." Sariel threw a strawberry at my brother who ducked and grinned happily when it hit Isabella who began complaining loudly in Italian.

"Okay," Dylan countered. "Why did the paper aeroplane cross the road?"

Seth frowned. "Um…dunno. Why did the paper aeroplane cross the road?"

Dylan grinned. "It was stapled to the chicken." The courtyard erupted into laughter and Annie beamed happily at Dylan.

Sariel and I had, by unspoken but mutual agreement, dropped each other's hand on the way downstairs and had split up somewhere around the area of the kitchen. I had grabbed several thousand calories worth of bread and then networked my way to sit with Seth, Jude, Annie and Dylan. I'd spoken to Paul on the way by – promising to join the usual suspects for a dip in the cave pool during siesta – 'without the whole making-out stuff' I'd warned him to much eye rolling and good natured ribbing.

Adrian had stopped me to apologise for not making himself known to me before the bonfire meeting. Armaros had apparently told him to keep schtum in case Seth and I learned of his abilities, became mentally unbalanced and tried to do him in (or something similar). I tried very hard to sound sympathetic instead of sarcastic when I told him that a little competition was healthy and I wasn't being at all sarcastic when I told him that his trick with the sword had been incredible. He practically glowed with happiness and shook my hand repeatedly.

"Okay, I've got one," Jude said, talking around a mouthful of banana. "What animal goes 'ooooh'?"

We all looked at one another. Dylan frowned in concentration, making Annie giggle. Out of the corner of my eye I saw Samyaza stop to speak with Sariel.

"A cow with no lips!" Jude said enthusiastically. Annie and Seth roared with laughter. Dylan looked unconvinced. "You can't make the 'mmmmooooo' noise unless you use your lips," Jude explained to him. "See? Mmmmmmmooooooo."

This was the cue for the whole table to break out into 'mmmmooooo' noises, with Dylan trying to look at his own lips as he made the noise. I might have joined in but Sariel and Samyaza were heading in my direction with identical serious expressions on their faces. Damn. What was this about? Naturally the first thing that came into my head was that Sam had found out about....last night… and Sariel and I were now in big trouble.

"Emily," Sariel began, shifting from foot to foot. I hastily stood up beside him and glared at Samyaza.

"It's perfectly natural, y'know," I hissed at him. "I mean, you lot have all done it and nobody's mad at you." Sam blinked at me. His mouth opened and closed like a fish for a few seconds.

"Er…Sam and the others were wondering if you would mind answering a few questions about y'know, your life and where you see things going from here, why you think you might have been chosen and your beliefs. And stuff." Sariel looked at my blank expression. "Y'know…before the others make their decision?"

The penny dropped with a thud. "Oh!" I grinned at them both. "Yeah, yeah. Sure. No problem. I thought that you were…" I giggled at Sam's confused expression and then cleared my throat and pulled myself together. "Right, yes. Um, when would suit?"

Sam was looking at me with concern. "Well, we don't want to get in the way of the usual routine. We were thinking that perhaps after lessons and training today? Before dinner?"

I nodded. "Yes. Fab, that would be great. Lovely. Look forward to it."

With a nod to Sariel, Sam wandered off again, glancing back at me every few seconds. When he was finally through the kitchen door I moaned and dropped my head onto my chest. "I'm an idiot."

Sariel was chuckling. "That was priceless. You're a comic genius."

I punched him half-heartedly on the arm, trying hard not to smile. It was kind of funny. Sariel faked a 'death-by-arm-punching' and then ambled off. I watched him go, finally understanding the expression about hating to see someone go but loving to watch them leave. Jeans just had to have been designed with Fallen Angels in mind; I mean the way they hugged his...

"Huh, hmmmm," Annie broke into my musings and I jumped. "A-ha!" she exclaimed, pointing at me.

"80's pop group. Cute lead singer." I quipped. Annie's eyes narrowed. "Sorry, thought we were still on the whole joke thing. Y'know 'mmmmmoooo' and all that." She frowned. "So, er, I have another one; why did the echo get detention?" Annie tapped her chin with her finger and studied me hard. The others were watching our little exchange. "No ideas? None? Okay...the echo got detention for answering back. Geddit? Tee hee. Ha ha."

Annie's eyes widened and she stood up suddenly, almost knocking Dylan's coffee off the table. "Carson. Garden. Now."

She marched off and Dylan turned his wide brown eyes to me. "I didn't think it was that bad. I mean, kind of juvenile but..."

"Juvenile?!" gasped Seth. "After the whole chicken crossing the road thing and her moo-ing all over the show,"

Jude poked him on the arm. "My joke was funny," she complained.

"Er, yeah, funny. Um..." I left Seth to talk his way out of that one and followed Annie after draining the rest of Dylan's coffee while he was building an argument about his comedic timing.

She waited in the garden just beyond the courtyard and her face was thunderous as I walked slowly over to stand beside her. "Hi," I said. "Another nice day then." Annie scowled and folded her arms. I sighed. "Ok, ok. What have I done now?"

I braced myself for a lecture on...I dunno; older men, safe sex, global warming, the use of apostrophes. Something. So when she threw her arms around my neck and began to giggle I immediately wondered if olive trees give off a kind of weird semi-narcotic. Anyway, I preferred the hug to a lecture so I squeezed her back happily. She pulled away and grinned at me. "You're glowing," she said with a breezy smile.

"I am?"

"Yep. Practically neon." She pulled me across the garden to a shady spot and sat down, patting the ground beside her. "So?"

I laughed. "So..."

"Yes, so...y'know, as in so did you and Sariel..."

"Yep."

Annie laughed and clapped her hands. "I knew it! The way he looked at you when you were walking across the courtyard this morning, the way you practically glided over the floor."

"I did not glide." I scoffed. "He was looking at me?"

"Did too. And yeah, he looked all right. It was so romantic." She sighed theatrically. "So, I take it this means you're a couple?" Well, that stopped me in my tracks. Were we? "You know, like boyfriend and girlfriend?" She dropped her head to one side and stared at me quizzically. "Is this a difficult question or something?" Her face fell. "Oh. My. God. Was it a one night stand? Please tell me it wasn't 'cause I have to tell you that you two are so cute together and he's so gorgeous and..."

"It's not that, and don't let Dylan hear you call Sariel gorgeous. He'll get all depressed and needy. It's just that...well...he's this totally hot but mega-ancient ...being. And I'm a seventeen year old nerd with Demon problems and combination skin. Doesn't really sound like a happily ever after scenario, does it?"

Annie scowled. "You're being so negative. He likes you, you like him. Yes?" I nodded. "So what's the problem?"

I sighed. "Too many variables?"

Annie shook her head and hooked an arm through mine. "Not everything can be solved by maths, Emily."

"Really? I'm joking, I know, I wasn't being...well, I just don't know where it goes from here." I sighed and started pulling grass out of the ground beneath us. "He told me he loves me." I said in a tiny voice.

Annie swung to look at me. "And when were you going to share that little nugget of information?" She didn't wait for an answer, just hugged me again. "Well, there's your answer. He loves you so the variables don't matter. Just be happy."

I smiled at her. "I am."

Isabella called us from the kitchen – Marvin had arrived so it was almost time for lessons to begin. Annie and I scrambled to our feet and dusted ourselves off. We began chatting about the day ahead – would the Angels join us for lessons? Or maybe for training? I hoped so; just the thought of Sariel being there gave my tummy a warm feeling. We were both looking forward to the swim at siesta and I was wondering whether to wear my usual swim suit or take Annie up on her offer of a bikini when she said, "So, how does the fact that you and Sariel have slept together affect Asmodeus's dastardly plans for your eighteenth?"

I stopped walking. Oh, crap.

CHAPTER FORTY-NINE

Marvin was in fine form and wearing the most incredibly garish pair of shorts yet – neon pink, orange and green mixed into a kind of psychedelic tornado of a pattern that made my head spin every time I looked up at him. He had decided to team these monstrous creations with a crisp white cotton shirt and, if my eyes weren't deceiving me, he had also decided to bead part of his beard. Bizarre.

Our lessons ranged from Physics to Business Studies by way of English, Religious Education and Politics. Marvin encouraged discussion and debate, believing that such an atmosphere opened the mind and exercised the old grey matter much more effectively than simply reading a textbook. There were benefits, although the conversations could sometimes become quite heated – Dylan was a firm believer that time travel would someday be possible due to the laws of quantum physics. Adrian, however, thought that this was a load of old bunkum (well, he used a French expression but I'm pretty sure it meant the same thing) and accused Dylan of being so wrapped up by his Star Wars obsession that he was ignoring reality. Annie had to intervene before Adrian said something that would really fire Dylan up – like Obi Wan Kenobi was a secret storm trooper or something – and thankfully Marvin decided that the time was right to move on to Business Studies.

And so the morning flew by and it was lunch time again. Sariel greeted me with a warm grin as I sat down opposite him at the kitchen table. For a change the place was fairly quiet.

"So where is everyone?" asked Dylan, accepting a large plate of orecchiette.

"They are in debate," Isabella told us, filling glasses with apple juice and offering some calzone to Sariel who declined.

"In debate?" Annie speared some pasta.

"Yeah, y'know about whether Adrian or Emily's the golden child," Seth said with a chuckle. "And then Eddie Murphy will have to rescue them from Asmodeus or something."

"You have a serious movie problem," Jude told him, but her

expression was affectionate.

Adrian was frowning and chewing on his lower lip. "So when will zey decide?" he asked softly. Lisa clucked like a mother hen, slung an arm around his shoulder and whispered something to him in their native tongue.

"They will vote on it tonight when we gather together again," Sariel told him gently. "Are you worried?"

"Oui," Adrian told him sadly. "Eet is a very serious zing for me. Zis was to restore my family's honour, you know?" Sariel nodded. "I do not zink we will ave another chance."

Paul dropped into a seat, wiping a dusty arm across his forehead. Isabella frowned at him but he flashed her a grin and showed clean palms so she set a plate down in front of him too.

"How many of your family have been trialed?" Jude asked.

Adrian sighed. "My fazzer say I am the fours." He looked up the table towards where I was sitting. "Ow could God choose the child of a Demon and not choose the descendent of Joan?" He asked. I turned to snap at him but stopped myself. I could tell by his face that he wasn't being nasty or judgmental. He was just asking the question.

I shook my head. "I don't know that He did, Adrian. Maybe neither of us is what the Angels are looking for." From the corner of my eye I saw Sariel frown. "Or maybe we both are and there are others like us. Maybe we're supposed to work together."

Heads nodded around the table.

"So what are you 'golden child' types supposed to do?" asked Dylan, getting to the crux of the problem as always.

"I don't know," I told him honestly. "Hopefully these guys can tell us. I'm going to get my mum first anyway."

"Will zey let you?" Lisa asked, she sounded amazed.

"Why wouldn't they?"

She shrugged. "Well, if you are zis special portent, won't they want to make sure nozzing appens to you? Would zey let you run off and fight Demons when you are the thing that could send zem back to paradise?"

I looked over at Sariel, he was listening closely to the debate.

"Would they?" I asked.

Sariel made a face. "I don't know. This is the first time in our existence that someone has been found who can..." he looked around the table, "...communicate directly with us. I mean, communicate as we do. That's huge. It was always expected that it would be, um, someone ..."

"Religious." I finished for him. He nodded and smiled.

"It was expected that they would know some of this already, perhaps be privy to additional information."

"So really Adrian and you are both a bit of a letdown since neither of you know the next steps." Paul said glumly.

No-one had any more to say about that and thankfully Annie started talking about our swimming date. I motioned to Sariel that I wanted to talk to him and carried my plate and glass to the sink where Isabella took them from me with a happy smile. We wandered out into the courtyard and then out the back gate, following almost exactly the path Isabella had led Seth and me the night before.

We were just through the first set of Olive trees when Sariel grabbed my arm and swung me to face him, planting a kiss on my stunned mouth.

"I missed you, m'amata," he whispered.

I grinned, "It's only been a few hours." I wrapped an arm around him happily though and we walked for a few minutes, simply content to be together. The sun beat down and the olive trees shivered in a light breeze. Sariel steered me to the right and into a wide gap which, he explained, was a fire break. In the event that some of the trees caught fire the break was intended to stop it spreading into the whole crop and would also ensure that firefighting equipment could be moved quickly to an affected area.

From our vantage point, the processing plant and workers apartments were visible with little ant-sized people moving here and there. A truck pulled into the compound and Sariel's eyebrows rose. He checked his watch.

"Something wrong?" I asked.

He shook his head. "Probably not. It's just unusual for a delivery to come at this time. It doesn't matter. So, what did you want to talk about?"

I sighed. "It seems a bit daft now."

Sariel rolled his eyes. "You do not do 'daft', Emily. What is it?"

"Well, I was just wondering. Now that I'm not...um. I mean now that I'm a woman..." I paused and then gave him a playful punch on the arm. His face had creased into a smug grin. "Hey, behave. This is serious."

Sariel pulled me into a hug again. "I'm sorry, I'm sorry. I couldn't help it. You just sounded so young for a moment."

"Yeah, well, I'm not. I'm almost eighteen, almost an adult."

He sighed. "Let's not have this conversation again. I am perfectly aware that you are not a child, Emily. Remember?" He grinned and I felt my face flush. "Awww, you look so cute when you blush." I punched him again and he nimbly leapt away before jumping back and pinning my arms to my sides. "Ouch, those punches are getting pretty powerful. You've been practicing." I nodded, wriggling to try and free myself and show him exactly how powerful my punches could be. "Calm down little wild cat." I struggled harder. "You want to beat me up now?" I glared at him. "Maybe I'll give you the chance at training."

I quit my ineffectual wriggling and blinked at him. "That sounds like a challenge."

Sariel's head fell back and he roared with laughter. "If you could see the way your eyes are dancing," he said, releasing me. "Am I in trouble later?"

I giggled. "Big, huge, major trouble."

Sariel checked his watch again. "Time we got back I think. Lunch is over. You have some cave exploration and I have to go to work for a few hours. I'll see you later? At training?"

I nodded and opened my mouth to ask something, or maybe say something but several kisses later all rational thought had left my brain and all I could think about was the next time I'd be able to get him alone.

CHAPTER FIFTY

Splashing around in an underground lagoon is possibly the most perfect way to spend an afternoon siesta. Especially when you're surrounded by your friends and keep winning water fights. Ok, so it was a bit childish to be swimming around underwater and pulling people under but it was fun! Besides, Antonio and two of the other younger children had come along too so we were doing it for them. Honestly!

Paul and I ended up sitting together for a while on the rocks at the side of the water to catch our breath. Seth was constantly being chased by the young ones but was adept at evading them. Dylan wasn't so lucky and ended up under the water more than anyone else, getting pulled up and then cuddled by Annie each time probably made up for it though.

"So," Paul began after a few minutes of watching the others. "You and Sariel, then? Want to share?"

I sighed. "It's complicated."

He made a face. "It always is, principessa. Try me. I promise I'm not as dumb as I look."

"Well, he's an Angel. I'm a half-Demon. He's ancient and gorgeous. I'm a nerdy schoolgirl. Are you seeing a trend here?"

Paul grinned and his fangs flashed. "You're missing the flip side of your argument?"

"I am? Enlighten me, oh great one." I leaned back and tried very hard to keep my expression from being too unimpressed.

Paul sighed. "He's a 'fallen' Angel and you may be a half-Demon but from what I hear, you've been blessed by a gift that can only be given by an Archangel. Right?" I nodded. "Surely the Archangel blessing cancels a bit of the half Demon thing out? And yeah, ok, Sariel's been around a while but he's spent most of his existence either being tortured by Demons or serving them, right?"

"Where is this going 'cause there's no real…"

Paul held up a hand. "My point is that he hasn't exactly been much of a playboy. Yes?" I nodded grudgingly. I'd never thought about that. "And, in case it's not entirely obvious, he may be ancient but he only looks about 20, 22 at the most."

I raised an eyebrow. "These are all good points, Paul. But I'm waiting for the sucker punch. You know, the bit where you start talking me out of the relationship?"

Paul laughed. "Oh, I thought about it, principessa. I most certainly did. But in the end, I know that what I want from a girl is no long term thing. I'm a love 'em and leave 'em kind of guy. You are not a one night stand kind of girl. Believe me; I can spot them at fifty paces."

"Wow," I said, shaking my head with exaggerated wonder, "You really are full of yourself, aren't you?"

He made a face. "I know my prey, principessa. That's no bad thing. And I also know what and who I am. How many guys can admit that to themselves, never mind other people?"

He had a point but I was about to put forward a decent counter-argument when Antonio swam over and begged us to come back to the game – Dylan was tiring, apparently, and they needed new victims. Before long the three children were pleading with us, their voices filling the cavern with echoes. Paul slipped off the rock and back into the water. "You know that if you ever tire of your Angel that I would be willing to step in and show you a good time, right?"

I laughed. "Keep swimming fang boy."

CHAPTER FIFTY-ONE

In front of a phalanx of watching (and no doubt judging) Angels, our trainers worked us hard. Several Angels had chosen to work out with us – Danel, Samyaza, Uriel, Sariel and three others. We were in the garden to the side of the Casa and in the shade of a number of tall, leafy trees but sweat was still pouring down my back within half an hour. And that was just the warm-up.

We worked on hand-to-hand combat, employing moves from all kinds of disciplines – Bruno was especially fond of martial arts techniques whereas Don just seemed to be a fan of some kind of hellish pit fighting. We punched and kicked and blocked and bruised each other for almost an hour and then Don called a break. I limped to the wall of the house and slid down it, certain that I was leaving a smear of seat wherever I went. Seth had flopped where he stood, lying prone on the grass and breathing heavily. Jude pulled him to his feet grinning cheerfully. If I'd been able to muster the energy I might've wiped the smile off her face with my fist but it seemed like a lot of effort just then.

Sariel brought me a bottle of chilled water. He was sweating too but still looked like he could've wiped the floor with Bruno and Don together and still had time to invent a new energy source for the planet. He sat down beside me, resting his arms on his knees and we sat quietly for a few moments as feeling began to slowly return to my leg muscles.

"Here we go," Sariel whispered under his breath, rising to his feet. Huh? I looked past him and sighed.

Armaros was leading a small group of maybe four others in our direction with a look of smug anticipation on his face. Outwardly Sariel and I looked calm and composed but inside I was shaking. If Armaros looked smug then he was bringing trouble to us. Sariel was gripping his bottle of water a little too tightly but he smiled at our visitors. "Not taking part in the training?" He enquired.

Armaros pursed his lips. "Some of us are taking the whole decision making process seriously, brother." He said, earning nods from his homies. They all had identical 'busy-doing-serious-stuff' expressions which made the whole situation suddenly seem a lot less scary.

Sariel waved a hand towards the ground. "Shall we sit?"

Once everyone was comfortable Armaros turned to me and smiled. I intended to smile back, really I did, but instead I felt an eyebrow rise in amusement. Armaros' smile turned to a sneer.

"So, Emily. We were wondering if we could ask a few questions?"

"Samyaza has already asked for time to question Emily later," Sariel told him pleasantly. I could hear the underlying edge to his voice and several of the others glanced sharply at him.

"We are aware of Samyaza's plan," one of them said in a haughty baritone, "However, it is unlikely that there will be time for all of us to ask all of our questions to both the…participants. Therefore we decided to approach with some fundamental queries."

I peered around our little group to where Adrian was lying on the grass, beside a rather pale looking Dean, chatting to Paul and Seth. "Should I ask Adrian to join us?" I asked.

The homies turned to look at Armaros for guidance in a move that was so Stepford-wifey that I almost choked. "That won't be necessary, thank you," Armaros said smoothly. "We will talk to Adrian separately." More nods around the circle. "Now to our questions? We were wondering how you think it possible that you, a non-believer, could possibly be chosen to lead the Fallen home above a young man whose family have been involved with the church for centuries and who are deeply religious and pious people?" He sat back on his heels like a viper who believes he has just delivered a killing strike.

So that was how it was going to be. Beside me Sariel leaned forward. I laid a gentling hand on his shoulder and smiled at the expectant faces in front of me. "Before I answer, gentlemen, perhaps we could be properly introduced?"

Armaros snorted. "You really do have an obsession with knowing names, don't you?" He laughed loudly, turning heads around the garden.

I laughed too. "Absolutely," I told him. "I like to know the names of anyone accusing me of not being good enough for God's work when I seem to remember hearing a story in school that said God went out of his way to look for non-believers. I think the comparison made was lost sheep being returned to the fold. Would that be correct?" I addressed my question to the youngest looking of Armaros' hangers-on who nodded unhappily. I held out a hand to him. "I'm Emily, pleased to meet you."

"Er, Rameel. So you believe that God has chosen you himself?"

I frowned. "You think Archangels act without God knowing about it?"

Rameel made a face. "Some believe that the Fallen committed 'unforgivable sin' and will never receive salvation from God. Others believe that Michael holds our fate – a mission given to him by God who couldn't be seen to return us to Heaven himself."

"Who thinks that you committed 'unforgivable sin' and why?" I asked, interested in spite of the fact that I couldn't quite believe I was having this conversation.

Rameel gestured around. "Some of us believe it. And some of the others who...we couldn't save." He glanced briefly at Sariel. "As to why some believe it? Well, Angels already know the secrets of heaven. We have stood in the presence of God. For us to know all these things and still to commit sin is...unforgivable."

I thought about that. "God the Father," I murmured.

""What?" asked one of the others. "Um, Asael, by the way. What do you mean 'God the Father'?"

I grinned. "I was thinking about how that phrase suddenly made more sense to me. You are His children and you acted exactly like children."

"In what way?" Sariel was leaning forward now, his eyes were wide but his face was unreadable. I reached automatically for our link to see what he was feeling and felt it blocked a hundred different ways. I scowled. Obviously they were suspicious that Sariel was helping me. Didn't they think that I was capable of working things out on my own?

I shook it off and came back to the discussion. "Parents tell their children what's right and wrong. All the time. We know from a young age that stealing is wrong, that staying out beyond curfew is wrong, that treating your brother with respect is good, whether he annoys you or not, that smoking, drinking, flirting with boys… whatever…are wrong. And what do children do? They try most of them anyway. It's part of growing up. Right? You push boundaries. Some kids do it more than others. Most of 'em get caught. And then what happens?" I looked around.

"They get punished," Sariel said softly, a note of amusement in his voice.

"Exactly." I said happily, fully into my theory now. "The parent has to dole out a punishment to show the child that what they did was wrong. It's common sense. You get punished for something and you're less likely to do it again. But the parent is doing it for the good of the child. And it doesn't mean that they aren't still loved and cherished." I sighed. "Of course spending an eternity in hell for showing people how to build pyramids is way more harsh than being sent to your room for chugging milk from the bottle."

"We are Fallen because of lust," said Rameel, his face flushing.

I shook my head. "No, sorry, I don't believe that. God was a smart dude. He wouldn't have given you all the working bits if he hadn't intended you to use them. The secrets of Heaven thing though? Yeah, I would imagine he'd be pretty pissed at that."

Armaros flinched. "I don't think profanity is required." He growled.

I nodded. "I apologise, I didn't mean to offend you."

"And so back to the original question perhaps?" Armaros said, glaring at Rameel.

"Yeah, sorry. Went off on a tangent there," I scratched my head.

"She does that a lot," Annie said. I looked up in surprise and gulped. We had attracted a crowd. They had gathered around in a loose semi-circle and all were listening intently. Don was standing just to my left, his arms folded across his broad chest and his face taut – a nerve jumped in his jaw. I looked back at Annie who glanced at Don, caught my eye and grinned.

"So, the original question was…" Armaros began.

I nodded. "Yeah, yeah, I remember," I told him. Ok, so it was rude of me but he was seriously spoiling what had actually been a good day. "Adrian and I were actually talking about this earlier."

"You were?" Armaros looked disgusted, he looked angrily at Adrian who was sitting on the grass just behind Lisa.

Adrian flinched a little but nodded. "Oui, er, yes, we spoke of it. I was…confused. And concerned for the reputation of my family."

"You thought you had failed?" Asked someone.

Adrian sighed. "I am uncertain." He admitted, not looking at Armaros whose face had turned several shades of unhappy.

"Yeah, so anyhoo. We talked about it and, well, to be honest, I don't know what the dude upstairs would or wouldn't do. I guess I'm not that well acquainted with him. I mean, we did religion at school so I know the parables, miracles and all that jazz but I don't think I'm qualified to second-guess Him." There were nods and thoughtful expressions all round.

"Tell them what you thought," Adrian spoke up. He nodded encouragingly.

I sighed. "Well, I was just wondering if maybe we're supposed to, y'know, work together. Like Heaven's version of the A-Team." I grinned.

Dylan put up a hand and everyone turned to look at him. Jude giggled. "It's not school cutie," she told him.

Dylan blushed to the very tips of his ears, "Er, yeah, sorry," he dropped his hand again and cleared his throat, "I just wanted to ask a question."

"Shoot," I told him.

"Er, well, I wanted to ask the …Angels," he said.

Armaros puffed up with self-importance. "We will hear your question, young man," he said in an equally pompous tone.

"Uh-huh. Yeah, ok. So I was just wondering why you guys are the ones making the decision on who is the…what is it? Portent? Chosen one? …anyway, I mean none of you really know what this chosen portent thingy is supposed to do when it gets here so how can you judge who it is?" There was silence. Dylan looked around at the stunned expressions on the Angels' faces. He rocked back on his heels. "Um, yeah. So that's what I was wondering."

Armaros's face was now almost purple. If he hadn't been an immortal Angel, I'd have been seriously concerned that we were about to have a heart attack victim on our hands. He stood up and pointed a finger at Dylan. "How dare you! You sit here in the presence of Angels. And you ask if we are qualified to judge a messenger from God?" Spittle flew from his mouth and his lips compressed into a thin line of contempt. "We are His children. We have lived for longer than your pathetic race have existed, we have lived among you, suffered at your hands, been tormented by the evil that you visit on one another, watched you welcome Demons into your souls as you destroy the planet that He gave to you and we have waited through the endless years for our salvation to be sent to us. No, we don't know what form that salvation will take and no, we don't know what we will eventually have to do to regain His favour but do you know what we have that you and this Jezebel can never have?"

I blinked at Armaros. Did he just call me a Jezebel?

Armaros was still on a roll. "We have faith, faith that our Heavenly Father will show us His messenger when the time has come. Faith that He will guide us to make the right choice. And Faith that His messenger will lead us home." Armaros took a shaky breath and sat down. Several of his little group clapped him on the back and whispered to him.

Dylan let out a long breath. "Oooookay. Um, thanks." He said quietly.

I stood up, brushing grass off my shorts, and turned to Don. "Can we spar now? I'd like to hit something."

Don grinned and began organizing everyone into pairs. Armaros caught my arm as I walked past. "I wasn't finished," he growled.

I shook off his hand. "I have a question of my own, Armaros." I tried to keep the anger out of my voice but failed miserably. "When you were watching the human race committing all these atrocities that you mentioned; while the Demons were getting stronger and dragging your brothers and sisters away; while they were ripping off their wings and torturing them until they couldn't take it anymore; while the earth was getting destroyed; Where exactly were you and what were you doing to stop it? Maybe that's why you've been here so long, because God is waiting for you to get off your ass and help his human creations instead of looking out for numero uno."

I walked away, leaving Armaros seething behind me and his groupies falling over themselves to calm him down. Samyaza was standing at the edge of the garden. He looked over at me thoughtfully as I walked past to join Sariel.

Sariel was grinning. "What?" I asked, irritated. "I made a good point."

He nodded. "I never said you didn't, m'amata."

"So why have you got that smirk on your face?" I finished pulling on the mitts that Don insisted we spar in and began limbering up. "I am pitying whoever has to fight you this afternoon," he told me, moving quickly out of reach.

CHAPTER FIFTY-TWO

In the end I didn't spar with many people – maybe because I pulverized the few that Don paired me with. I cut Seth down within three minutes, scoring my three points with a flurry of body punches, a knee to the groin and finally a low sweep that took his legs from under him and left him gasping on his back. Lisa was next. She was a girly fighter – all delicate little dancing moves and soft punches. I earned my three points by simply keeping her off balance and feigning punches towards her face, landing gentler hits to her stomach and kidneys while she had her hands up protecting her supermodel looks.

Adrian was a tough fighter – we'd sparred before a few times and I enjoyed the challenge of figuring out his moves. He danced in and out of my reach, staying just far enough away to make me work for each shot, hoping to tire me. And, after seeing the mess I'd made of Seth, he stayed well away from my knees and legs, grinning as he nimbly avoided a sweep. In the end I beat him by using his moves against him – I copied him until he began to tire and then moved inside his reach to make each point before backing away again.

Don made me sit out and rehydrate while he set Seth on Dylan – it didn't last long, Seth landed a good shot to Dylan's shoulder which numbed his right arm and a shot to his stomach which doubled him over. As Seth moved forward to claim his third point, Dylan ran off screaming and leaving everyone else in fits of laughter. Lisa and Annie sparred and almost made me sick with laughter – both of them were just too girly, asking each other if they were ok after each shot and twirling like ballerinas before getting tangled up in each other's legs. Don named that one a draw.

Jude took turns with Seth and Adrian, scoring points simply by being the more aggressive. She may have been fierce but she wasn't a clever fighter – Adrian managed to score two points while Seth managed one, although he was probably going easy on her.

Bruno paired up some of the Angels – both he and Don had

to work together to keep track of the scoring 'cause Angels fight fast and furious. It's weird. I mean, hearing that the guys around you are warriors is one thing but actually seeing them in action is a whole other ball game. Uriel took on Danel and then Samyaza; leaving them both eating dirt within seconds. She looked like a scary Amazonian warrior with her dark hair whipping around her head in a plait as her long legs and swift fists dealt solid blows.

Helping Danel up she laughed at his face. "What's the matter, brother, did you forget that I always beat you?"

Danel grinned and shook his head. "No, sister. I am just always surprised at how fast you do it." She laughed again and hugged him.

To my surprise Armaros' buddies Rameel and Asael stepped up to have a go too, with some of the others shouting encouragement. Rameel was the smaller of the two but faster with his fists whilst Asael favoured a kind of block and thrust style of fighting – like Adrian he was content for his opponent to tire themselves out. It was a close match with Asael finally coming out the victor with a score of 3-2.

Bruno glanced around. "Any other challengers?" He asked.

Armaros stepped forward, shrugging off his jacket. "I challenge Sariel," he said loudly. Bruno frowned and glanced towards Sariel who gave a slight nod. I swallowed but said nothing. This was a challenge that Sariel had to answer – even I could see that. With a grin in my direction, he stepped forward and walked to the centre of the garden, stopping opposite Armaros.

Bruno stood between them, "No weapons," he said, looking from one to the other and then raising his arm high above his head. Sariel and Armaros nodded and Sariel rolled his shoulders, letting his arms drop to their sides. Someone sat down beside me, someone-else moved up on the other side, a hand slipped onto my shoulder. I kept my attention on the fight.

"This will be a good lesson," Uriel whispered into my ear.

I was about to ask what she meant when Bruno stepped back and dropped his arm. The match had officially started. Armaros circled slowly to the left, licking his lips and flexing his fingers.

225

Sariel stood like a statue, waiting for the first move. When it came a collective gasp echoed around the garden. Armaros had moved with the speed of a striking cobra, his fists were a blur as he lunged forward. Just as quickly, he stepped back again and went back to circling. Bruno glanced to Don, they conferred quietly for a few seconds and then Bruno made a downward slash with his right hand, "No points. All blocked."

There were muted cheers and a few boos around us. Uriel laughed softly. "Sariel could do this all day. Armaros is too keen. He doesn't wait for the right moment, he strikes too hard and too fast. Sariel will wait and stay calm. This is how it is to fight Demons. They are clever but they are also impatient to cause pain and see blood spilled. Like I said, this is a good lesson." I glanced at her then, feeling as though something had just fallen into place, something I wasn't even aware of needing to know. I felt around the edges of that idea and came away empty handed. I frowned, knowing that the feeling would stay with me until I figured it out – like a tough maths problem. One question did come to mind though.

"Will we fight Demons?" I asked her, turning my head back towards where Armaros was gearing up to attack again - it was obvious from the way his feet moved a little faster, his fists came away from covering his face and he held his breath just before he launched himself across the ground. The man had more tells than a bad poker player. Sariel side-stepped at the last moment, sending a fist into Armaros' side as he flew past and went sprawling on the grass.

Beside me Uriel laughed aloud. "That was brilliant!" she yelled punching the air. Armaros scowled at her as he dusted himself off and went back to his place. Uriel moved closer to me. "If we do then we will fight together," she whispered before raising her voice to make a loud cat-call as Sariel slipped off his shirt. I knew that I should be asking something else but whatever it was got lost in the moment as I got distracted first by Sariel's tattoos and then all his exposed skin. I was still admiring the little hollows where his shoulders met his neck when he moved on Armaros. His shoulder muscles rippled as he slipped low inside Armaros' defenses and his fist connected with Armaros' thigh. Sariel was back to his starting position before Armaros dropped to the floor – dead legged as Don called it. It didn't score a point but it meant that Armaros would be hobbling for a few minutes. We all clapped, earning another scowl from Armaros which made my smile widen in response.

Bruno called order and the match went on – Armaros moved in ever-decreasing circles, attacking with frenzied annoyance. Sariel blocked everything, slipping out of his reach time after time, dipping and ducking faster than Armaros could reach him. He made no further attacking moves.

"What's he waiting for?" I whispered to Uriel.

"Armaros wants to defeat Sariel very badly," She answered.

"You think?!" I snorted.

"Sariel has nothing to prove. Like I said, he could keep this up till a fortnight next Tuesday if he wanted."

Isabella appeared at the edge of the garden. She looked elegant and beautiful in a mid-length camel skirt and deep green wrap-over top. Her eyes passed over the garden and she smiled happily. "Dinner will be ready in half an hour. Finish up please, Sariel," she shouted.

"Ah," said Uriel. "Now we will have some fun."

Sariel smiled at Isabella and then turned his attention back to Armaros. "Let's not keep the lady waiting, brother," he said. "I don't know about you but I'd like a shower before dinner."

He moved before my eyes had even registered the fact. There was the dull smack of skin on skin and then he was back again and Armaros was blinking stupidly, one side of his face red from the power of Sariel's fist.

"Point!" called Don.

"Confirmed," said Bruno with a grin. "To centre gentlemen," He raised his hand again, stepped back and dropped it.

Armaros blurred into action; his leg spun in a roundhouse aimed at Sariel's head but Sariel was no longer in front of Armaros. He struck from behind, a simple but powerful blow to Armaros' left kidney. Armaros crumpled to his knees, grimacing.

"Point!" yelled Bruno happily.

"Confirmed," Don said. They high-fived each other as Sariel helped Armaros to his feet.

"Good match, brother," he told him.

Armaros managed a grin. "The war's not over. Brother" He limped off in the direction of the house and Sariel came to where Uriel, Seth, Jude and I were waiting. The others began to drift away, chatting noisily among themselves.

Sariel pulled his shirt back on and grinned at me. "So? Still think you could beat me?" he asked.

I shrugged nonchalantly. "If I really wanted to. Would be a shame to mess up those pretty tattoos though."

Sariel laughed. "I see. So you'd be concerned for the wellbeing of my ink?"

"Absolutely." I folded my arms and grinned at him. "I could still beat you, though."

Sariel laughed and swung me into his arms. "Oh, really? And how would you do that m'amata?"

"Obviously I'd have to find a way to distract you," I said softly, looking up into his twinkling eyes.

He sucked in a breath. "I seem to remember that you have remarkable powers of distraction," he told me and I felt a shiver run though me, remembering the kiss on the train and at the door of my room…and this morning. He kissed me soundly on the lips as I melted against him, enjoying the heat of his body and the taste of him.

Someone coughed loudly and we pulled apart to find Seth and Jude staring at us with wide eyes. Uriel was smiling happily.

"Er…will we get ready for dinner?" Seth stammered.

Sariel rubbed a hand through his hair. "Yeah, I definitely need a shower." He looked at me, opened his mouth to say something and then obviously thought better of it. He let go of me and nodded to Seth. "Yeah, so I'll go and get a shower then. Later?"

Seth nodded a little distractedly. "Yeah, later."

"I'll go too," said Uriel glancing at Seth and giving me a

supportive grin.

"Great," I said. "Thanks." I called after her. She waved back at me and I turned my head back to Seth.

"Well, want to explain now or later?" He asked.

"Are you insane?" Jude asked him. "She has to explain now. Give her any more time and she could, like, make up some story or something."

"A story?" Seth looked incredulous. "How can there be any other explanation then the fact that they're…a couple now."

I nodded and began to walk off. "Er, where are you going?" Seth asked.

"You're way too smart for me, Seth. You figured it all out already. See you at dinner." I walked on into the house, leaving Seth complaining loudly behind me. Well, that wasn't so difficult.

CHAPTER FIFTY-THREE

I was walking across the hall towards the stairs when a little whirlwind almost knocked me down. Antonio was so excited that he was practically vibrating as he and I disentangled ourselves and I caught my breath while he danced from foot to foot.

"Whoa, there, Tony. Slow down. Is Sir Alex at the front door or something?"

Antonio giggled. "Sir Alex is too busy to come here to Casa Cielo, Emily. This is molto meglio. You have un pacchetto postale." He bounced up and down again a few times.

"A what?"

Antonio rolled his eyes and then thrust a small brown package into my hands. "See? This came today. Are you going to open it?" He grinned and nudged me enthusiastically. "Is it un dono? Did one of your friends in England send it to you? Is it an engagement ring from the Padrone?"

"Er..." Did everyone know about Sariel and me now? I squeezed the little packet and felt four hard edges. So, no engagement ring then. I willed Antonio to calm down a little bit so I could think. "This is for me?" I turned the package over in my hands carefully. There was no return address and no post mark, just my name written in black marker. "But no-one knows I'm here..."

"Che succede?" Isabella stepped out of the doorway to the kitchen. She looked from me to Antonio and then to the parcel in my hands. She frowned and her eyes caught mine. "Are you sending some post?" She asked me, her face frowning with concern. "It might be a little...unwise...to let people know where you are."

I shook my head. "No, this came for me. Antonio brought it."

We both turned to look at Antonio whose happy bouncing had stopped. He looked back at us and his face fell. "Sono nei guai?" he asked in a shaky voice.

Isabella smiled and knelt in front of him, putting her hands on his shoulders. "No, no. You are a good boy, Antonio. You are not in trouble. Tell me, who gave this to you?"

Antonio sniffed and looked up at me with sad eyes before

turning back to Isabella. He bit his lip and his brow crinkled as he thought about it. "A tall man with brown eyes. He was a worker I think. His clothes were all dusty."

Isabella nodded and smiled at him. "That's good, Antonio. Have you seen this man before?"

Antonio thought again and finally shook his head. "No, I don't think so. He was un estraneo." He paused. "Was he a bad man?"

Isabella ruffled his hair and pulled him into a hug. "I don't know, Antonio. But you have been a good boy and you are not in trouble, you don't need to worry. Okay?" Antonio nodded shyly. Isabella smiled at him again and then whispered loudly, "Maybe you should have a treat for being such a good boy. You know where the Padrone's cookies are?" Antonio's face lit up like a firework display and he nodded enthusiastically, running off immediately to claim his reward.

Isabella stood up, pulling a phone from the pocket of her skirt. "What do you think?" she asked and I could hear the tension in her voice. She tossed her phone from hand to hand and chewed her lip.

I lifted the package to my ear and gave it a little shake. Isabella squeaked and grabbed my arm, her eyes wide. "What if it...? What if we..? Kaboom!"

I grimaced. Ok, I hadn't really thought about the bomb possibility. I mean, yes, we were hiding from big, bad, grumpy Demons but still, would Asmodeus really send a bomb? I mean, he wanted me to be in one piece when he sold me, right? Unless of course he'd found out about last night already. Was that even possible? The thoughts cannoned around inside my brain for a few seconds and then I reached for my link with Sariel, letting it go almost immediately when another thought came to mind.

"Er, Antonio said a worker delivered this, yes?" Isabella nodded, still watching the package anxiously. I wasn't quite sure how to say what I was thinking without sounding like Queen of the Huge Egos. "Er, is Paul working today?" I asked and felt a blush heat my face from the toes up.

Isabella looked at me for a moment and then understanding

filled her expression. "Ah, you think maybe he is still...having feelings?"

I shrugged. "Well, it makes more sense than Daddy dearest sending a bomb."

Isabella sighed. "Agreed. Although Asmodeus is not the only Demon out there and you know how competitive they are. You are still in danger from the others too, Emily. Never forget that."

I nodded, suitably chastened. "Then we need some more advice." I reached for the link again. *Sariel?*

Just need to find a shirt and I'll be down. You got ready fast!

Well, I haven't made it upstairs yet.

What's happened? Has Armaros been asking more of his questions?

No, no. It's just that...well, I got post.

You got...? I'm on my way.

In the end Uriel, Gadel, Sariel and Don converged on us within seconds of each other. The package got passed around and squished, pulled, shaken and sniffed (that was Don) by everyone before it was handed back to me. The others began debating what to do with it while I stood with it in my hands wondering how many pieces we would be blown into and if Angels could survive getting blasted apart. Isabella gasped and I looked up in surprise. While my brain had been thinking about body parts joining up again, my hands had gone their own way and opened the parcel.

Sariel chuckled. "Well it's not a bomb then," he said.

"What's not a bomb?" Dylan was standing at the bottom of the stairs watching us all with a stunned expression on his face. "There's a bomb?" He ducked down and began crawling on his hands and knees towards the kitchen. We watched him in silence for a few seconds until I shook my head and pulled him up off the floor.

"What are you doing?" I asked.

Dylan sighed and gave me a don't-be-an-idiot look. "I'm going to get Annie and Seth, of course."

"Why? Are they bomb disposal experts now or something?"

"No, don't be ridiculous. But if there's a bomb then we need to decide what to do with it, right? And we always talk about these kinds of things together."

I nodded. He had a point.

"You've been sent bombs before?" Don asked looking at me as though he was only really seeing me for the first time.

"Er, no. It's just like he said - we always talk things though together, y'know." I grinned at Dylan who grinned back happily.

"Yeah, and Annie probably does know how to disarm a...what kind of bomb is it?" He looked at the little packet in my hand.

I shrugged. "No idea. It just feels like...wait a minute!" I shook my head and laughed. "Why are we even having this conversation? It's not a bomb. We were just worried that it was but I opened it and nobody got blown up so it's ok."

Dylan frowned. "You opened it without knowing that it wasn't a bomb?" I nodded, feeling stupid. "So you don't actually know that it's not a bomb? It could be rigged to go off when you remove the...what did you say it was?...from the packet."

I looked down at the parcel, feeling scared all over again. "I don't know what it is. I haven't looked yet. Can they really make bombs that do that?"

Dylan nodded, his face tense and serious. "They can pack explosives into anything, Em. And they can make them go off exactly when they want them to."

Sariel sighed and took the parcel out of my hand. He reached in and pulled out the slim plastic case inside while Dylan dropped to the ground again screaming and putting his hands on top of his head. The kitchen door opened and everyone came spilling out, faces worried and curious.

Annie stopped and studied her boyfriend. "Emily, why is Dylan lying on the floor screaming?" she asked calmly.

"He's worried about the bomb," I told her.

"Wait," Jude spoke up. "There's a bomb?"

"Let's not get into this again," said Uriel shaking her head. "We were concerned that there was a bomb but no-one's been splattered over the walls yet so it seems to be ok." She turned to look at Sariel. "Am I lying?" she asked with a grin.

Sariel had opened the case and was staring at it. He looked up at me and I caught the tension in his eyes at once.

"What?" I asked a little bit desperately. "What is it?"

He reached it out to me. Inside the small case was a regular-looking DVD with 'Watch me' printed on it in black marker. My heart sank into my trainers. This didn't feel right at all. I turned to Isabella. "Got a DVD player?"

CHAPTER FIFTY-FOUR

We gathered in the living room at the front of the house. The air conditioning fan whirred above our heads and Isabella had opened all the windows to combat the heat from so many of us crowded together,

Uriel, Isabella, Seth and I had taken the sofa in front of the mammoth TV with Sariel, Jude, Annie, Dylan, Samyaza, Adrian, Lisa and Dean crushed around and behind us. Don and Bruno joined several of the other guards at the back of the room and the door where Armaros, Gadel, Danel and some of the other familiar faces were pressing in on one another. We were all tense and, even though I felt warm, I could feel the goose bumps on my arms. Part of me was still a little worried in case I played the DVD and it turned out to be some declaration of undying love from Paul. Now how embarrassing would that be?

I was just about to push 'play' when Paul himself elbowed his way through the door. He caught my eye and nodded before going to whisper something to Isabella. She listened to him intently and then patted him on the arm and took her mobile from her pocket, gripping it tightly in her right hand.

Sariel's hand dropped onto my shoulder, making me jump. I giggled. "Oooh, nerves are getting the better of me."

It's okay, Emily. Whatever this is, we can deal with it.

I nodded and pushed 'play'.

For the first few frames the camera danced hap-hazardly down a dark corridor, giving us brief glances of oil paintings on the walls and the odd item of antique furniture. Sariel's hand stiffened on my shoulder as our camera operator opened a set of imposing doors and went inside. There was the echoing sound of a throat being cleared, the camera steadied and focused on a figure sitting calmly behind a large mahogany desk. I had the strongest feeling of déjà-vu. The room and the desk were very familiar. I had almost figured it out when the figure lifted its head and I groaned.

Asmodeus looked into the camera and grinned.

Around me, the room erupted with gasps and exclamations

but I ignored them, concentrating on the man rising from behind the desk and still chewing over why the room was so familiar. It clicked with me as he walked slowly around to stand in front of the desk, folding his arms and glancing around as though giving us time to take in who he was and where he was.

I turned to look at Sariel. *Rick Farlow's study, right?* Sariel nodded grimly. *And the pack?*

Sariel blew out his cheeks and shrugged. *They're Were, Emily. Asmodeus wouldn't have got within 20 miles of them without at least one of them picking up his scent.*

On the screen, Asmodeus had begun to speak. "Hello, Emily. Hope you're having a lovely time in Italy, I'm sure you're making lots of new friends." He chuckled. "Your mother and I are missing you and Seth very much. Oh, wait, you won't have heard – I'm now legally your guardian, your mother and I got married on Tuesday and my lawyer had her sign your care to me." He waggled his finger at the camera. "I have to tell you that I'm a stickler for discipline so your recent behavior has been somewhat of a disappointment."

"Oh, blow it out your ear," I mumbled, earning a giggle from Dylan. Seth and I looked at each other worriedly. Was he lying? Seth's face was very pale, and his hand gripped mine tightly.

"So," Asmodeus continued. "Do you recognise where I am today?" He spread his arms out and swung around a little. "Pretty impressive den for a wolf, isn't it? I have to say, I'm mightily impressed although if I was to criticize anything it would be the style of the rest of the house – it's a bit uninspired." He leaned close to the camera. "Must be the wife's taste." He winked.

"Anyway," he continued. "I thought I'd drop by for a visit, introduce myself face to face. I mean, it's only neighbourly since the cub made a bid, don't you think. Of course that's a little by the by now, isn't it?" He looked deep into the camera, his dark eyes glittering. "We'll get back to that, Emily. Be sure of it." For a moment his gaze burned into mine from the screen and I gulped loudly.

He knows. How could he know already? I couldn't help that my voice had taken on a whiny tone.

It's ok, Sariel's voice was calm and strong inside my head. Our link hummed with warmth and I relaxed a little.

Asmodeus smiled and leaned forward. "I'll be honest, I came to take back the knife. You remember it, don't you?"

"Damn right," I whispered. "Wish I'd kept a hold of it."

Asmodeus sighed theatrically. "Unfortunately there doesn't seem to be anyone home and I've had my people search the house and grounds extensively but the knife seems to have vanished again. I was so hoping that Rick and I could have a little chat, maybe figure out who took the knife to begin with and why." He waggled a finger again. "I think you were on to something that night, Emily – you remember our discussion? When you and Sariel sat down with me for a chat? Someone was stacking things up against me, hoping to take over maybe? I'd certainly like to know who's waiting to stab me in the back this time." He sighed again and stood up, straightening his jacket and running a hand through his hair. He turned away from the camera, heading back to the chair. Was that it? Speech over? I dared to let a little spark of hope flare in my heart. Asmodeus stopped walking and turned back to the camera.

"Goodness me, I almost forgot." He walked back around the table and leaned back against the table again. His face was calm but serious. "Now, Emily, I hear you've been a very naughty girl." I sighed. Here we go. "I can't tell you how devastated your mother and I were to hear that you've been whoring yourself to an older man. And not just any older man, no – one of the Fallen." Asmodeus shook his head and tutted. "You know what this means, of course." I knew that I should be blushing about now, that the eyes of everyone in the room were probably turned to Sariel and me in shock, horror or astonishment; but my attention was riveted on the man in the screen and in the darkening of his features as his anger slowly rose. "You have done me out of a lot of money, Emily. You have embarrassed me in front of my peers and you have called the good name of my House into question. I will not stand for this."

Asmodeus had begun to breathe harder, his eyes widened

and a vein throbbed on the left of his forehead. "I will have entertainment for my friends on the thirtieth of August and if I can't have you then I will have the next best thing." I looked at Seth in horror, wondering how I could protect my brother. Seth's face was a mask of terror, his eyelids blinked very fast. Jude had begun to cry. Sariel leaned forward and squeezed my arm.

We won't let them take him, he told me.

None of us were expecting Asmodeus next words. "I will have my Fallen Angel back."

We all snapped our attention back to the screen. Asmodeus was smiling again; his eyes were full of laughter. "No," my voice cracked on the word and I turned to look wildly at Sariel. His face was unguarded for just a moment and expression was one of shock and fear. He covered it up immediately with the carefully calm mask that I remembered so well from the first few times I'd met him. "No." I said again.

"Here's the deal," Asmodeus was saying. "If Sariel hands himself over then I will allow you, your friends and your mother to live. If he doesn't then I will drag you into the depths of hell – you remember the place, Emily? – and I will introduce you to more pain and torment than any being has ever endured. Make up your minds fast." He leaned back towards the camera and his eyes seemed to seek me out. "Knock, knock, Emily."

"Who's there?" said Dylan. Annie shushed him. "What? This could be like a Demon knock knock joke. I've never heard one." Annie shook her head and her face was sad, she pulled Dylan away, talking to him in a soft, urgent voice.

There was a commotion in the doorway and three men came in. All were dirty from the olive plantation and all were carrying guns. Isabella stood up and ran to them. "What is it?" she asked quickly. They spoke in rapid Italian, gesturing around them and pointing to Sariel and I. Isabella turned an anguished face to us "Sariel, you must get out of here. There are Demons on the grounds."

"What?!" Uriel was on her feet and heading for the door as chaos erupted and people began running. Sariel spoke urgently to Don who nodded and came to stand on my left. Uriel came back into the room. Her eyes found Sariel's and I knew they were communicating silently. I pushed away a momentary flash of irritation as Sariel's head dropped to his chest for just a moment. I realized that I was standing but I didn't remember getting up from the sofa. Everything was happening too fast, I was losing track of what exactly was going on.

Tell me. Sariel looked up at me. He reached out and pulled me into a hug and I wrapped my arms tightly around him, feeling tears coming to my eyes although I wasn't certain why I was crying. *We're going to run again, right?*

He shook his head. *No, no running.*

Then what…? I pulled back to look at him. The mask was still in place – his face was impassive but his eyes were filled with a million emotions. I searched them for some sign that he wasn't thinking what I thought he was thinking. I opened my mind, felt the others rush in too and let them come, shoving them to all the corners and concentrating on our link. It was there but he was trying to block me a little and so I pushed. Hard. There was a moment of resistance and then Sariel's mind was open to me and I staggered under the weight of it all. His concern for his friends, his family; his fear for himself – how long could he stick Asmodeus's torture; plans to rescue my mother; plans to get Seth and I away; hope for the future; fear for the future and behind it all I felt a stronger emotion directed right at me and I recognized it ; Sariel loved me.

I cried then, knowing what he was going to do and why. I heard myself shouting at him but couldn't quite make out the words, knew that my fists were pounding on his chest but he just held me, whispering into my hair and trying to kiss away my tears.

There was a loud explosion in the hallway and we all took cover as screams echoed through the house. Uriel and Danel stood up, coughing in the smoke and dust filled air, as a tall figure entered the room and I gasped as Daeshan smiled at Sariel.

CHAPTER FIFTY-FIVE

Don sat down beside me and handed me a doughnut. I ate without really tasting it – my rumbling stomach said that I was hungry but my ability to enjoy the fuel that I put into my body seemed to have gone. It had taken a lot of other things with it too.

I looked up and down the subway station. There were a lot of people there – most were native New Yorkers, but there were a large number of tourists poring over maps and snapping photographs, and, of course, there was us. We were spread out from one end of the platform to the other in discrete knots of two or three. Uriel was the only one who stood alone – she had her back to a concrete post on the far right so that she could watch the whole area. As usual she was being chatted up – she didn't mind (it was a good cover) and the guy was cute but I could see her eyes pass over us all every few seconds. He would be history once our train arrived.

It was six days since Daeshan had taken Sariel. Six days since my world had collapsed around my ears yet again – it was getting to be a habit – and it was all a blur.

I knew that we'd escaped through the tunnels, that there had been a lot of walking to get to the coast where Isabella and Mario's gorgeous boat was waiting. Mario himself was at the helm. I remember he spoke to me for a long time once we'd set sail but what he said is lost somewhere in my memory. Sariel had asked Uriel and Don to look after us and I know that they'd had their work cut out - Seth and Jude wanted to hunt down every Demon in existence for a while and had loud arguments with Uriel; as far as they were concerned we were heading in the wrong direction. Asmodeus was in England and we were heading for America. Lisa and Adrian were in shock – Dean had been in the wrong place at the wrong time, he'd died when Daeshan blew the front door off its hinges; Annie and Dylan were terrified – being on the run from Demons wasn't the giggle-fest they'd been expecting; Paul was quiet, which had been surprising, he had taken on the role of my silent protector – always by my side, not asking for anything more than to be there. And me? I don't know what I was. I stayed inside my head for as long as Sariel would allow it, lying on the grass beside him in the Garden of Eden he had created in his mind.

We talked about anything and everything – wars, books, movies, Angels, Heaven, whether Apple was better than Microsoft, writers, actors, plays – or at least everything except what Daeshan was doing to him. And if his hand tightened in mine more often as the time went on, and his body shuddered or he cried out in pain? We didn't mention it. It never happened.

One morning I woke up and Sariel was gone, our link was blocked and Uriel was waiting for me. She was staring off into the trees and turned to look at me when I sat up. "He stayed with you here for as long as he could, Emily," she told me sadly, "But he can't keep the link open any longer. It takes too much energy to keep his pain from you."

"But I can't feel anything," I told her angrily.

She sighed. "I'm blocking for him now."

"He'll be ok," I said, wondering if I was asking her or telling her.

Uriel swung her long legs around so that she was facing me. "He'll try, but we both know how close he's been to…changing. I'm not sure if he can …"

"HE CAN!" I shouted, standing up and whirling away from her. "He can and he will."

And so I had come back to the real world and found myself in a small hotel on a motorway. Don was watching me from a chair in the corner and I was lucky that he could move fast – he took one look at my face and launched himself towards me with the room's waste bin in his hand, reaching me just as everything I didn't remember eating for the past few days came back up.

And now here we were in New York City – skyscrapers, yellow cabs, vast numbers of people making their way from one side of the city to another at a pace that suggested they were all being chased by Demons too. I loved and hated it in equal measure imagining my mum being there as a young woman not much older than I was now – before she met Asmodeus and everything went pear shaped – and wishing I could have shared this experience with both her and Sariel.

I sighed and accepted a drink of water from Don. I'd finished the doughnut although I couldn't remember how it tasted or even whether it had been plain, jam-filled, custard, vanilla, chocolate or a combination of them all. I leaned against Don's shoulder and whispered a thank you, grinning as he ruffled my hair and then gave me a rather powerful pretend punch on the arm.

I glanced towards Annie and Dylan. They were chatting quietly together and his arm was slung casually around her shoulders. Annie was wearing jeans and a plain white shirt, Dylan wore sweats and a matching jacket. They looked like they belonged here – another young couple waiting for the subway to take them home.

Paul was standing talking to a young girl in a short denim skirt. Her blonde hair was in pigtails and she was wearing a sheer blouse over a black bra. Paul looked to be enjoying the conversation if his smile was anything to go by – although he was being careful not to grin too widely; nothing puts the ladies off like a flash of fang, I thought unkindly. His eyes met mine for the briefest of seconds and I immediately felt guilty for the compassion I saw in them.

I looked for Seth. For a few moments I couldn't see him and panic began to bloom in my chest. I sat up, feeling Don tense beside me. Uriel's eyes flicked over towards us and she lifted her chin slightly in question.

And then a large woman in a polka-dot dress and huge red hat moved forward to look down the track and I saw him. Jude was making him laugh and his smile was wide and goofy and beautiful. He looked my way and I saw how forced the smile was, how lines of strain had woven their way around his mouth and how much fear he was carrying on his shoulders.

I gulped. I'd let them down.

Back at the house, while I was wailing and pounding him with my fists, Sariel had been telling me how to survive and how to keep the others alive too. "Be strong," he'd told me. "You are the glue that is holding everything together and Asmodeus knows that. He wanted to tame you, to bring you into his house and instead you almost killed him but he still can't believe that you could do all that alone. He thought your mum was your strength so he took her. That didn't work and so he is taking me.. You're better than that. You're stronger than that. Go forward, Uriel will lead you where you need to go. Find out what you're here to do and do it." He'd sighed and given me one last, fierce kiss. *Thank you for giving me something to fight for. I love you.*

The station PA system hissed with static and some of the passengers began to move – getting ready for the next train to be announced. The static hissed again and music began to play. The Plain White T's were singing 'Delilah'. I drew in a shaky breath.

On the platform the waiting passengers looked at each other in confusion and then delight; some laughed, some began to sing along. The woman in the polka-dot dress swayed her enormous hips in time to the music. I could feel the eyes of the others on me and realized that I was crying. The music died away and the announcer's slightly stunned voice told us that the express to Lexington Avenue would be arriving in two minutes.

Uriel stepped away from her admirer and moved to stand beside me. "He is letting us know that he's still there," she said happily.

I sighed and wiped my face, shaking my head and feeling my heart break all over again. I straightened my back and faced Uriel. "No," I told her gently. "That was Sariel's goodbye. We're on our own."

ACKNOWLEDGEMENTS

Thanks as always to the usual suspects – Shauna, Bex, Debbie and Irene for all the reading/feedback/coffee – and also to the new victims…er…I mean 'lovely beta readers', Shaun, Carol and Linda for the correcting of mistakes and pushes in the right direction.

To the lovely Principessa Sara – grazie for helping me to get all the Italian words and phrases correct this time! I really appreciate it.

And to my family for putting up with my insanity and inability to cook/clean/attempt to act normal while my head's full of dastardly Demons and gorgeous Angels. Love always xx

I hope that you enjoyed 'Demon's Revenge'
Look out for the final installment in Emily's story
- 'Demon's Blood'
which will be available in 2013

Connect with me online:
Email me: aly3008ish@gmail.com
Find me on Facebook
Follow me on Twitter: @aly3008
Visit my website: ashleymccook.co.uk
Read my blog: Ashley McCook's Space